Duty and Doubt

Eleanor knew that she *should* convince her niece Aurora that the Earl of Huntley was not the unpoetical person of practicality and purpose that Aurora disdained, but rather the answer to any young lady's fondest dreams.

Eleanor knew that she *should* convince the earl that Aurora was not the overly romantic, quite immature young thing he had his doubts about, but rather a ravishingly desirable bride who would make him happy forever.

But when Eleanor looked into the earl's deep hazel eyes, her certainties melted into one overwhelming question:

Should she betray her family's trust—or her own treacherous heart. . . ?

────── AR AFFAIR OF HONOR ──────

SIGNET Regency Romances You'll Enjoy

AN AFFAIR OF HONOR

HONOR

AMANDA SCOTT

A SIGNET BOOK

NEW AMERICAN LIBRARY

For
Terry
with love

NAL BOOKS ARE AVAILABLE AT QUANTITY DISCOUNTS WHEN
USED TO PROMOTE PRODUCTS OR SERVICES. FOR INFORMATION
PLEASE WRITE TO PREMIUM MARKETING DIVISION, NEW AMERI-
CAN LIBRARY, 1633 BROADWAY, NEW YORK, NEW YORK 10019.

SIGNET TRADEMARK REG. U.S. PAT. OFF. AND FOREIGN COUNTRIES
REGISTERED TRADEMARK—MARCA REGISTRADA
HECHO EN CHICAGO, U.S.A.

SIGNET, SIGNET CLASSIC, MENTOR, PLUME, MERIDIAN AND NAL BOOKS
are published by
New American Library,
1633 Broadway,
New York, New York 10019

First Printing, September, 1984

1 2 3 4 5 6 7 8 9

PRINTED IN THE UNITED STATES OF AMERICA

I

It was a summer day bright enough to set rainbows playing upon the breaking waters beneath Brighton's chalky cliffs. The lace curtains in the cheerful, expensively appointed morning room stirred with the motion of a gentle, easterly breeze that drifted through the open first-floor windows of the tall, white-trimmed brick house at Number Twenty-seven Upper Rock Gardens.

Although the breeze carried with it the inevitable crisp tang of the sea, the architect who had assisted Brighton's city fathers in their effort, some fifteen years earlier, to bring the popular little fishing village up to the standard expected by the steadily increasing summertime surge of royal and noble visitors had not been so lacking in good taste as to present the residents of Number Twenty-seven or those of its equally distinguished neighbors with a view of anything so mundane as the town's crumbling chalk cliffs and broad, desolate expanse of blue sea. Therefore, the principal rooms of the homes in Upper Rock Gardens overlooked nothing more unusual than a tidy, cobbled street such as one might find in any fashionable, inland town.

Though the soft breeze stirred the delicate morning-room curtains and even fluttered the swordlike leaves and showy blossoms of the huge, yellow irises arranged in a stoneware bowl on the low table in front of the window bay, it was not strong enough to disturb either of the morning room's two occupants. The elder of these, a fluffy-haired, pink-gowned lady with nearly fifty-five summers to her credit, was the Lady Agnes Lindale. At the moment, Lady Agnes sat upon a gray settee in the window bay, a piece of fancywork resting forgotten in her lap, as she watched with increasing impatience while the lovely young woman sitting opposite her at a parquetry writing table dealt with the morning post.

An errant ray of sunshine penetrated the space between two of the shifting lace panels and dust motes danced along its path as it set auburn highlights glistening in the young woman's thick, high-piled chestnut hair. Silence reigned, broken only by the occasional screech of a gull outside, until Lady Agnes stirred restlessly.

"For pity's sake, Nell! Do you mean to tell me what your sister has to say, or do you not?"

Miss Eleanor Lindale lowered the single-page missive that she had been scanning and looked up to reveal startlingly blue, heavily lashed eyes set deeply above well defined cheekbones in a charming, oval face. She smiled cheerfully at her mother.

"Forgive me, Mama. It must seem an age and more since I began," she replied. "I have merely been attempting—and not at all successfully, I might add—to conjure a meaning out of what appears to be the devil's own web of copperplate."

Lady Agnes's face was turned discreetly away from the morning light—so revealing of one's all-too-rapidly advancing years—but Nell could discern her impatient frown well enough. "I cannot think why it should take you so long," her ladyship said fretfully. "Your sister writes a very elegant hand."

Nell chuckled but glanced doubtfully at the page of weblike lines which she had been attempting to decipher. As she did so, the furrow forming between the straight, narrow brows that gave such emphasis to every expression of her candid blue eyes cleared magically. "Ah ha!" she pronounced on a note of distinct triumph. "It is the *rains* that were early. Do you know, Mama, I had stared and stared at that word before, but by merely glancing at it just now, it suddenly became quite clear. At first, all I could make of it was *onus*, but one knew that could not be right. Though, to be sure," she added musingly, "what on earth early rains have got to do with anything . . . Oh, I see. Something to do with the lower crop yield having put Crossways all out of frame. As if a few bushels more or less of whatever it is he grows on that monstrous estate would matter a cracked groat to a man with pockets lined as deeply as his are."

"Eleanor!"

Miss Lindale glanced up at her indignant parent just as Lady Agnes stretched a well tended hand toward the elegant silver-gilt vinaigrette placed conveniently upon the polished oak table at her right. Withdrawing the crystal stopper, she waved it gently beneath her straight little nose, a gesture that brought a rueful twinkle to Nell's expressive, dark-rimmed eyes.

"I do beg your pardon, ma'am. I should not have said such a thing. At least," she amended candidly, "I should not have said it so bluntly." She flicked the letter. "But Clarissa puts me all out of patience. She does indeed write an elegant fist, but she has crossed and recrossed her lines till I cannot tell where one thought ends and another begins."

"Well, it cannot matter, after all," Lady Agnes replied vaguely as she replaced her vinaigrette on the table. "Clarissa always writes very much the same thing, does she not? If one of the children has not fallen out of a tree, another has thrown out a rash, and the expense of the doctor's visit has all but reduced the family to bread and pig's knuckles for supper. Let her but try to hold house here in Brighton," she added with an air of weary but patient endurance, "and I daresay she would soon cease to cavil about the expense of keeping up an estate in Kent."

Only half listening, Nell frowned again. "She does mention the expense of something. One moment, whilst I . . ." She broke off, turning the sheet more toward the light and peering at it through narrowed eyes. "Oh, of course. A *London Season* would be an outrageous expense. It looked like *louder session*, you know. No one, you will be relieved to hear, dearest ma'am, has fallen or gone ill. She concerns herself with Rory."

"Rory, indeed," Lady Agnes sighed, airing an old grievance. "The child is the Lady Aurora Crossways, and so she should be called. I cannot imagine what my poor papa would have had to say to *such* a nickname."

"Even Grandpapa must have agreed—had he ever had an opportunity to express himself on the subject—that to have called any child with Rory's shaggy plaits and eternally muddied petticoats Aurora would have been outside of enough," Nell said with an indulgent smile. "Perhaps, however, the little ragtag gypsy who last visited us will have outgrown her hoydenish ways. It is time for her come-out, you know. By heaven," she added, her tone changing to one of exasperation as she returned to her task, "I do wish Clarissa might have seen her way clear to adding a second sheet to this letter, instead of crowding all this lot onto a single page!"

"She is merely being frugal," Lady Agnes stated repressively.

But Nell could not be repressed so easily as that. "Clarissa is an unconscionable pinch-penny and nothing else," she retorted. "There is no point whatsoever to this sort of economy. She cannot have feared you might be put to so much as a ha'penny's expense for the extra sheet, because Crossways has not left Kent and, as you see, was there to frank this letter for her. So it is merely that Clarissa could not bear the pain of parting with a second sheet of her precious letter paper."

"Well, perhaps she does carry her sense of economy a bit far sometimes," Lady Agnes admitted reluctantly, "but——"

"At least she comes by such strong notions honestly enough," Nell teased, hoping to stop the impending lecture before it began.

Lady Agnes stiffened, much like a ruffled partridge. "If you mean by that impertinent remark to imply that your own mother is a nipfarthing, Eleanor Lindale, I'll thank you to——"

"I would never say anything so improper, Mama," Nell protested with a chuckle.

"Well, you certainly *should* not. Not that Kit has not said that very thing to me."

"He never did! What a shocking bouncer, ma'am. To accuse your only son of such a thing. Kit would never speak so to you."

"Well, it was by way of being the same thing, I'm sure. He said I had nip-farthing notions. You know he did," Lady Agnes insisted indignantly. "And merely because dear Sir Henry and I do not choose to loosen the pursestrings at his every least whim."

Nell remembered the incident in question clearly—her handsome young brother angry and frustrated; her mother indignant and full of righteous reason; her mother's man of affairs volubly censorious. But although her eyes danced at the memory, she managed to preserve a tolerable gravity of countenance.

"To a gentleman of nineteen summers without a penny to bless himself, I daresay that the matter of a new shirt is something beyond a mere whim, dearest ma'am, and for you to suggest that your dressmaker might simply mend the lace and add new collars to his old shirts was hardly a notion destined to please him.''

"And why not, may I ask?" demanded her ladyship. "I daresay Millicent might even have added *new* lace—particularly if she was careful to use only goods unemcumbered by that odious import duty—and the result would still have cost a deal less than it cost to allow that disgracefully expensive tailor of Kit's to make an entire new shirt. I cannot approve of such extravagance.''

"No, ma'am, and how shocking that you should have been saddled with two such expensive offspring as Kit and myself, with nothing at hand to discharge the burden but that dreadful pittance Papa left for the purpose.'' She said nothing about Lady Agnes's reference to smuggled lace, of course, for smuggling had become so prevalent a fashion that most people felt they were losing some of the best opportunities that life had to offer if they did not acquire some duty-free goods. But Nell's eyes were twinkling wickedly by now, and since they both knew to the farthing what a very comfortable independence Mr. Lindale had left to his widow, there was little Lady Agnes could say in reproof. She had recourse once again to her vinaigrette, instead.

"Kit did get his shirt, did he not?" she pointed out, albeit a trifle weakly. "Three of them, actually. I am persuaded I could not be so unnatural a parent as to wish to *deny* my darling children the necessities of life.''

"No, indeed," Nell agreed, adding irrepressibly, "Moreover, as I recall that particular incident, there was little else to be done once poor Kit showed you how his old shirts were quite bursting at the seams.''

"In a better world, one might expect one's son to stop growing at a reasonable age," Lady Agnes mused with a long sigh. Then she gave herself a small shake and added more firmly, "But there is nothing at all wrong in having a well ordered sense of economy, my dear. Though you may tease me and complain of dear Clarissa's frugality, it would do you no harm to cultivate such careful habits yourself. No man wishes to take a spendthrift to wife.''

"Mama, for pity's sake, I am no spendthrift. I am, however, five-and-twenty years old, so it is perfectly clear that no man wants me for his wife, spendthrift or not! I have been placed irretrievably upon the shelf, and well you know it.'' She grinned again, easily stifling her annoyance that the subject had once again risen its head to plague her. ''I shall spend my declining years being an expensive prop to my adorable, if overburdened, mama.''

''Fiddlesticks!'' retorted Lady Agnes, ignoring provocation for once. '' 'Tis early days yet, my love, for well you know you've had little chance to find a suitable husband. I have forever been telling you these past two years that you should put yourself more in the way of meeting eligible gentlemen.''

Smiling, Nell shook her head. ''I cannot think it would have done me the slightest good, ma'am. What self-respecting gentleman would give me a second glance in a roomful of blushing, seventeen-year-old debutantes?''

''Nonsense,'' objected her ladyship stoutly. '' 'Tis not as if you are ill-favored, my dear. You were quite the prettiest girl in London or Brighton the year you made your come-out.''

''Ah, but shy and inarticulate in company, ma'am, so I didn't take. And there was never a second chance.''

''So unfair,'' sighed her ladyship. ''No other family of my acquaintance has been so cursed. Six deaths in as many years. And so ill-timed. Each new one coming just as we were about to put off our black gloves.''

Nell nodded agreement. ''And except for dearest Papa,'' she added, hoping to clear the troubled frown from her mother's face, ''not one of them was worth the effort of putting them on.'' Lady Agnes looked up in immediate protest, and Nell laughed. ''Come now, Mama, and admit that my sentiments, though highly improper, are perfectly sound. Uncle Edgar was a crusty curmudgeon who never cared a wink for anyone but himself.''

''Very true,'' agreed Lady Agnes, ''and it was unpardonable of him to leave all his money—*family* money at that—to that disgraceful woman from Somerset who had the unutterable temerity to call herself his housekeeper. Housekeeper, my—''

''Indeed,'' Nell chuckled, pursuing the subject with relish. ''And Cousin Frederick's carriage accident can only have been providential, since he was but a skip and a hop ahead of the bailiffs. Only think of the scandal he might have brought down about our heads had he lived much longer than he did!"

Lady Agnes shuddered delicately. "True enough, I fear. It did seem somewhat hypocritical to wear mourning on his behalf, though I had got quite accustomed to my blacks by then. Nonetheless, my dear, it was very sad when Aunt Hester passed on."

"Perhaps," Nell mused. "I never knew her as you did, of course. To me, she was merely a rude old lady whose breath smelled of peppermint and whose clothes emitted clouds of snuff whenever she moved."

"Filthy habit, that. All very well for gentlemen, of course, and both Sir Henry and Mr. Brummell do take theirs with such a natty air. But I cannot approve of the habit for a gentlewoman."

"Of course not, ma'am. And even you will be hard-pressed to explain why we were all plunged into deep mourning when Aunt Agatha's second husband died. He was a sour creature and no connection of ours at all. I should have thought six weeks of black gloves would have answered the purpose well enough."

"And so it should have," Lady Agnes agreed. "But you know very well that your Aunt Agatha would have been offended if we had not observed all the proprieties. Besides," she added with a sigh, "you could not have danced in black gloves, and by the time the six weeks had passed, the Season here was over anyway. And the following year, poor Mr. Pallworthy went to his reward. Your aunt would never have forgiven us if we had behaved shabbily then, for not only was he our first cousin, but he had been the vicar at Parkhurst— and thereby her confessor, you know—for years and years."

"Sometimes," Nell said thoughtfully, "I cannot think how Aunt Agatha came to be your twin, Mama."

"Why, in the usual fashion, of course, my dear." The twinkle that lit her ladyship's eyes gave her a sudden resemblance to her youthful daughter. "Not but what I don't follow your meaning well enough. I may be a nipfarthing, but no one would ever accuse me of being cross-grained."

"No, indeed," Nell agreed promptly. "Why, you are quite the kindest, most generous-hearted person of my acquaintance. And Clarissa agrees. I daresay she would not so much as consider sending poor Rory to spend six weeks with Aunt

Agatha. Only think how nipped about and confined the poor child would be!"

"Agatha wouldn't have her," Lady Agnes stated flatly. "Not for *one* week." She paused with an arrested look, then bent a suspicious eye upon her daughter. "Are you suggesting that we are to have that doubtful pleasure, Nell? For I must tell you——"

"Is it not wonderful, Mama?" Nell interrupted quickly. "And just when you have been saying that I should go about more, too. For you must have guessed that Clarissa means to launch Rory here in Brighton. At least," she amended, "she means for me to do so."

"Why on earth, if she means the girl to come out this year, did she not do the thing properly in London?" demanded Lady Agnes. "I am sure Clarissa never said a word about any of this to me."

"Since Rory did not turn seventeen until mid-June," Nell explained patiently, scanning the letter in order to be certain of getting her words right, "Clarissa felt she was too young to make her come-out during the London Season. She also"— this on a wry note—"mentions the expense. I daresay she thinks it will be cheaper here."

"Well, of course it will cost less if she means to do it from Upper Rock Gardens," replied Lady Agnes a bit tartly. "In London, she would have had to hire a house, and that would have been dreadfully dear."

"Crossways can afford it, however."

"I did not say he couldn't, Nell. How you do take one up! Does Clarissa expect me to absorb the expense of this visit?"

"Of course not, Mama. Crossways will underwrite everything while Rory is here."

"There will be a good deal of upheaval, Eleanor," her ladyship said dampingly. "And I hope you will not want me to endure the exertion of a dress ball or any other large entertainment here in the house."

"Clarissa does not mention it, ma'am, nor do I imagine she would expect it of us. Only let me write to tell her you will agree to let Rory come. I confess I should rather enjoy taking her about."

"Why on earth is Clarissa not doing so herself?"

"Something to do with the dowager. Let me see . . ." Nell skimmed the letter quickly. "Yes, here it is. The Dowager Countess is enjoying one of her distempered freaks—not a very elegant turn of phrase, is it. Nonetheless, she has commanded their presence in Chatham by the end of the month.''

"Clarissa and Crossways, but not Aurora?"

Nell chuckled. "I daresay Rory may have refused to go. You know how often Clarissa has complained about her mama-in-law. She has said, too, more than once, that Rory cannot abide the woman.''

"Probably old Lady Crossways tried and failed to teach that chit to mind her manners.'' Lady Agnes was sitting upright on the settee now, her vinaigrette forgotten for the moment. Her eyes narrowed. "I should not wish to appear unfeeling, Nell, but I cannot but think that having that girl here will very likely put us all at sixes and sevens. She does not know our ways, after all.''

"No indeed,'' Nell agreed. "That is the purpose of one's come-out, is it not? To learn the ways of so-called polite society? And Rory will learn quickly enough.'' Lady Agnes continued to look skeptical. Indeed, the lines near the corners of her mouth looked even a bit mulish. Nell studied her for some moments before a twinkle crept into her eye and she demanded, "Do you think Rory cannot learn, Mama? Because you think her a slowtop, or because she had the misfortune to be born in Kent and not in Sussex? Confess it! You do think that, don't you? She is your granddaughter, ma'am!''

Lady Agnes winced, but she recovered quickly. "She may be a member of the *family*,'' she stated, emphasizing the final word, "but she is still a foreigner, my dear, and say what you will, foreigners do not always adapt well to our ways.''

"Kent is the very next county, ma'am. It is not darkest Africa. And the ways Rory must adapt to are more or less London ways, now that the Prince of Wales has made Brighton such a popular refuge for his friends among the *beau monde*.''

"He, at least, is a gentleman,'' Lady Agnes said fondly. They had heard rumors to the effect that the prince was not altogether popular in London, but Lady Agnes, like most of Brighton's citizens, liked and admired the First Gentleman of Europe. He, by the mere fact of choosing their town for a retreat from his royal duties, had brought prosperity upon them all, and little could be heard against him in the erstwhile fishing village.

"Indeed, he can be all that is charming," Nell agreed. "But you have not answered me, Mama. Surely you will not deny Rory her come-out on the flimsy pretense that you fear she will disgrace us with her Kentish manners."

"I suppose you and Clarissa will do as you please," Lady Agnes said wearily, making use once more of her vinaigrette. "But do not expect me to take charge of the girl. You will have to attend to that. And be certain Crossways agrees to a Dutch reckoning," she added more firmly, the vinaigrette poised in midair. "There are always expenses one does not anticipate, and I shall not wish to be expected to justify every odd ha'penny."

"No, indeed, ma'am, nor would he expect it of you. It is Clarissa who would make such demands, if such demands were ever made. However, I can safely promise that she will not plague you on that head. Then, you agree?"

"Agree to what?" The pleasant masculine voice speaking from the doorway behind her startled Nell, but she turned to the newcomer with a delighted smile.

"Kit, how was your ride?"

"Invigorating," the young man replied, crossing the room with a quick stride, then bending to kiss his mother's powdered cheek. "What sort of agreement is she attempting to wring from you, ma'am? Shall I stand your champion?"

"Dear boy." Lady Agnes looked fondly upon her son, and indeed, he was a sight to gladden any mother's heart. Well above medium height, handsome young Christopher Lindale possessed a figure that made his tailor the envy of his trade. Though broad enough of shoulder so that no wadding was needed, he was not yet so broad as to tax his man's skills when it came to the smooth fit of his coats. Kit had changed out of his riding dress and appeared now wearing a well-cut coat of forest green over tan breeches and well-polished Hessians. His light brown hair was stylishly swept back from his forehead. His neckcloth was elaborately tied, and if his shirt points were a bit too high to be comfortable, he gave all the appearance of the fashionable young man about town.

"Well, Mama?" He glanced roguishly at his sister, his eyes—as blue as her own—twinkling with mischief. "Do you require a champion?"

"She does not," Nell replied. "I was merely seeking her approval of my own return to the social scene."

"Were you, indeed?" Kit lowered himself to an armchair, taking care not to crease his coat and disposing his long legs before him with practiced ease. He cast a skeptical glance at Nell. "I am more than seven, sister mine. If that were all, Mama would be cast into transports. Where's the rub?"

"There is no rub," Nell chuckled. "Merely a treat for all of us."

"We will hope so," muttered her ladyship *sotto voce* to her vinaigrette.

"You'll see, Mama. I think Clarissa is doing us a kindness. We shall all enjoy the festivities much more seeing them anew through Rory's eyes."

"Rory!" Kit's posture underwent a sudden change as he registered wary alertness. "Not that upstart blond baggage with the flyaway plaits and rude manners!"

"I'm quite sure the plaits will be gone, Kit," Nell laughed. "After all, Rory is turned seventeen. No doubt she will be much as I was at that age, full of eagerness and anticipation of delights to come."

"Well, if she's as tongue-tied as you were, you may call me a Dutchman," Kit retorted. "Why on earth does Clarissa want to fire her off here? Brighton is scarcely the proper place for a young thing to be trying her wings."

"There's nothing wrong with Brighton," put in her ladyship loyally. "And if there are some persons who come from *other places* who do not know how to keep the line, I am sure Nell will know how to send them to the rightabout."

"Nell! Why not Clarissa?"

"She and Crossways are wanted in Chatham," Nell replied evenly. "The dowager thinks they do not visit often enough."

"Not sick, is she?" Kit's face expressed sudden alarm.

"No, of course not. Why should she be?"

"With our luck it would be just like the old lady to pop off and plunge us all into mourning again."

"Oh, no, she *couldn't*," moaned her ladyship.

"Kit, for heaven's sake! Mama, don't be a goose. We should not even be forced into black gloves. She is only Clarissa's mama-in-law, after all."

"Well, she is the gypsy's grandmother, so you cannot expect her demise to leave us entirely unaffected," Kit returned.

"You could scarcely squire the chit about if the old lady cocks up her toes."

"Don't call her the gypsy!" Nell snapped, annoyed by his attitude. "She has a perfectly good name. And the fact of the matter is that Lady Crossways is not on her death bed. You," she added tartly, going for the throat, "are merely irritated because you are used to being the center of attention yourself, Kit."

"And why not? After all, she is likely to put this house in an uproar, and you'll both be expecting me to lend my escort—probably to the dashed assemblies at the Castle and the Old Ship as well. And just because she's a dashed female, no expense will be spared to furbish her up. Ha!" he exclaimed as a new thought occurred to him. "I'll wager that's why Clarissa's saddling you with the charge. Only one set of gowns that way. She surely won't expect to pay for yours, Nelly dear, but she'd dashed well have to tart herself up if *she* brought the chit out. This way, most of the expense will fall upon Mama. I call it dashed unfair."

"Kit, do stop thinking of yourself for once," Nell begged. "No, no," she added when he made a gesture of protest, "that's precisely what has thrown you into such a pet. You are afraid Mama's purse will have to be opened for Rory and that your pockets will suffer accordingly."

"Well, and why not?" He hunched a shoulder, looking more like a sulky schoolboy than a young gentleman of nineteen summers. "I should have been allowed a proper come-out in London, and well you know it. But, no, Mama and Sir Henry said I was too young, so I must make do with the delights of Brighton. But only such delights as they approve of. And now you will be wanting me to dance attendance on this young chit—two years younger than I am myself—and everyone will be falling over to puff her off so that she can find a proper husband. If you were at all concerned about my welfare, Nell, you'd see that her coming here will be a dashed nuisance."

"Stuff," retorted his unsympathetic sister.

"Children, don't bicker," pleaded her ladyship. "You will give me the headache. Really, Nell, it is most unkind of you to tease Kit so," she added reprovingly. "You ought to have told him at the outset that I shall not be obliged to disburse so much as a penny on Aurora's behalf. And you, Kit," she went on, effectively stifling the smile that was beginning to spread across his handsome face, "you should be ashamed to speak so of Sir Henry, when you know he has only your best interests at heart."

Nell watched to see how her brother would respond to the rebuke. Sir Henry Sinclair, his principal trustee, was ever a thorn in Kit's side. Sir Henry was no doubt a very wise man when it came to handling finances, but he possessed no tact whatsoever when it came to handling the boy. Nell knew he was much more likely to lecture than to sympathize. Lately, he had been hoping, vocally and constantly, that Kit would prove himself a gentleman during the upcoming Season. But since Kit's head seemed to be as full of potential card tables and cockfights as it was of canapés and country dances, Nell had no great hopes of his making it through the Season unscathed by at least one or two of Sir Henry's fiery lectures. He frowned now, but contained his often uncertain temper.

"I am sorry if I offended you, Mama, but Sir Henry is an old woman. I am not a child to be constantly guarded and scolded, but he treats me like one. I daresay he will tell me I should be grateful for the diversion of my—Lord, she's my niece, ain't she?" He shook his head in wonder at the thought of having a niece two years his junior. "Well, he will be sure to say as much, anyway. I'm going to Harry's." And, with a bitter glare for his sister's benefit, he got to his feet and left the room.

She glanced at Lady Agnes. "I hope he doesn't mean to be difficult, Mama."

"Kit?" Lady Agnes considered the possibility with knit brows. "I daresay Sir Henry's right, you know. Or would be," she added when her daughter looked perplexed. "If he had said what Kit said he said. Oh, dear. I mean it would not be a bad thing if Kit were to find Aurora diverting. Not that it would do as a match, of course."

Nell grinned. "I don't think we need worry about that possibility, ma'am. Although it would be very nice if I could manage to find a suitable husband for Rory while she is here." The mischief was back in her eye. "Just think of all the money I would save Clarissa. She wouldn't have to spring for a London Season at all if I could get Rory riveted here. Perhaps," she added, further scandalizing her parent, "I have a turn for economy after all. Do you not think so, Mama?"

II

The next two weeks were busy ones for Nell, and while the time passed quickly by, she found herself growing daily more excited about the prospect before her. She had not seen her niece for nearly six years, for it had not been thought necessary to drag the young girl to any funeral since Uncle Edgar's and that only because he had died right here in Brighton. But as Nell struggled to remember the scrubby twelve-year-old who had set them all by the ears with her pranks and mischief, she smiled. By no stretch of the imagination could she conjure up an image of Rory as the shy, nearly tongue-tied sort of debutante she had been herself.

No, indeed. There would be no need to coax her into company. On the contrary, it would no doubt be necessary to curb the child's enthusiasm, because it would not do for her to acquire a reputation for being fast or, worse, flirtatious. But Nell worried only briefly over such possibilities. She had not realized until the opportunity presented itself how much she desired a more active social life. She had indeed been serving as a comfort to her mama. For nearly two years. For there had been nothing really to stop her going back into society the year after Cousin Pallworthy's demise. Lady Agnes had certainly recommended it. However, she had also looked faintly alarmed whenever Nell had received an invitation that tempted her in the slightest.

Lady Agnes enjoyed, if not actual ill health, at least a languorous disposition. The series of deaths in her family had served only to encourage a natural inclination to indulge her solitary habits. Without her husband's encouragement, Lady Agnes had discovered little desire to decorate the social scene by herself. An occasional ladies' card party was all she exerted herself to attend. But her spirits required constant support. And if Nell suggested leaving her to her own devices for an evening, although she would certainly encourage the outing, she would also wonder rather sadly how she would go on without Nell's companionship. Nell had made the attempt once or twice but had found it difficult to pursue her own pleasures while her thoughts kept returning to Upper Rock Gardens.

Pursuing a social life without her mother's active support proved to be nearly impossible anyway. Even at the age of four-and-twenty, as a single lady she had required suitable escort. Her brother was still too young for the office, and although many friends from earlier days were married and might have served her, she was made to feel disconcertingly like a third wheel on the few occasions that she had accepted their invitations, and she had quickly been convinced that such arrangements would not answer.

It seemed to her one day in the midst of her preparations for her niece's arrival and the rapidly approaching Season that, had she truly wished to return to an active social life at an earlier date, she might have made more of a push to do so. But in all honesty she had to acknowledge that she had not wished it. Such doings had suddenly seemed childishly foolish. She had felt out of place and old at twenty-four. Not just old, she amended to herself with a slight smile, but quite ancient in fact. Some of her married friends had also seemed childish, as though their mental growth had stopped while hers had gone on. If marriage did that to one, she had decided dispassionately, she could do as well without it. She had her books, her music, her needlework, and her riding to occupy her time. She had also, thanks to Lady Agnes's disinclination to bestir herself, had a house to run. She had not been bored. But now, it was as if she had a real purpose in life. Though she had not been able to attend the balls and assemblies alone, as a spinster lady she could well serve as chaperon to her niece. She could renew old acquaintances, wear lovely gowns, and generally amuse herself; and, at the same time, she could oblige her elder sister and her niece. Even Lady Agnes could scarcely cavil at being left alone when Nell would be engaged in such an admirable activity. In the past weeks since Clarissa's letter had arrived, with Nell's own experience as a dreaded example, it had occurred to Lady Agnes that her granddaughter should be safely wedded as soon as possible.

The day appointed for the arrival of the Crossways family came at last, and while instructing the chambermaid in the final preparations of Rory's bedchamber, Nell found her thoughts straying once again to the problem of finding a suitable husband for the girl. With the Prince of Wales's Own Regiment of Hussars stationed right here in Brighton, there were, of course, any number of eligible gentlemen available, even if one did not consider the stream of summer visitors that had already begun to descend upon Brighton.

It was expected to be a busy Season. Many tourists had stayed away in recent years, fearing French invasion, but the successful outcome of the Battle of Trafalgar the previous fall had put an end to such worries, and every nook and cranny in Brighton was expected to be full this year. The prince himself had been in town for nearly a week, with his friends and followers arriving daily.

Nell did not doubt that a suitable husband for her niece could be found among these visitors or even among the permanent residents of the town. But the thought of being solely responsible for sifting the suitable from the unsuitable she found a trifle daunting. Back in the days when Mr. Wade, master of ceremonies at the Castle Inn, and Mr. Hicks, his counterpart at the Old Ship, had been at the height of their power, she might have depended upon them to guide her. But of later years their power had begun to wane. Rory might meet some young gentleman at Donaldson's Library or along the esplanade who had not condescended to sign the visitors' book—a social solecism of great magnitude in days gone by, but nearly acceptable behavior now—and such a gentleman would therefore be quite unknown to either of the masters of ceremony.

Sir Henry Sinclair might assist her, of course. Lady Agnes certainly turned to him often enough, and Kit, of course, was greatly dependent upon him. But Sir Henry was a gentleman inclined to be overly conservative in Nell's opinion. Surely, if she turned to him once, he might expect her to bow to his authority rather more often than would be consistent with either her own or her niece's comfort.

Of course, once she had renewed her own acquaintance with various members of the *beau monde*, there would doubtless be any number of persons to help her. Comforted by that thought, she put her worries aside and turned her mind instead to the pleasure she would enjoy while watching her niece try her wings. The matter of a husband, considering Rory's ample fortune, would no doubt take care of itself quite satisfactorily. It never once occurred to Nell that the matter might already be well in hand, but she was brought to realize her error immediately upon the arrival of the Crossways party.

She was reading aloud to Lady Agnes in the morning room when the pretty chambermaid who had helped prepare Rory's bedchamber entered to inform them that the visitors were, at that very moment, descending from their carriage onto the flagway.

"Please, my lady, Mr. Pavingham says he will need Jeremy to deal with her ladyship's baggage, and so he sent me to tell you they have come and will be up directly." Lady Agnes inclined her head.

"Thank you, Katy," Nell said, laying her book aside as she rose to her feet. "Tell Pavingham to show Lord and Lady Crossways and the Lady Aurora into the drawing room, if you please."

"Yes, Miss Nell." The maid disappeared through the door, and her muffled footsteps could be heard on the carpeted steps as she hurried back downstairs.

With a quick glance into the oval mirror on the wall near the door, Nell smoothed her slim, pale yellow skirt and pinched her tiny puffed sleeves into shape, then twisted a chestnut side curl firmly into place. A damped forefinger tidied an eyebrow, and she was ready. She smiled at Lady Agnes.

"Shall we go down, Mama? I confess I am anxious to see how Rory has turned out. And to see Clarissa and Crossways, too, of course."

Lady Agnes smiled vaguely as she gathered her vinaigrette and lace handkerchief. Thus armed, she preceded her daughter to the landing. On the first step, she turned.

"Did Kit say when he would join us, dear? I am afraid I don't remember. We've scarce seen the wretched boy all week."

"He didn't say," Nell replied, her own irritation with her errant brother carefully masked under a placid tone. "He knows perfectly well that Clarissa and Crossways must leave directly after dinner, however, so I daresay he will dine with us.''

"I wish they would stay the night," Lady Agnes said fretfully, turning to continue her way downstairs.

"Well, they won't, so don't press them to do so," Nell warned. "You know Crossways has requested that dinner be put forward in order that they shall be able to reach London before midnight. He has business to attend to there before they go on to Chatham.''

"I know," her ladyship returned over one shoulder. " 'Tis merely that—Clarissa, darling!'' Her tone changed dramatically when the doors into the drawing room were flung open by the young footman, Jeremy. Lady Agnes held out her hands—vinaigrette, lace handkerchief, and all—to her elder daughter.

While they exclaimed their greetings, Nell noted only that her sister had grown plumper since their last meeting before her attention was claimed by the fact that there were four people in the room, and not three as she had expected. Despite her desire to renew her acquaintance with her niece, her gaze was drawn, perforce, directly past the young girl, toward the darkly handsome gentleman behind her.

He was easily six feet tall, and his lean, muscular body was clad in buckskins, highly polished top boots, a buff waistcoat, and a dark brown coat. It was apparent, even to Nell, that his tailor possessed a skill far superior to that of her brother's man, for the dark coat was perfectly cut to fit a pair of the broadest shoulders she had ever seen and then nipped in again to hug the gentleman's lean waist and narrow hips. No ordinary tailor could have achieved such splendid results. The extraordinary breadth of shoulder gave the dark gentleman the appearance of being slightly top-heavy, but the buckskins did nothing to conceal the rippling muscles in his thighs and calves, so one could not doubt that his long legs would capably support his magnificent torso.

Nell realized she was revealing unmaidenly curiosity by staring at the gentleman's fine form and, with heightened color, lifted her gaze to his face. His thick, dark hair was brushed forward so that tapering locks and heavy sidewhiskers framed his tanned, strong-featured countenance. His jaw was pronounced, and the chin that rested upon the well starched folds of his neatly tied cravat gave the appearance of being firm to the point of stubbornness. His wide, straight mouth was, in Nell's opinion, well formed, though his lips showed a marked tendency to twitch just as her gaze came to rest upon them. Hastily, she forced herself to look away, noting only the way his dark brows seemed to knit together in a natural frown above deep-set hazel eyes and high, well-defined cheekbones before she smiled an absent-minded welcome at her sister and the Earl Crossways. Nevertheless, a sharp tug at her memory seemed to suggest something familiar about the stranger's face. It was Clarissa's high-pitched laughter that finally recalled her to her senses.

"Really, Nell, you look quite bemused. I told Huntley you would remember him, but he was as sure as he could be that you would not."

"Huntley?" Uncertainly, she looked back, only to find her gaze locked with a pair of twinkling eyes. The memory chord was plucked again, but the memory itself eluded her.

"Yes," Clarissa replied, clearly delighted. "Mama . . . Nell, forgive my manners, won't you, and pray allow me to make known to you the seventh Earl of Huntley, our darling child's betrothed husband."

Nell was still perplexed. The name meant nothing to her.

"Philip Radford at your service, Miss Lindale." He bowed, watching her closely with a lurking twinkle still evident in those deep-set eyes. His voice was low and a little gruff, but having heard it she wouldn't have needed the name to guide her. She remembered the voice, and the sound of it took her back over the years to her own short-lived social whirl.

Making her curtsy, she awarded him a dazed smile, striving to conceal the mixture of emotions washing over her at the memories his voice had stirred, and trying at the same time to discover a hint of the boyish face she remembered beneath the heavy sidewhiskers and the thick mop of hair. At that moment the penny dropped.

"Did you say Lord Huntley and Rory are to be wed?" she asked, astonished to hear her own voice firm and clear.

"Indeed, yes," Clarissa replied. "Philip and Crossways signed all the necessary papers before we left home, but our darling has insisted upon a proper come-out, and Huntley has kindly agreed to indulge her wishes. Fortunately, he has business in the area, so it will be an excellent opportunity for them to become better acquainted, will it not?"

"Indeed." Nell's voice did not sound quite so firm this time. She glanced doubtfully at her mother.

"I should think they would already know each other if they are betrothed," that lady stated, putting Nell's own thoughts into words.

"Well, we don't, Grandmama," said the Lady Aurora flatly, speaking for the first time. Nell's eyes were brought to focus upon her niece at last. Though she could still see vestiges of the ragtail hoyden of bygone years in the slightly narrowed, golden eyes and the stubborn tilt to the pointed little chin, she had to admit that Rory had turned out better than anyone might have dared to hope five years before. She was taller than Nell, and her slim-skirted, spotted muslin frock concealed none and, in fact, emphasized all of her slender, well-curved young body, from her high, full breasts to her rounded hips and long, tapering thighs. Her thick golden hair had not fallen victim to the merciless cropping so much in fashion with the younger set, but had been allowed to fall loosely in natural ringlets about her pretty, marble-like shoulders. Her only hair ornament was a bright red ribbon, matching the wide sash that nipped her dress in just under those magnificent breasts. Red gloves, sandals, and reticule completed her outfit. She swung the reticule by its tie-strings as she gazed directly at her grandmother and continued in a matter-of-fact tone of voice.

"Huntley's estate marches to the north of Papa's, and they determined between them to consolidate the two by making this match. So, it is merely a marriage of convenience, you see, and that is why his lordship has graciously agreed that I might cut a dash before settling down as his countess in Kent."

"Very gracious, indeed," commented Lady Agnes weakly.

But Lady Crossways took her at her word. "You may well say so, Mama, but then Huntley is always considerate." She smiled condescendingly at the dark gentleman, a gesture that caused Nell's own lips to twitch slightly.

Clarissa appeared to have changed very little over the years, except for her increasing waistline. But the added pounds seemed to have kept the lines of age at bay, for her rosy complexion, despite her thirty-five years, was as flawlessly smooth as ever. The present penchant for narrow, Grecian gowns did little to enhance her figure; however, she used her elegant India shawl to advantage, its deep folds and drapes doing a good deal to conceal the faults of her figure. Her light blue, dark-rimmed eyes were as lovely as ever, and no one could deny that the artless tumble of red-gold curls à la Titus was anything but vastly becoming to her.

Nell realized Huntley was watching her and felt sudden warmth invading her cheeks, but if he meant to speak to her, he had no chance, for her brother chose that auspicious moment to make his entrance, followed shortly thereafter by the arrival of Sir Henry Sinclair, who had been invited to dine. The latter gentleman's appearance on the scene, though he claimed to have arrived before his appointed hour, reminded Lady Crossways that she and her daughter required some time to freshen up before dinner. Crossways and Huntley likewise begged their hostess's indulgence and retired with Kit to change for the meal. Nell took her sister and niece upstairs, thus leaving Lady Agnes to entertain Sir Henry as best she might.

"Still just as fusty as ever," stated Clarissa once they had entered the pretty yellow bedchamber allotted to Rory.

"Do you mean Sir Henry?"

"Of course. Who else? 'Pon rep, Nell, I am astonished the old gentleman don't still powder his hair. He wears it long enough." She patted her own stylish curls with an air of self-satisfaction.

"He has been very kind to us," Nell said evenly. There were two other women, unknown to her and clearly of the serving class, already in the room, and she did not wish to continue such a conversation in their presence. "I do not mean to change my gown, Clarissa, but I'm certain my hair needs attention, and my woman will be waiting. So if there is nothing further you require . . ."

"Run along, my dear. Alice and Sadie will see to our wants, I assure you. But first let me say how pleased I am that you have agreed to show Rory just how to go on. The pretty puss has been cast into transports these weeks and more at the very thought of seeing Brighton under her favorite aunt's guidance."

Nell gave a wry smile. "Since I am her *only* aunt . . ."

The Lady Aurora chuckled appreciatively. "Aunt Nell, I

think we shall deal together famously," she said, stepping forward with both slim hands extended. Nell found her own clasped warmly within them. "I was so afraid you'd be an antidote, but I can see at once that you are nothing of the sort."

"Th-thank you." The words rode on a gurgle of laughter. "I think that must be a compliment. I shall certainly accept it as one. Now, do bustle about, you two, or Mama will soon be in a fret. Cook does not approve of odd dining hours, you know, and will be in a rare taking if you are not standing ready when her dinner is announced."

Clarissa's high-pitched laughter sped Nell on her way to her own room where she found Madge, the tirewoman who had served her since her come-out, awaiting her. Quickly, she seated herself at the dressing table, relaxing while Madge's skilled fingers dealt with the fashionable tangle of curls and plaits that adorned her head. Removing pins and brushing ruthlessly, Madge chattered as she always did, but Nell knew from vast experience that it was mostly rhetorical and required nothing more of her than an occasional murmur of interest. Thus, she was able to indulge her own thoughts without fear of offending her maid. That she might, as mistress, simply tell Madge to hold her tongue never occurred to her, which was just as well, for after years of similar indulgence, it would probably have done little good. Madge would merely think her out of temper and try to scold her into a more cheerful frame of mind.

Fortunately, such drastic steps were unnecessary, and as the brush strokes became a sort of underbeat for the drone of Madge's chatter, Nell found her thoughts returning to the seventh Earl of Huntley. There had certainly been more of a change in him than the mere change of title, she thought.

Philip Radford had been about twenty-four when she had first met him. He had been handsome enough then, too, although his looks had been a good deal more boyish and his hair, minus the sidewhiskers, had been tied back neatly at the nape of his neck. Of all the young men she had met that Season, he, with his easy sense of humor, expressive, penetrating eyes, and friendly smile, had made the greatest impression. He had been kind and attentive, easier for her to talk with than most of the others, and he had made her feel quite grown up. She thought they had become excellent friends, despite the fact that he had been merely the younger son of an earl and therefore not precisely the sort of young man her parents might have expected her to marry. Her grandfather, after all, had been a marquess, and that fact added to her father's very respectable fortune meant that Nell could look where she chose for a husband. It did not matter, however, for Philip Radford had not offered for her, and neither he nor any of the others had made an attempt to seek her out after her father's untimely death. She had no idea what had become of him, and she had managed after a passage of time to convince herself that it did not matter.

But now she recognized a strong sense of curiosity. What *had* he been doing these past years to change him so? The heavy, dark brows knitting together in a near shelf over those still expressive eyes seemed almost alarming now where once they had been merely interesting. Initially, to be sure, there had been that twinkle of amusement at her failure to recognize him. But the twinkle had faded rather quickly, replaced by a more cynical glint. He spoke little and seemed a good deal more at ease conversing with Lord Crossways, Sir Henry, or even Kit than he did when speaking to his intended wife or to the two older women. With Nell, he had exchanged not so much as a word after the introduction. It would be interesting, she thought now, to see if he would speak to her at dinner.

Madge brushed her hair up into a twisted knot at the crown of her head and confined it there with two jeweled combs and a slim braid of Nell's own hair. As a final touch she combed out a few curling tendrils to frame her mistress's face, then stepped back to view the results of her handiwork, while Nell checked to be sure her pearl eardrops were firmly fixed in place.

"That will do nicely, Madge," she said, smiling into the looking glass. "I shall want my lace scarf, and then you may go. I'll ring when I'm ready to retire."

"Certainly, Miss Nell." The woman returned the smile, then turned away to do her bidding. A moment later, looking precise to a pin with her lovely lace scarf caught up at her elbows, Miss Lindale descended the stairs to join the others in the drawing room. The gentlemen had preceded her, and Lady Crossways and Rory followed some five minutes later.

Scarcely thirty seconds after their arrival, Pavingham entered to announce that dinner had been served.

Sir Henry, nattily attired in proper evening dress, with his curling gray hair confined at the nape of his neck with a black silk ribbon, took his place opposite his hostess at the foot of the table. Crossways, of course, was seated at Lady Agnes's right hand next to Nell. Rory sat at her grandmama's left, while her mama and Huntley flanked Sir Henry. Kit sat opposite his younger and next to his elder sister. Nell concealed a little smile at the table arrangement. Unless Huntley's manners had suffered a great deal in the time that had passed, he would be forced to converse with her even if the conversation did not become general. She bided her time while helping herself to dishes from the first course as they were offered to her.

Crossways' attention was claimed almost immediately by his hostess, whose company manners were always above reproach. Nell overheard Lady Agnes saying quietly that she hoped the early rains hadn't depleted his crops entirely. His reply was lost to her, however, when Jeremy presented a dish of oyster patties and turbot garnished with crisp fried parsley sprigs, gherkins, and lemon butterflies. Nell helped herself to a slice of the fish with overlapping gherkin slices, then nodded to the maid carrying the fish gravy in a heated sauce boat. No sooner had Katy spooned some over her fish, however, than Huntley spoke to her.

"You are looking well, Miss Lindale."

"Thank you, my lord," she replied politely. "Do try some of the turbot. 'Tis excellent."

"No doubt. I prefer the oyster patties, however. Do you care for some of this spinach soufflé?" He indicated the side dish nearest his elbow.

"Thank you, sir." She allowed him to serve her, but when their eyes met, she felt as if his gaze went straight through her, numbing her. It made her feel nearly giddy, like a young girl again. Color rushed to her cheeks before Huntley's gaze slid away. It was a moment before she could speak. "I-I trust you had a pleasant journey." The moment the words were out she wanted to kick herself. What an inane thing to say! She had been out of the schoolroom for years and was practically mistress of her own home, yet she sounded quite as shy and tongue-tied as she had consistently sounded during her come-out. Despicable behavior!

Huntley answered her smoothly enough, saying that the journey had been no more wearing than one might expect. "The town seems already quite full," he added.

"Indeed, yes," she replied, smiling. "The Duke of Marlborough's house is nearly overflowing. They say that his highness has already complained of the noise, saying they will have to acquire better manners before Mrs. Fitzherbert arrives."

"Maria has not yet arrived, then?"

"Not yet, but both she and little Minnie Seymour are expected on Sunday week. It begins to look as though she will be able to keep the child, after all, you know."

"So I heard. The guardian angel wins through at last." He raised an eyebrow. "What do you think of that case, Miss Lindale?"

Nell was perfectly willing to discuss Maria Fitzherbert's efforts to adopt the eight-year-old child entrusted to her care some years earlier by friends. It was a topic that had fascinated her for some months. Other powerful members of the Seymour family, for many reasons, had been unwilling to agree to the adoption and had steadily refused to leave Minnie with the prince's mistress for longer than certain specified periods of time. At one point the prince himself had even offered to settle ten thousand pounds on the child if the head of her family, Lord Hertford, would agree to leave her to the care of himself and Mrs. Fitzherbert. Unfortunately, the offer had only made matters worse. Nell had not understood why at the time, but Huntley explained with a grin that it was because of an earlier friendship between a Seymour lady and the prince.

"The family feared his gift might be misconstrued, you see."

Nell chuckled. She had known only that the offer had been declined, the official reason having been that young Minnie would one day possess a fortune of her own.

"I think it was very kind of Lady Hertford to help them," she said.

The chief objection to Mrs. Fitzherbert, as everyone knew perfectly well, was her religion. There was widespread public prejudice against the Church of Rome, which manifested itself when a lawsuit ensued for custody of the child. It was not until Mrs. Fitzherbert was able to enlist the support of her friend, Lady Hertford, that a compromise had been reached. Lady Hertford was said to have coaxed her lord into claiming guardianship of the child, and once it had been granted by the Court of Chancery, she convinced him to allow Mrs. Fitzherbert to act as his deputy.

"Prinny certainly dotes on the child," Huntley said now.

"Indeed," Nell agreed. "There can be no doubt that he and Mrs. Fitzherbert both love her dearly. It would be cruel to separate them, especially in view of the fact that Minnie's spiritual welfare has now been entrusted to a bishop of the Church of England."

"Thus offsetting any Roman tainting at Maria's hands?" The cynicism had returned. His voice, though pitched low, was harsh.

Nell's eyes widened. "You speak as if you think I disapprove in some way, sir. I assure you I do not. Only those who do not know how kind she is have dared to question Mrs. Fitzherbert's motives."

"And she has been kind to you?"

"Indeed, sir. Mrs. Fitzherbert is kind to everyone."

Huntley looked as if he would like to pursue the conversation, but his attention was claimed at that moment by Sir Henry. Nell turned back to find Lord Crossways attending to his dinner. She felt oddly breathless, and it seemed strange to realize there had been others nearby while she conversed, however briefly, with the dark gentleman sitting so disarmingly near her. When he had turned to answer Sir Henry she had for a moment expected to find herself alone. It was very odd indeed to see her sister chatting with her brother and Lady Agnes deep in conversation with young Rory.

Jeremy appeared at her shoulder to clear the first course, and a moment later he was back with a roast of beef to begin serving the second. She spoke again from time to time with her dark neighbor, but the group at the table was a small one, and it was not long before the formal atmosphere waned, and when Clarissa complimented Nell on her lovely scarf, the conversation promptly became general.

"I own, I should like very much to have one made in a similar pattern," Clarissa went on, "however, I daresay such delicate lace must come very dear."

"Oh, no," Nell replied with a chuckle. "It was duty-free, you see."

"Came to the house in a loaf of bread, if you please," Kit put in with a laugh. When Rory demanded more information, the others realized that the topic was not precisely suitable for the dinner table, and Nell deftly turned the subject, but not before she noticed that Huntley's eyebrows were sternly knitted again.

Directly after dinner, Lord Crossways made their apologies and both he and his lady bade their daughter a fond adieu. Huntley departed with them in order that they might give him a lift to the house in the Marine Parade which he had hired for the Season, but before he left, he made it plain to both the Lady Aurora and Miss Lindale that they would be seeing more of him in the immediate future.

"Perhaps you will accompany me in a walk along the cliffs tomorrow," he suggested.

"We should be delighted, sir," Nell replied.

Next to her, Rory muttered under her breath, "Perhaps."

III

Having said their farewells in the entry hall, the three ladies returned to the drawing room, accompanied by Sir Henry and Kit. The latter, moving to stir up the fire, seemed slightly on edge, and it soon became clear to Nell, if not to anyone else, that her brother had made plans for the evening ahead that did not include an hour or so of idle conversation in his mama's drawing room. She had noted earlier that he scarcely exchanged so much as a word with their niece, so, deciding that his manners needed a sisterly nudge, she smiled at him and took her seat in an armchair near the hearth, directing Rory to take its mate.

"Kit, I cannot recall whether you and Rory met each other at the time of Uncle Edgar's funeral or not," she began.

"Not then," he answered, shooting a curious look at her. "I was at Eton, recovering from an ague or some such thing. But she was still here when I came down for the long vacation."

He did not sound as if it pleased him much to recall the fact, but Nell plodded determinedly on.

"Ah, yes. How foolish of me. You were both quite young then, of course. Do you remember Kit, Rory?"

"Of course I do," that young lady replied, grinning. "He pulled my hair, put earthworms in my boots, and presented me with an apple-pie bed so many times I grew accustomed to investigating my sheets each night before retiring. A perfectly charming fellow."

"And what about you, my girl?" Grimacing, Kit straightened, still holding the poker, and turned to face her. "Who put thistles under my saddle? And salt in my tea! And who exclaimed well within Papa's hearing that dear Kit had been ever so clever as to knock Colonel Hanger's wig off with a dirt clod from twenty paces?''

"But the colonel *must* have been at least twenty paces away!" Rory protested with a mischievous laugh. "A noteworthy accomplishment, especially in one's uncle."

"Well, Papa was *not* twenty paces away when you applauded my skill, and I daresay you were perfectly well aware of that fact.''

"Of course I was. But that was the very same day you had chosen to put three spiders down the back of my dress. I daresay you'd have received a far worse thrashing if I had told Grandpapa about that shocking prank.''

Nell looked at her brother with lifted brows, daring him to respond to such a home thrust, but he only shrugged and moved to replace the poker.

"I say, Aunt Nell, must I call him Uncle Kit?"

Before Nell could reply to this provocative query, Kit turned a stern eye upon their niece. "It will be as well for you if you do, miss, and show proper respect into the bargain."

Rory wrinkled her pretty nose at him. "Well, I daresay I shan't do either. You don't look very much like a proper uncle, you know, and I'll wager you won't act like one either. Did you design that waistcoat yourself?" Sweetly innocent, she turned golden eyes up to gaze at him with well-feigned interest.

Kit cast a swift glance toward his mother and Sir Henry, but they were in the process of settling down to a friendly game of piquet and were paying no heed to the young people. Thus reassured, Kit straightened his shoulders and tucked a thumb into his waistband, striking a pose that clearly showed his pride in the article in question, a dashing bit of gaily embroidered lilac silk.

"My tailor actually designed it, but I suggested the colors and the motif. I flatter myself to think it a rather successful venture.''

"Well, I think all those birds and butterflies flitting about in a lavender sky look pretty silly," Rory said flatly. Her gaze was still all innocence, and her hands rested demurely in her lap, but Nell knew in that moment that her niece had actually changed very little in the years since her previous visit.

Kit glared. "Do you think so, indeed?" His words were dangerously calm.

"That is exactly the sort of pattern I'd imagine on one of those French *incroyables* one hears about. All you need to complete the image is a curly topknot in place of your windswept locks."

It was too much. "A fop! You have the nerve to take *me* for one of those painted little pixies? I'll have you know, my girl, that this waistcoat is all the crack, and one of those—those jelly babies wouldn't have the sense to wash his linen, let alone turn himself out as natty as this. Why——"

"Enough, Kit," Nell chuckled. "Can't you tell when you're being roasted?"

"Roasted!"

"To a turn, my dear. Rory," she added, turning her attention back to the grinning girl, "it clearly has never been properly impressed upon you that whatever else you might say to a gentleman, on no account must you make a May game of his sartorial taste."

"Oh, but it *has* been impressed upon me, Aunt Nell. Why, I am persuaded that Mama has said any number of times that, on no account, must one criticize what a gentleman chooses to w——"

"That does it!" snapped Kit. "If you want me, I shall be at Harry's. Or else," he added airily, "Harry's man will know where to find the pair of us."

Striding between them, he kissed his mother hastily on the cheek, said a polite good night to Sir Henry, and made good his escape, probably, thought his much-tried sister, to one of the gaming hells rapidly springing up on the Steyne or along Ship Street. She eyed her niece with amusement.

"Do you mean to set us all by the ears again, Rory?"

"No, ma'am, only Kit." The golden eyes twinkled. "He responds so very satisfactorily, don't you agree? If I had said such a thing to Huntley, he would very likely have frowned and growled something about being sorry his appearance had offended me."

Before she could stop herself, Nell asked, "Does he frown so much then, your Lord Huntley?"

"Oh, ever so often! I think he does not approve of me. You *cannot* imagine, Aunt Nell." Rory sighed deeply. "Just think what it will be like to be buried away in Kent with a man who frowns at one whenever one turns around, and who looks like he is frowning even when he is not. Those eyebrows!''

"I remember I was used to think them interesting," Nell said thoughtfully. "You do not?"

"Interesting! Morbid is what I think them. Besides, he is very old, is he not?"

"I should not imagine him to be much above two and thirty," Nell replied on a note of indignation.

"There, 'tis precisely as I expected," Rory stated, much as though her aunt's words merely clinched the matter.

Nell glanced at the other two occupants of the room. This conversation intrigued her, but it would never do for Lady Agnes or Sir Henry to hear Rory speaking so improperly.

"I daresay you would like to get settled into your bedchamber, my dear," she suggested tactfully. "I shall take you up to see if you have need of anything that has not already been provided. I presume your maid has remained with you," she added as an afterthought.

"Yes, she has," Rory answered, getting obediently to her feet. Her eyes were twinkling again. "And my groom as well. Joe is at the stables, however, and I sent Sadie to have her supper and told her she need not return until I ring. So we can enjoy a comfortable coze, Aunt Nell. We shan't be interrupted."

Minx, Nell thought. But she did not grant her niece the satisfaction of a verbal response. Instead, she made polite excuses to the cardplayers and led the way upstairs.

"Is is not slightly improper to leave Grandmama alone with Sir Henry like that?" Rory asked, lifting an eyebrow.

Nell chuckled. "I think Mama can take care of herself," she replied. "She has known Sir Henry most of her life, after all. He is like an older brother to her."

"Does he chuck you under the chin and call you Miss Sly Boots? That is what my papa's brother does to me whenever he chances to visit us."

"Does he? Well, I am thankful to say that Sir Henry never steps beyond the line of what is pleasing."

"How dull for him."

On the point of entering the pretty yellow bedchamber, Nell glanced back at her niece, but Rory did not seem to sense that she had been impertinent. Instead, she appeared to be perfectly sincere, even a little concerned for the old gentleman.

A fire crackled cheerfully in the white-marble Adam fireplace, casting a dancing glow onto the delicate foliated pansy bouquets and *guilloche* border of the elegant Axminster carpet. The high, carved bed stood against the righthand wall, safely distant from the pair of tall windows, where yellow velvet curtains had been drawn to shut out any creeping draft of the dangerous night air. A pleasant jasmine scent wafted through the room from the pair of glass oil lamps burning on either side of the bed, and the yellow velvet spread had already been turned down. It was a cozy room, Nell thought, one that ought to please her charge. She glanced at Rory and was rather startled to discover that she, rather than the bedchamber, seemed to be the object of her niece's interest.

"Is all to your liking, my dear?" she inquired gently.

"Indeed, 'tis most charming. I shall feel quite at home." Rory moved gracefully to sit in a yellow velvet slipper chair drawn up to the marble hearth. "Do sit down, ma'am."

Nell drew up the dressing chair. "Shall I ring for tea?"

"Not yet, if you please." She paused, looking down at her hands. "Shall I have to apologize to Kit, Aunt Nell?"

Chuckling, Nell smoothed her skirt, then shot her niece a direct look. "Do you think you should?"

"Well, I don't think I said anything so very terrible, after all, and I'd just as lief not, if you don't say I must."

"I am not such a dragon, Rory. Kit can deal for himself."

The younger girl breathed a sigh of relief. "Thank heaven. I feared you might be a trifle fusty, after all. I am ever so glad you are not. Tell me what we shall do tomorrow."

Willing enough to pursue a harmless topic, Nell smiled. "First of all we must go to Donaldson's Library."

"Library! Aunt Nell, I am not in the least bookish." Rory's expression indicated that she was seriously alarmed.

Nell laughed. "My dear child, you do not understand. In the daytime, the social life here absolutely revolves around the circulating libraries. They are not mere bookshops as they are in London or other towns. Indeed, one *can* read at Donaldson's, I suppose. One may certainly buy or borrow the latest novels, plays, and poems. And one may also purchase supplies for painting and sketching and other such pastimes. But, to a much greater extent, Donaldson's is like a public club. One visits the place in order to meet other people and to gossip, to write letters on the piazza, or to look through portfolios of the latest scandalous caricatures. And besides all that, one can try a new piece of music on the harpsichord, take a ticket for a raffle, or even make up a table for loo or some other game. The first thing you must do, of course, is to inscribe your name in the visitors' book.''

"Visitors' book?" Once she realized that her aunt did not mean for her to spend her time reading improving works, Rory had begun to relax. By now her interest was piqued.

"Yes, indeed," Nell replied. "Once you have done that, we can visit some of the nearby shops. You will find all manner of things, such as rare china, lace, millinery, ribbons, muslin, chintz and cambrics, even tea. I daresay the prices may shock you, too—not that things are dear, for they are not. Indeed, some things are nearly dagger cheap. I have it on excellent authority that most of the goods sold in the shops along the Steyne have been smuggled in from France."

"Smuggled!" Rory's eyes lit up.

"So I have been told," Nell said, grinning at her delight.

"How exciting it would be to meet a real smuggler!" Rory exclaimed. "Or, better still, to ride along on a smuggling venture."

Nell returned to earth with a bang. "Nonsense," she said briskly. "I am persuaded that you would find such a journey vastly uncomfortable. Now," she continued hastily, fearing her lively niece would dispute that opinion, "a day or so after you have signed the visitors' book, Mr. Wade will come to call upon you here. He is the master of ceremonies at the Castle Inn, which is across the square from the prince's Marine Pavilion. Assemblies are held at the Castle every Monday, you know, but one needs an invitation in order to be admitted. Mr. Wade will attend to that and will also see that you always have a partner."

"I have been to small private parties at home, and Mama took me to an assembly in Tunbridge Wells once, even though I was not properly out, of course," Rory said. "There was a Mr. Brooke there who attended to such details, but I never required an introduction from him. I do not seem ever to lack for partners, Aunt Nell." The statement was made with simple pride, and looking at her lovely niece, Nell did not for a moment doubt its veracity. A young woman as beautiful as the Lady Aurora Crossways would need little assistance from the Mr. Wades of the world. Rory had paused and seemed now to be deep in thought.

"What is it, dear?"

"I was just wondering if it would be necessary to inform Mr. Wade that I am betrothed," she replied candidly. "Must he know, ma'am?"

"Well, I see no reason to volunteer the information if you do not wish it. But if he should ask you, you must tell him the truth. Why would you want to keep such information a secret, dear?"

"Because I shall discover a good deal more pleasure if people are not constantly reminding me that I already belong to Huntley. I mean to enjoy my freedom as long as I am able, Aunt Nell, and people will be always on the watch for me to misbehave if they know I am spoken for, will they not?"

It was certainly the way of the world. Nevertheless, Nell could not deny that she would be grateful for anything that would ensure Rory's good behavior. The more she heard, the less certain she was that she would be able to keep her lively niece in line. Clearly, Rory was accustomed to going her own road. Her naive assumption that she could do as she pleased if no one knew of her betrothal was nearly frightening. Nell was wise enough, however, to realize that it would do little good to begin their relationship with a stern lecture. Besides, there were other matters she wished to discuss, and the opportunity at hand was too good to miss.

"Rory, dear, do you mind if I ask you something rather personal?" The girl shook her head, albeit with a hint of wariness in her expression. "I cannot help noting from your conversation that you are not particularly enthusiastic about this match. Surely, it is not being forced upon you?"

"Of course not. But 'tis the custom among persons of our station, is it not, for parents to select their daughter's husband?"

"Yes, of course. But your parents dote upon you. I find it hard to believe you were not consulted in this important matter."

Rory frowned. "I suppose I was consulted. Papa said he thought, being that Huntley was past the age of foolishness, that he could be brought up to scratch, which sent Mama into transports of delirium, so I could not but realize that the match is an excellent one. I shall be a countess, you know, and the pin money he has promised me would make you stare, Aunt Nell. He is vastly rich, you know. Though he was not such a fool as to scoff at the chance to acquire Papa's estates, of course.''

''But you do not love him, Rory,'' Nell said gently.

''Of course not. Nor he me. That would be very unfashionable, would it not? I expect I shall find romance elsewhere, however.''

Nell stared at her, shocked at last. ''Romance?''

''Well, of course,'' Rory replied, wide-eyed. ''Does not every woman long for romance?'' Nell allowed herself a bemused nod, not trusting herself to speak. Rory went on. ''I own I should like to be really, truly in love, but I doubt it is in my nature. The minute I think I am in love—and I have thought so many times, you know—I discover something about him that puts me right off. Like my drawing master, for example. He was a delightful man. Handsome beyond permission and a voice that could charm anyone, but I soon discovered he had no sense of humor. And Hailey, Papa's groom. A great sense of adventure. He was full to the brim with ideas and had a wonderful sense of humor. But I soon realized he would be quite out of place at an assembly or even in Mama's drawing room. So I fell out of love immediately.''

''Wh-what does poor Huntley lack?'' Nell asked weakly.

''Oh, any number of things,'' Rory responded without a blink. ''He is not at all romantic, you know. He becomes utterly cynical whenever anyone mentions the advantages of rank, though Papa certainly would not have entertained the notion of a marriage between us had he still been a mere younger son instead of a wealthy earl. And he makes not the slightest effort to win my regard. He treats me, in fact, like a child, and not even a favorite child at that. My behavior shocks him from time to time, and he has an unfortunate tendency to bellow when he is displeased. He does not understand that I am constitutionally incapable of sitting quietly and sewing seams as his mother must have done. Why, the first thing he told Papa after the betrothal papers were signed was that I must no longer be allowed to ride about the estate without a groom to attend me. Can you believe such fustian? I own I was vastly annoyed with him. And with Papa as well. For what must he do but agree with the idiotish man! I ask you, Aunt Nell.'' Rory spread her hands in a gesture that, in anyone else, might have been meant to indicate helplessness. But Nell did not think her niece was at all the helpless sort.

"Surely, no well-bred young lady rides unaccompanied in the country," she suggested for lack of anything else to say.

"Well, I didn't dress to look like a young lady at such times," Rory said flatly. "Whenever I rode alone like that, it was because I wished to ride astride, unhampered by skirts and conventions alike. I wore boy's clothing. Besides," she added hastily, "on my papa's very own estates, who would dare to accost me?"

Who, indeed? Nell thought, ruthlessly stifling her shock at the thought of her niece in boy's clothing. If anyone could take care of herself, she was willing to believe Rory could. She regarded that young woman with fascination. In the reflected firelight Rory looked like a vibrant, golden girl. Her hair glittered with gilt highlights. Even her simple white muslin gown seemed to pulse now with an orange-gold life of its own. Surely, no man could look at such a girl and not be besotted. She seemed nearly magical, a sort of fairy princess. No, not a fairy princess, Nell amended. Fairy princesses were by nature generally gentle, submissive sorts. Nell doubted that there was a submissive bone in Rory's body. His lordship would certainly have his work cut out for him. She wondered if he had half a notion of what lay ahead of him.

She realized Rory was waiting for her to comment. "I am certain you must feel perfectly secure on your papa's estates, dear, where everyone knows who you are. But I do hope you will not attempt to ride alone or improperly attired while you are staying with us. Not only Lord Huntley, but everyone else would stare to see you behave so improperly."

"Well, I brought my mare, for I was persuaded we should ride from time to time. I hope we may do so often."

"Of course we shall, if you like. There are some splendid rides along the cliffs, or we can ride to Brighton Downs one day if you think it would amuse you to do so. I enjoy riding very much."

"Brighton Downs," Rory repeated thoughtfully. Even as Nell saw the pit yawning before her, the golden eyes sparkled with enthusiasm and the lithe young body in the slipper chair showed even greater animation than before. "Is that not where the prince's regiment is encamped?"

"It is," Nell replied, carefully keeping her voice even. "We shall not ride near the encampment, however."

"Oh." The single word expressed a good deal of disappointment.

"For heaven's sake, Rory, surely you would not wish to parade before a bunch of unruly soldiers!"

"Well, no, not common soldiers, Aunt Nell, but there are officers as well, are there not?"

"Now, see here, young lady," Nell began sternly. But when her niece only looked interested to hear what she would say next, she broke off with a laugh. "I daresay now you are roasting me. But it will not do, you know. In your own village, where you are known, your behavior must generally be excused, but here in Brighton I beg you will be circumspect. Pranks will not be well accepted, and your behavior, good or bad, will reflect upon both your grandmama and myself. I hope you will remember that before you do anything improper."

"Oh dear," Rory said. "Then you, too, expect me to do outrageous things. I know that Huntley fears the same thing."

"I don't expect anything of the sort," Nell returned. "But from what I have heard and seen so far, I believe you to be as high-spirited as you were at twelve, and I'm persuaded that you rarely think before you act or speak. And that," she added when her niece looked stricken, "is plain speaking, indeed." She leaned forward, holding out a hand. "I have accepted the duties of a chaperon, my dear, but I am truly not a dragon. I do hope we shall be friends."

Rory flashed her a brilliant smile and grasped the outstretched hand warmly. "We shall be, Aunt Nell. I just know we shall be. And I shall try very hard not to do anything that will bring discredit to you or to Grandmama. I may still roast Kit occasionally, may I not?"

"With my goodwill," Nell laughed, giving Rory's hand a quick squeeze. "It may help prevent him from putting himself on too high a form." She got up and moved to pull the bell. "I believe I shall ring for tea now, dear. I know the hour is not yet far advanced, but you have had a tiring journey and will wish to be at your best tomorrow. An early night will be good for both of us. I doubt that we shall see many of them in the days ahead."

"Shall we be very busy, ma'am?"

"Indeed we shall. Once word gets around that I am sponsoring my beautiful niece, we shall have more invitations than we shall be able to answer."

"Shall we be invited to the Pavilion?"

"Oh, dear." Nell paused, with her hand on the tapestry bell pull, staring at her niece in dismay. "It never occurred to me to ask Clarissa whether she meant that for you or not. However," she added quickly when Rory moved to protest, "I daresay she would have mentioned it if she objected." She pulled the bell. "Just see that you remember to show proper respect to Mrs. Fitzherbert if you should chance to meet her."

"The prince's mistress?" Rory looked more excited than shocked by the possibility.

"Here in Brighton many look upon her as the prince's true wife," Nell told her. "She is very kind, and many think she has not been fairly treated. 'Tis all on account of that infamous Marriage Act, you know. Her marriage to the prince was never annulled, because it was not considered to be legal in the first place—not having the King's blessing and all."

"Were they actually married, Aunt Nell? I heard 'twas nothing but fudge."

Nell nodded. "We believe so, at any rate. 'Tis on account of Mrs. Creevey, Mama's good friend, telling us last autumn—I believe 'twas just before the action at Trafalgar, you know—that Prinny had suffered a curious slip of the tongue. He was telling Mrs. Creevey how he had spent the day quietly alone with Mrs. Fitzherbert at her house on the Steyne, which—and these were his very own words, mind you—was certainly very *unfashionable*. Now, does that not show that he, at least, believes himself to be her lawful husband? For how else could he possibly have thought his actions unfashionable?"

Rory went into a peal of laughter, startling the maid who entered just then with the teatray. "Oh, Aunt Nell, 'tis unanswerable proof, to be sure."

"Well, we thought so," Nell replied with a smile. "Put the tray on that table, Katy. We mean to help ourselves." The maid bobbed a curtsy and left them to investigate the covered dishes. "Oh, good. Cinnamon muffins," Nell said. "Cook makes excellent muffins. Do have one."

"What about the Princess Caroline of Brunswick, then?" Rory asked once she had buttered her muffin.

"We do not see Prinny's wife here or his daughter, either,"

Nell replied simply, pouring them each a cup of hot tea. "Indeed, he seems a good deal less interested in poor Princess Charlotte than in Mrs. Fitzherbert's little Minny. You will often see him with them as they stroll among the visitors on the Steyne or drive in his carriage along the esplanade."

Rory frowned suddenly. "You told Huntley we would drive with him on the esplanade tomorrow," she said slowly. "Must we?"

Nell sipped her tea, watching her companion over the rim of the fragile cup. She did not reply until she had replaced the cup in its saucer. "We must. He wants to get to know you better, my dear, and I must say that considering you will soon be his wife, I should think you would agree that his intentions are admirable and do all in your power to help him achieve his purpose."

"He did not even say what time he means to call for us." Rory sounded sulky.

"Never mind that, child," Nell said comfortably. "I daresay that if we do not chance to meet him at Donaldson's Library, he will contrive to send a message here to the house. He is a gentleman who is perfectly capable of dealing with such minor details."

Rory sighed and reached for another muffin.

IV

The following morning dawned crisp and clear. When the middle-aged chambermaid who brought Nell her morning chocolate opened the moss-colored velvet drapes in her bedchamber, bright rays of sunshine spilled across the mellow-toned Holbein carpet, almost touching the embroidered flounce of her bed. The bedchamber, not being one of the principal rooms of the house, looked both to the south and to the east and, situated as it was on the second floor, presented a fine view—on sunny days, at least—of bright chalk cliffs and sparkling blue sea.

Sitting up, Nell stretched and pulled off her cap, pushing the resultant tumble of curls back over her shoulders as the maid plumped pillows behind her.

"Open a window, Mary. 'Tis a lovely day."

"You'll catch your death, Miss Nell." But, moving obediently to do her mistress's bidding, Mary did not speak as if she entertained any expectation of her words being heeded. Nell grinned at her stiff back.

"Hundreds of people come to Brighton every year for the sole purpose of breathing our wonderful air, Mary."

"Be that as it may, Miss Nell, that air is damp, and you know quite as well as anyone that damp air carries ague and a plague of other nasty things. Windows was meant to be shut."

Nell chuckled. "Is Lady Aurora awake yet?"

"Dunno, I'm sure, miss," Mary replied, adjusting the sash to admit as little as possible of the gentle sea breeze. "That maid of 'ers be a saucy piece o' goods, 'n all. Said 'er ladyship preferred 'er own people about 'er, 'n would I be so good as to leave the chocolate on the landing side table fer 'er

44

to take in when 'er mistress be ready. I never saw the like afore, Miss Nell, 'n that's God's own truth, that is.''

"Oh dear." Nell regarded the chambermaid with dismay. Mary had been with the family quite as long as either Cook or Pavingham, which was to say since before Nell herself had joined the Lindale household. When Nell was old enough to make her come-out, it had been suggested that Mary might well serve as her tirewoman. But Mary herself had declined the honor, saying that she knew her place well enough, thank you, and Miss Nell deserved the best, which in Mary's opinion meant a proper dresser. She had therefore greeted Madge's arrival in the household with her fullest approval. But, whether she knew her place or not, she took full advantage—often—of the fact that she had known her mistress from the cradle, and Nell knew that if she was to have any peace at all, she must soothe Mary's obviously ruffled feelings at once. "Was she rude to you, Mary?"

"Not to say rude exactly, Miss Nell.'' The maidservant was already coming down from the boughs. "She's just a bit full of 'erself, is all. I'll warrant 'er young lady spoils 'er a mite.''

"Well, I shall speak to the Lady Aurora, if you like," Nell said pacifically. "I daresay young Sadie has taken a bit more upon herself than her mistress has any notion of." Her eyes twinkled suddenly. " 'Twould doubtless serve her well and good if you were to *allow* her to do everything for her mistress.''

Mary grinned, catching her meaning at once. "It would at that, Miss Nell. I daresay we'd soon 'ave that wench begging fer mercy if she was to find 'erself 'auling water and wood up them narrow back stairs. Laying fires, changing the bed . . . ah, 'tis a beautiful vision I'm enjoying just now, Miss Nell.''

"I see that I can safely leave the problem in your capable hands, Mary. I rely upon you to see that she does not complain of ill treatment to her mistress, however. I'd as lief not have the business dropped back in my lap, if it is all the same to you.''

Mary laid the chocolate tray gently across her mistress's lap. "Never you fret, Miss Nell. I can deal with that baggage if anyone can. Just you leave 'er to me. Shall I be sending Madge up when I go downstairs?''

"If you please," Nell agreed. "Tell her I shall want her in

twenty minutes. Until then, I mean to enjoy the peace and quiet. I daresay the time will come that I shall look back upon these unencumbered moments with great longing."

Mary rolled her eyes heavenward. "Like that, is it, miss?"

"I'm afraid so, Mary. Indeed, I am very much afraid so."

Shaking her head in sympathy, Mary departed, leaving her mistress to relax against her pillows, savoring the sweet hot chocolate. What on earth, Nell wondered, watching steam rise from the cup in her hands, had she let herself in for? Any young woman who could mention Philip Radford in the same breath as a groom who would fail to bring an acceptable aura to her mama's drawing room would bear watching. A good deal of watching.

Not common soldiers, Aunt Nell, but there are officers as well, are there not?

Nell shuddered at the encroaching memory, devoutly praying that Rory had indeed been speaking in jest. What lurking devil had spurred her to mention the Downs at all? Was it not only natural that the one word should lead an impressionable young girl's thoughts directly to the military?

After all, Brighton Camp was by far the most famous military encampment along the South Coast. For some ten years and more, parades, grand reviews, field days, and sham battles on the Downs had been part and parcel of each succeeding Season's delights. The resident townspeople had come to regard them as entertainments got up expressly for their benefit, rather than for the serious purpose of military training, and they turned out right along with their summer visitors on these occasions in every sort of conveyance. Barouches, landaus, landaulets, sociables, curricles, tandems, and even fish carts—all were crammed with spectators and loaded with provisions for a merry day's outing on the Downs. It was not always possible, however, for these entertainments to be conducted with strictest military discipline and decorum. As the result of any number of unfortunate incidents over the years, Brighton fathers consistently discouraged their daughters from associating with the military.

The Prince's Own was indeed stationed on the Downs, just as Rory said, and that glorious Hussar regiment was easily the most popular in the Army among fashionable young men. Almost every one of the officers was a personal friend of the Prince of Wales, and even the famous Beau Brummell once numbered among them. They kept their own blood horses, their own swift curricles, and even—some said—their own dashing ladies. Their military duties being by no means arduous, they had plenty of time to join in the social activities of the *beau monde*, so nearly every young woman who came to Brighton dreamed of being escorted by a smart young cavalry officer in a dazzling scarlet or blue uniform. And since the assemblies at both the Castle Inn and the Old Ship were extremely popular with those young officers who were privileged to receive invitations, Nell had no doubt that her beautiful young niece expected to have her pick of the lot.

An image of Lord Huntley suddenly flitted across her mind, and Nell drew a long breath. How on earth was she to guard his intended wife for him? For she had no doubt from what she remembered of him that he would expect her to do exactly that. It did not matter that Clarissa and Crossways undoubtedly expected the same thing. They had shirked their own duty by casting the office onto her inadequate shoulders. Let them reap what they had sown. But Huntley was a different case entirely. He had had little choice in the matter and must therefore place his dependence upon Nell. Of course, he would no doubt be willing to help her. The thought let her relax again. Surely, he could be depended upon to protect Rory from herself. It would be simply a question of keeping her well enough occupied so that she would have little time to get into mischief. Nell smiled at the thought that she had previously worried about the difficulty of finding suitable young men to interest her niece. Now she found herself hoping they would be in short supply.

She was not given much more time to ponder her difficulties, for Madge soon entered and began to lay out her clothes. Less than an hour later Nell entered the breakfast parlor neatly attired in a walking dress of russet sarcenet with a striped tunic and kid boots. Her mother and brother sat at the table, the latter rising to greet her entrance, then seating himself quickly in order to reapply his attention to his high-piled plate. Nell regarded the cup of tea that occupied, in solitary splendor, the space before Lady Agnes.

"Not feeling quite the thing this morning, Mama?"

"Oh, I'm perfectly stout, dear." Lady Agnes smiled wryly. "Indeed, I am a trifle too stout. In no time at all I am persuaded I shall be quite as fat as Clarissa, for Millicent has had to let out three of my new gowns. I thought perhaps I might have a little dry toast if the tea does not satisfy my hunger sufficiently.''

"Nonsense, Mama, you will never be fat, and you must eat something more substantial than that. Fasting cannot be good for you. You will make yourself ill.''

"Well, you know I always have a glass of wine and a biscuit at midday, Nell. I daresay I shall do well enough. And only think of the money Cook can save if I don't eat so much.''

"I think it would be wiser simply to ask Cook to return to plain fare for a time and to forget the rich sauces you enjoy so frequently. I am persuaded 'twould do you far more good than starving yourself, ma'am.''

"Oh, Nell, we could not do that. Why, whatever would that young French kitchenmaid find to do if Cook ceased to require her lovely sauces? You know we hired her particularly for the purpose.''

"Aimée is grateful to have a position, Mama. After the dreadful ordeal of escaping from her homeland to a strange shore with two tiny children in hand, she would scrub floors and still be happy.''

"But her family is a noble one," protested Lady Agnes. "It seemed somehow almost suitable when she was merely providing us the benefit of her exquisite sauces. But to ask her to scrub floors . . . no, no, Nell. I couldn't.''

Nell chuckled. "I never said you should, ma'am. I merely said she would not refuse. Our family is also a noble one. You, after all, are the daughter of a marquess, are you not?''

"You know I am, dearest," her ladyship replied complacently, "and whatever anyone might say, I did not marry beneath myself when I married your dear papa. His birth was respectable and his fortune made him perfectly eligible. But what has that to say to anything?''

"Merely, that if circumstances required it of you, I have no doubt that you would have scrubbed floors in order to keep your children from starving after Papa died.''

Lady Agnes looked doubtful. "I shall not dispute your word, of course, my dear. But I confess I am most grateful that I was never put to such a test.''

"I am also grateful to have been wellborn, Mama, and in a civilized country where people do not cut off one's head merely because one chances to be well off. But Aimée and her babies are safe now, and if Cook were to ask her to help with mere plain cooking, she would not object. Now, do let me help you to some of this ham. I am persuaded that you will enjoy it.''

Lady Agnes agreed that perhaps a small morsel of ham, a bit of cheese, and perhaps even a very small chunk of bread thinly spread with butter would not cause her to burst the seams of her lovely lavender morning gown. Liberally following her directions, Nell soon placed a plate before her and set another for herself.

''Where is her ladyship this morning?'' Kit inquired, sitting back in his chair and nodding when Jeremy asked if anyone would care for more hot tea.

''I don't know, I'm sure,'' Nell replied. ''I believe she will be down when she is dressed. We are going to Donaldson's this morning.''

He shook his head. ''You will have your hands full, Nell.''

''Don't be nonsensical. She is already betrothed. It is merely a matter of making her known to the *beau monde*. Rory will behave with propriety, my dear. It would please me, by and bye, if you would not provoke her.''

''I? Provoke *her*? Seems to me the boot was on the other foot last night.''

''You were scarcely conciliating, Kit.''

''See here, Nell, if you mean to begin the day by reading me a lecture——''

''I mean no such thing, Kit, and I apologize if it sounded like that.'' She smiled coaxingly. ''What are your plans for the day?''

He shrugged. ''I expect Harry and I will think of something.''

''I cannot conceive why you should wish to spend so much of your time with Harry Seton,'' Lady Agnes said, narrowing her eyes. ''I am persuaded that neither your papa nor Sir Henry would approve of the association. Mr. Seton appears to me to be the sort of young man who would sit in a window with his telescope trained on the ladies' bathing machines.''

A slight flush on her brother's cheeks informed Nell that this pastime was not altogether unfamiliar to him, and she judged it time to intervene in the conversation. ''Mr. Seton has been a good friend to Kit, Mama. You know he has. I expect they will join the rest of the world in a stroll on the Steyne. Will you not, Kit?''

He smiled at her gratefully. "I expect so. Will you both excuse me now?''

"What, not leaving on my account, are you, Uncle Kit?"

Rory stood in the doorway, a vision in narrow turquoise-and-pink stripes. Her lovely hair was bound with fillets, à la Greque, and her slimly tailored walking dress showed her trim figure to advantage. She grinned at her uncle, already half out of his chair.

Kit straightened. "Good morning. I trust you slept well.''

Nell hid a smile. Clearly, her brother was determined not to be drawn. Rory stepped forward to inspect the dishes laid out for breakfast "I slept very well, thank you. Good morning, Grandmama, Aunt Nell. Are there any sausages? I adore sausages.''

"Under the silver cover on the left,'' Kit directed. "Good day to you, ladies. I'm off.''

"I hope I didn't scare him away,'' Rory said sweetly as she took her place.

"Don't be absurd, child,'' Lady Agnes said with a warm smile. "Gentlemen are always in a rush to begin the day, don't you know.''

Rory returned the smile and brought her plate to the table, declining Jeremy's offer of tea and requesting chocolate instead. "Shall we go to Donaldson's directly after breakfast, Aunt Nell?''

Nell nodded, her mouth full of Yorkshire ham.

" 'Tis a fascinating place, Donaldson's,'' offered Lady Agnes. "I purchase my paints there.''

"Goodness! Do you paint, Grandmama?''

"Mama paints elegant little things on velvet and satin,'' Nell told her.

"How clever of you! Is it very difficult?''

"Well, not if one finds the proper paints,'' Lady Agnes explained. "So many of the dyes are quite wrong and will run or bleed or simply fade away. That is why I go to Donaldson's. Their supplies are always to be relied upon.''

Once breakfast was over, Nell and Rory collected their hats and gloves, and Nell ordered the landaulet.

"I frequently walk,'' she explained, "but Mama would prefer that we take the carriage.'' She paused in the entry, waiting for Rory to finish pulling her pink kid gloves on. It would never do for a lady to be seen departing the house while still in the act of donning her gloves. Soon they were both ready, however, and Pavingham escorted them to the waiting carriage with a properly stately air.

The carriage took them by way of Edward Street to the Steyne, past the Duke of Marlborough's house and past Mrs. Fitzherbert's house with its three arched bays and distinctive first-floor balcony. The balcony was deserted when they passed, but Nell explained that Mrs. Fitzerherbert and the prince often sat there together or with friends and nodded graciously to such passers-by as might merit their notice.

They were set down at the door of Donaldson's Library, and Nell instructed her coachman to collect them again in an hour.

"That will allow plenty of time for you to become acquainted with the best of the little shops hereabouts. Is there anything in particular you desire to purchase?"

"Only some green ribbons, if I can discover the correct shade," Rory replied. "I have a bit of the material I want to match in my reticule."

It was a matter of but a few moments for Rory to inscribe her name and direction in the visitors' book. Looking about the library afterward, she professed herself charmed by the decor, but Nell noted that her glances fell a good deal more readily upon the various young men visiting the place than upon the books, art supplies, or card tables. She hid a smile.

"Shall we look for your ribbons now?"

Rory, gazing in rapt admiration at a tall, dark-haired young gentleman in the dashing blue and gold uniform of the prince's regiment, did not seem to hear her, so Nell patiently repeated her suggestion.

The younger girl turned quite pink and glanced sharply at her. "Oh, yes, of course," she replied quickly. But she could not resist a look back over her shoulder as they passed out of the library.

"That is not the only uniform you will see, my dear. The town is quite heavily littered with them."

"Uniform?" Rory shot her a saucy grin. " 'Tis not the uniform but the young man in it, Aunt Nell. Was he not the most shockingly handsome gentleman you have ever clapped eyes upon?''

"You only think it is not the uniform," Nell replied gently, stifling an impulse to remind her niece that she was betrothed. "In my experience, nearly every young man looks extraordinarily handsome in a uniform. And those Hussar kits are particularly becoming. Just you wait till you see one of them in full dress with his pelisse and silver lace."

Rory looked dubious, but she did not argue, and they moved on to visit the shops. They soon found her green ribbons, made a good many other trifling purchases, and then Nell suggested they simply stroll for a while and enjoy the sights.

Rory had already exclaimed her astonishment over the changes wrought in the prince's Marine Pavilion since her previous visit. The onion-domed roof of the stables seemed to her to be something straight out of a fairy tale. She glanced at it again when they emerged from the last shop.

"What a truly magnificent imagination his highness must possess," she said solemnly.

"What a very expensive imagination would be more to the point," remarked a dry but familiar voice from the flagway close behind them.

Rory muttered something under her breath, but Nell was grateful to observe that her charge was all smiles as they turned to bid good day to Lord Huntley.

"Good morrow, ladies," he said with a polite bow. "I chanced to observe you from across the way but decided to await your emergence from that tiny shop before accosting you." He glanced at their many parcels and lifted an eyebrow. "Have you emptied the shops?"

He was looking very well this morning, Nell thought with a small glow of pleasure as she replied in kind. He wore a well-cut coat of dark blue superfine over cream-colored pantaloons and tasseled Hessians. Once again his neckcloth was neat but not extravagant, and his waistcoat of plain light blue moiré silk was typically conservative. The only glitter about his person was supplied by the four gold buttons on his coat and his heavy gold signet ring.

Rory seemed to notice none of this sartorial elegance. She eyed him with mock—at least, Nell hoped it was mock—disfavor.

"It is quite like you, my lord, to think of the expense of that magnificent structure instead of its beauty. He is quite abominable, Aunt Nell. Do you know," she added, pouting prettily, "that he does not even approve of fairy-tale knights in shining armor?"

"My dear sir!"

"I never said I disapproved of them," Huntley corrected evenly. "I merely gave it as my opinion that you would not really enjoy being courted by one."

"I said"—Rory turned pointedly toward her aunt— "that I thought it would have been wonderful to live in those days and to have a handsome knight in shining armor sue for my favors. And he"—glowering now at Huntley—"said they must have smelled quite dreadfully after being cooped up for an hour or two in their armor."

Nell looked at Huntley, her eyes dancing. "You didn't!"

He smiled. "I did. And before this young lady manages to prejudice you further, let me hasten to confess that I also pointed out the probability that being confined in all that tin was bound to make a man itch."

A gurgle of laughter escaped Nell, but Rory merely scowled.

"I told you he is not in the least romantic, Aunt Nell."

"So you did, my dear. Well, my lord?"

"Correct again, I fear." He smiled again. Really, Nell thought, it was quite odd how that little smile could gentle his harsh features. At times it made his lordship look almost like the young boy she remembered. The absurdity of the thought brought a touch of extra color to her cheeks, and she looked away quickly.

"We must not stand like stocks," she said a moment later, glancing at the little watch pinned to her bodice. "My carriage collects us at Donaldson's in ten minutes, sir. Will you walk along the Steyne with us?"

"Gladly, Miss Lindale. I have been noticing a good many changes since I was last here. Doubtless, it has been interesting for you to watch the continuous progress of things."

"Indeed, sir." She was at ease again, and they were able to discuss the changes that had occurred over the years as they strolled along the broad brick path on the inside of the railings that separated the spacious lawns from the encircling carriage road. It was Brighton's most fashionable promenade, providing the same opportunity that Rotten Row provided in

London for the members of the *beau monde* to see and be seen. Almost every day the prince and Mrs. Fitzherbert and their friends, as well as many of the nobility, joined the general throng of visitors on the Steyne. Although it was the fashionable promenade, it had not always been the most delightful place for walking, Nell remembered, especially in the wintertime. In earlier years when the ground had been rough and often muddy or encumbered by the fishing nets spread around to dry, the grass had been patchy and uneven, and a stagnant pool of dirty water had stood almost perpetually in front of the Pavilion. In wet weather, the water of the Wellsbourne flowed into it and ran down the Steyne into the sea at Pool Valley.

She reminded Huntley of that nuisance, and he nodded. "I remember the year the prince and the Duke of Marlborough provided for the arched brick sewer to be built," he said.

"So they did," Nell said with a smile. "And in return the Lords of the Manor gave them permission to enclose a portion of the Steyne in front of their houses. I confess, I am astonished that this lovely expanse of grass has been allowed to remain. One would expect a main road to have been cut through here by now. Do you know that even the footpath connecting St. James's Street with Castle Square has been left as it was? But the little winding stream is gone. Do you remember the black pigs that used to graze along its banks, sir?"

"I do. And," he added with a wry grimace, "I remember as well that one had to watch carefully where one trod."

Nell chuckled. "Rory is quite right to say you lack a sense of romance, my lord. I thought the little pigs quite picturesque myself."

"I daresay. I prefer to think myself a realist, however."

Rory made a small sound closely resembling a snort, and Nell grinned at her. "We are leaving you out of our conversation, my dear. It is vastly unfair of us to discourse upon a subject of which you can know nothing. Pray forgive us."

"I don't mind," Rory said, smiling back at her. "I was trying to picture the place as it must have been in the olden days." Nell stifled a choke of laughter and looked quickly at Huntley, who was looking very much taken aback. But before she could comment, Rory went on, "Those houses look new, Aunt Nell. What could you see there before they were built?"

"Only the Downs, my dear, and a distant view at that. This whole central area was open, too, for the railings were not here then. And the grass itself was not so carefully mowed and evenly thick as it is now. Most of the changes, I must confess, have been for the better."

There were a great many people strolling about now on the smooth green lawn and the brick path, the ladies lovely in their clinging gowns, and the gentlemen more severe in their dark cloth coats and pale pantaloons. Rory saw her first real fops mincing along arm in arm, their pomaded locks confined in intricate topknots or braided and curled to compete with any of the women. Unlike the other gentlemen, they reveled in brilliant colors and startling effects.

There were others, too.

"Who on earth is that?" Rory demanded suddenly.

Nell, following the direction of her gaze, saw the object of her amazement immediately. He was a spruce little man driving a green gig. But it was not the color of his vehicle that was so startling. Rather it was the fact that everything else about him was tinted to match. He wore green pantaloons, a green striped waistcoat, a green coat, a green cravat, even a green watch string and green seals. His gloves, the livery of his servant, and his whip were all green as well. But the most astonishing fact was that his hair, sidewhiskers, eyebrows—even his ears and chin—had been tinted with green powder.

"That," said Nell with a laugh, "is Mr. Cope, one of Brighton's best-known citizens. He is, for obvious reasons, known as the Green Man. They say that even his rooms are painted and furnished in green and that he eats nothing but greens, fruits, and vegetables. Altogether a rather eccentric gentleman, I believe."

"Goodness," Rory said, staring at the Green Man as he passed by. Huntley pointed out the fact rather astringently, and she looked at him in amazement. "But he must want people to stare if he dresses so," she protested.

Nell thought it politic to intervene at that point. "I see my carriage waiting," she said, holding her hand out to Huntley. "We shall expect you this afternoon, sir."

He agreed, promising to call for them at two o'clock. On

an impulse Nell invited him to dine with them that evening as well.

"I should enjoy that very much," he replied. "Unfortunately, I am engaged to dine at the Pavilion tonight. Plans are in progress for celebrating his highness's birthday, which falls on Tuesday, as you know. You and Aurora will be attending the ball?"

"Indeed, we will, sir," Nell said, firmly stifling an absurd sense of disappointment at his refusal to dine with them. It was merely, she told herself firmly, that she had hoped to help further his acquaintance with his bride-to-be. However, there would be time enough for that, and Rory did not seem in the least dismayed by the prospect of dining without the pleasure of his company.

V

Lord Huntley's carriage rolled up before Number Twenty-seven Upper Rock Gardens promptly at two o'clock. Nell noted his arrival from her chair by the drawing room window. Setting aside her book and glancing at her watch, she observed aloud that his lordship was certainly the punctual sort.

In the straight-backed damask chair opposite her, Rory shrugged. "I daresay he is. I have not myself acquired the habit of punctuality, however, so I hope he won't expect it of me. Do we go down or wait for him to come up here?" She showed little enthusiasm for either course as she continued to turn over the pages of the ladies' magazine she had been perusing.

"Pavingham will not show him upstairs because he knows we mean to go out directly," Nell said equably, "so I think we should collect our hats and gloves. And I expect you will be glad of a pelisse if he means to walk along the esplanade."

Rory sighed but put her magazine aside obediently. A few moments later they joined Huntley in the small green saloon on the ground floor.

"You are very prompt, sir," Nell said, greeting him with a wide smile. "I hope you do not mind that we have kept you waiting a moment or two."

"Not at all, Miss Lindale," he replied in his quiet way. "I took the precaution of directing my coachman to walk the horses."

"I don't think Aunt Nell was particularly concerned about your horses, Huntley," Rory said, her words tinged very slightly with sarcasm. "I daresay she feared you might suffer from boredom." She moved to the looking glass to straighten

57

her hat and so missed the quick flash of annoyance in his lordship's eye.

Nell saw it, but when he turned to look at her, the annoyance had dissipated. Nonetheless, his gaze was oddly penetrating. "It was most kind of Miss Lindale to be concerned—if, indeed, she was—for my well-being. However, I should not be a very practical man if I were to neglect the welfare of my horses."

"Very true, sir," Nell said lightly. "My papa always put the welfare of his horses ahead of his own. Shall we go?"

Huntley's carriage could be seen approaching from Edward Street when they emerged from the house, and once they were all inside, the coachman directed his horses toward the Marine Parade. His lordship had graciously taken the forward seat, so Nell was comfortably able to point out the sights to her niece.

Just as she was showing Rory the baths at the corner where the Steyne met the Marine Parade, Huntley signaled his coachman to halt.

"Would anyone else like some gingerbread or an apple?" he inquired.

Rory stared at him as if he had spoken a foreign tongue, but Nell grinned, nodding her pleasure as she exchanged a knowing look with him.

"I should very much enjoy some gingerbread, sir. Do have some, Rory. Phoebe's gingerbread is practically a tradition."

"I am not very hungry," replied her ladyship, "but in any event, I should prefer an apple."

"As you wish."

Huntley jumped down and strode across the street, and a moment later, leaning out, Rory exclaimed, "I thought there must be a bakeshop, but he is purchasing your gingerbread from that peculiar old woman on the corner, Aunt Nell."

"So he is, dearest," Nell replied, unperturbed. "That is Phoebe Hessell, and she is no ordinary old woman. Indeed, she served in the Army for five years as a private soldier."

"But females do not serve in the Army!"

"Phoebe did. She was even wounded once. Her daring ought to appeal to that romantic heart of yours, Rory dear, for many years ago when her lover was ordered to the West Indies with his regiment, Phoebe contrived to follow him. As I understand it, she was a strongly built, deep-voiced girl of fifteen at the time, though I'll confess 'tis hard to imagine her so right now.'' She glanced again at the wrinkled old woman, who, despite the clement weather, wore a knitted woolen tippet, a huge shabby bonnet over a well-worn cap, and long wash-leather mittens, the ragged ends of which quite failed to cover her weather-beaten fingers.

"She is very old," said Rory softly, "and does not look as if she can ever have been very pretty." Indeed, the woman's large nose, dominating a small face that resembled nothing so much as one of her own apples well dried out, made such a possibility as youthful beauty seem unlikely.

"Nevertheless," Nell continued, watching Huntley as he paused to exchange a few words with Phoebe, "she followed her Samuel by disguising herself as a boy and enlisting in another infantry regiment. And not until Samuel was sent home, suffering from a severe wound, did she disclose the secret of her gender and obtain her discharge. Upon her return, she found Samuel in hospital and obtained permission from the authorities to nurse him. As soon as he was sufficiently recovered, they were married, and they lived together quite happily for some twenty years before his death."

"That is a romantic tale, but now poor Phoebe is forced to support herself by selling gingerbread and apples on a street corner," Rory said, shaking her head. "I think that is very sad."

"Phoebe likes what she does," Nell told her. "It gives her a chance to talk with her many friends and to make a little extra money, but her gingerbread is not what saved her from the Poor House. His highness did that."

"The Prince of Wales?"

"Indeed, it is merely one of many examples of his generous heart. When he heard of Phoebe's plight, he called her a jolly old fellow and arranged for her to be paid ten shillings a week from his own purse."

"Ten shillings!"

Nell smiled at Rory's outraged expression. "Not a vast amount by your standard, my dear, but ample enough for Phoebe's modest needs, I assure you. She never overlooks an opportunity to sing his praises. Now, do push open that door again, for here comes Huntley, and by the look of him, he has purchased Phoebe's entire supply."

It certainly appeared as if he had done that very thing, for he had a bulky parcel done up with string tucked under his arm. As he climbed into the carriage, he handed Rory a shiny red apple. Then, signaling to his driver, he leaned back against the squabs and grinned at Nell, looking like a mischievous schoolboy.

"I daren't open this while we are moving, or we shall have crumbs all over us. I thought perhaps we might find a place to stop near the Bedford Hotel. Then we shall be able to indulge our appetites properly."

Rory stared at him. "Do you like gingerbread so much, sir?"

"I like this gingerbread."

They passed Black Lion Street, Ship Street, and Middle Street, and soon the carriage was rolling along past the Battery. The row of new hotels facing the open expanse of sand and blue sea loomed ahead of them on the King's Road, but the carriage turned onto the esplanade, and Huntley signaled his driver to draw up alongside the wide lawn that separated the cobbled pavement from the dry stone wall above the beach.

"Now we may enjoy our treat," his lordship stated with satisfaction, beginning to undo the string.

"One has a lovely view from here," Rory observed noncommittally. "Would it be flying in the face of propriety if I was to get out and walk alongside the sea wall for a bit?"

"I hardly think—" Huntley began.

"Not at all, my dear," Nell said in the same breath. Then, realizing she was contradicting his lordship, she bit off her words and raised rueful eyes to him. "I am sorry, my lord."

He shook his head gently. "Not at all, Miss Lindale. No doubt I was hasty. This place is hardly St. James's or Bond Street, after all. Her ladyship will come to no harm here, I think. Moreover, Laxton will watch over her and see that no young sprig dares to accost her. Pray do not stray beyond his sight, Aurora."

"No sir, I won't. Thank you," she added as he opened the carriage door and stepped out to hand her down. He saw her safely to the flagway, then returned to his place.

"We can all stroll a bit, sir, if you think we should go with her," Nell said, suddenly conscious that she was alone with him.

"Nonsense. I want my gingerbread."

Without further ado, he removed his dark leather gloves and opened the package. Then, withdrawing a snowy handkerchief from his waistcoat pocket, he spread it over his hand, placed a generous square of gingerbread in its center, and handed it to Nell. Their hands touched.

"It smells delicious," she said, hoping she looked and sounded more poised than she felt. Her fingers, even beneath her York tan gloves, seemed to burn where Huntley's hand had met hers. This chaperon business had hidden pitfalls. She could not remember being alone with any man until now except for her father and brother. It would not have been thought seemly. If, for example, when they had met so many years before, Philip Radford had offered to take her driving in a closed carriage, she would certainly have been accompanied by her maid, even as she now accompanied Rory. No eyebrow would do more than twitch should anyone chance to notice her—a mere chaperon—in the carriage with him now, though it would occasion a good deal of talk if she were the one walking along the sea wall munching an apple while Rory dined *tête à tête* on gingerbread with his lordship in the carriage. Really, the rules of society were sometimes a trifle odd.

"I'll grant the delightful aroma, Miss Lindale, but one is expected to taste gingerbread as well as to smell it."

Nell looked up, startled. His eyes were twinkling, and she remembered how interesting she had thought his face in those days gone by. How could Rory think he looked to be always frowning? With a quick apology, she moved to break off a small chunk of the gingerbread, then paused, realizing she still wore her gloves. Carefully, she set the little cake and handkerchief in her lap, then peeled off her right glove. Her nerves seemed to have a mind of their own, and she felt all thumbs. It would not have surprised her in the least if, instead of lifting the morsel daintily to her mouth, she had dropped it or crumbled it or even missed her target.

Really, Nell, she scolded herself, this is most unlike you. Get a grip, my dear. She had been concentrating upon her task and now, looking up at him again, realized that he had been watching her. She felt rapid, telltale color creeping into her cheeks. She swallowed quickly.

"'Tis very fine weather, is it not, my lord?"

"It is. I believe we agreed upon that fact only this morning."

"So we did," she agreed, searching hastily for another tack. "Have you very much business to attend to while you are here in Brighton, sir?"

"A little. Mostly humdrum stuff."

"Then you will have time to attend the festivities. Do you go to the opening assembly at the Castle on Monday?"

He helped himself to another generous chunk of gingerbread. "I am not much in the habit anymore of doing the fancy, I'm afraid. That is one reason I thought it only fair that Aurora have a chance to enjoy herself before the wedding. It will not be very gay for her at Huntley Green."

"But surely you do not mean to retire from society once you have married, sir!" She tried to imagine her lively niece rusticating permanently in rural Kent. It was a vision impossible to achieve, even with her fertile imagination.

"I daresay we shall make an occasional visit to London," he said, more as if he were mulling over the thought than as if it were a decision he had already made. "I have a house there, in Berkeley Square. My mother is there now."

"You do not go yourself?"

"Occasionally, for a day or two, to see my tailor or to have a word with my man of affairs." He leaned forward, peering out the carriage window. "I hope she doesn't take it into her head to wander off."

"My lord, why on earth did you offer for Rory?" The words came before Nell had any notion she meant to speak them. Huntley stiffened slightly, and she dared not speak again, but waited warily for him to respond.

He relaxed again immediately, and when his gaze met hers, she saw amusement rather than irritation. "You haven't changed very much, have you, Nell? Your tongue still outruns your head."

"Oh, sir, pray forgive me. I should not have asked such an impertinent question as that."

"But you did ask," he pointed out. "Do you wish to know the answer?"

Honesty as well as rampant curiosity made it impossible to respond in the negative. She nodded her head. "And curiosity is so unbecoming in a lady of quality."

"Nonsense," he replied bracingly. "Honesty must always be becoming to anyone. And you are, as I recall the matter, always honest, Nell."

She had scarcely noted his use of her nickname the first time, but she couldn't fail to note it now. "I have not given you leave, sir, to call me Nell. 'Tis not seemly in view of my position as Rory's chaperon."

The hazel eyes glinted with a near metallic hardness. "Don't play foolish female games with me," he said, but his voice was surprisingly gentle. "You gave me leave eight years ago."

"But that was eight years ago, my lord. We were friends then. Now I feel I scarcely know you."

It was true. Philip Radford had been an open, cheerful young man with easy manners and the patience to set a shy young girl at her ease. He had been noted for his tolerance, his generosity, and his kindness. Lord Huntley, on the other hand, seemed harder, more reserved, even cynical, as if the world and time had shown him too much of life. He was still just as handsome, and she had caught fleeting glimpses of the sense of humor that had once been so easily expressed, but as for the rest, he might as well have been a rather chilly stranger.

"We could be friends again," he said now.

"Perhaps, and I hope we shall be," she replied warmly. "It would be most uncomfortable always going about together if we could not be friends."

He seemed completely taken aback for once. "Always going about! What on earth do you mean by that?"

"Well, surely you mean to escort your intended bride whenever she goes out for an evening's pleasure, my lord."

"No, I do not. There can be no reason for that. She will enjoy herself well enough—probably moreso—without my escort."

Nell stared at him, wondering at her own vivid disappointment. "You cannot mean that, sir," she said quietly. "How much credit do you suppose the *beau monde* will give your betrothal if you ignore your intended bride altogether?"

"I daresay the betrothal will survive," he replied. "It is to be a marriage of convenience, after all. And it would not be convenient to me to begin by being continually dragged to balls, soirées, and musical evenings."

Nell felt a sudden flash of anger but managed to stifle it before it did any more than add light to her lovely eyes. "Do you mean to tell me, sir, that you have no reason for marrying my niece other than to acquire her papa's estates? I own, I'd not have credited the friend I used to know with such cupidity.''

"I offered for her," Huntley replied in measured, even goaded tones, "because it seemed the most practical thing to do. My brother died without issue, and the title will die with me if I do not produce a son, a fact that has been thrown up to me incessantly over the past two years by both my mother and my elder sister. You should meet them before you condemn my actions. I promise you, they both frighten the wits out of me.''

He seemed perfectly serious, and the atmosphere in the carriage had intensified to the point where Nell felt a distinct need for a touch of levity.

"Termagants both?" she inquired, lifting her brows and smiling at what was so clearly a jest.

But Huntley gave the word serious consideration, his heavy brows knitting into one.

"Louisa is a termagant," he pronounced at last. "She is married to Sir Gerald Dalrymple, whose family has royal connections. Nevertheless, despite such solid nobility to support him, I cannot recall a single instance when Sir Gerald actually showed the temerity to dispute my sister's word. I daresay he goes in terror of her just as I do.''

"I've no doubt you are roasting me, sir," Nell replied, "and I know for a fact that your mama is no termagant, for I have had the honor of meeting her myself, you will recall. She is a very gentle lady. I remember she always wore pale gowns when everyone else was striving for a rainbow effect.''

"Oh, Mama still wears pale gowns," he agreed with a wry twist of his lips. "Louisa wins through by her assertive personality, but Mama enjoys even greater success with a mere lace handkerchief and a crystal vinaigrette.''

"Oh dear!" Nell chuckled appreciatively. "My mama is much the same, sir. Whenever things do not go her way, out comes her vinaigrette. And the hartshorn, as well. She waves the one under her nose and drinks the other and contrives to look very weak and ill-used. But surely you do not allow yourself to be governed by such tactics as that!''

"Alas, you do not know my mama at all, Miss Lindale. She has perfected the use of such common weapons to a pure art form. Feminine tears, I fear, quite unman me, just as they did my brother and father before me. So what with Mama always crying over the shocking fact that, despite her foresight in presenting Papa with not one, but two stout sons, the succession seems now doomed to fade away only because of my dreadful lack of a sense of duty, and my sister saying much the same, of course, and saying it much more loudly . . . It was she who suggested the Lady Aurora, since the Crossways lands would so admirably increase the size of Huntley Green.''

"But surely there were other, more suitable ladies."

"If by suitable you mean older, there was only one. Her papa's lands bound mine on the east. However, even Louisa did not feel we should pursue that connection once she discovered that the lady in question possessed a hook nose, a wart on her left cheek, and forty years in her dish."

Laughter bubbled up again, and Nell had all she could do to stifle it. As it was, a small gurgle escaped before she could stop it. "How . . . how kind of your sister."

He grinned at her. "It was, wasn't it."

"Well, it was." Suddenly feeling as if eight years had simply melted away, she grinned back at him. "I needn't ask you how your proposal was greeted at Crossways, either, for my elder sister is as much a trial to me at times as yours is to you. It is quite lowering to reflect that your wealth and property must have put any other consideration to flight. Poor Rory." The last words were spoken without thought, but Huntley seemed to take no offense.

"Why 'poor Rory'? She seems well enough pleased."

"But she has such a romantical disposition," Nell protested. "Surely she must yearn for a love match!"

"You forget that she was raised by your sister, my dear." The cynical look was back. "Aurora may yearn for romance, but she finds the thought of being a countess with endless pin money quite palatable, I assure you."

Nell thought over his words and was forced to admit that, from what she had so far seen of her niece, he very likely had the right of it. She sighed. It seemed so wrong. But really, when one came to mull it over, it was probably not wrong at all. Rory would have security, a very fine old title, and a no doubt indulgent husband.

Huntley suddenly leaned forward in his seat, and she realized that her niece was approaching the carriage. His lordship pushed open the door and jumped down to assist her, but paused suddenly and stared.

"What is *that* thing?"

Rory was all smiles. Her eyes sparkled, and her cheeks were flushed from the cool sea air. She wore her russet pelisse, and wrapped up in one of its folds was something she was handling with excessive care.

"Only look at him, sir! Aunt Nell, 'tis the dearest little kitten. He was shivering in a nook of the sea wall and mewing so piteously. I'm persuaded he must have misplaced his family."

"More than likely, a wise mother abandoned him," Huntley said. "Which is precisely what you will do, Aurora, if you've got any sense at all."

"Well, I haven't, then, for I should never do anything so cruel." She put her foot on the step and turned beseeching eyes upon her aunt. "You will not make me abandon something so helpless as this, will you, Aunt Nell?" She held out her prize, a bedraggled, very small, slightly damp, gray kitten. From the look of it, Nell thought, it could not be more than three weeks of age. Her brow wrinkled slightly.

"I doubt it will live, Rory. 'Tis so very small."

"Of course it will live. I shall make it do so. Is there any more of that gingerbread?"

"Mostly crumbs, but it doesn't signify," Huntley answered, waiting impatiently. "I doubt he can eat. He still needs his mother."

"Just let me try." She climbed into the carriage and, taking Huntley's handkerchief from Nell, spread it on her lap and offered the kitten one crumb. To everyone's astonishment, the little mite accepted it hungrily.

"It will make him sick," Huntley prophesied. "He needs milk. And he is probably flea-ridden as well. I shan't thank you, Aurora, if I find tomorrow that my carriage has been infested."

"Oh, don't be so fusty, Huntley. Get in. He will take cold if we do not get him home soon."

He obeyed, and they were soon on their way back to Upper Rock Gardens. Rory continued to feed her protégé crumbs from the napkin, and the kitten seemed equally as grateful for the last bit as the first.

"He has been starving," she announced. "Anyone can see

that. Once he has been well fed, he will be a beauty, won't you, my dear.''

''In my experience, stray cats rarely turn into beauties,'' Huntley said with a near sour expression.

Nell bit her tongue. It was easy to see that he was annoyed, but she could think of nothing to say that might alleviate his displeasure. It seemed such a trifling thing. Of course, if Rory truly meant to keep the little thing, it might not seem a trifling thing to Lady Agnes. She pointed this out gently.

''Pooh, Grandmama will not care a button. Once she sees him, she will know he belongs with me. And I shall see she is not troubled by him one bit. I shall attend to his feeding and care all by myself.''

Nell wondered how Rory thought such a thing would be possible with the busy social schedule they would have once the Season truly began. But the thought brought another upon its heels that nearly caused her to laugh aloud. Sadie. No doubt most of the care of the stray would fall upon her shoulders, and it would be interesting to know just what might happen the first time she asked any one of the Lindale servants to assist her. On that thought, she looked up, her eyes brimful of amusement, only to discover that Huntley was watching her again, an enigmatic expression in his own eyes. She was conscious of a wish that she could share her amusement with him.

''I believe we are nearly there,'' he said almost hastily when their eyes met. There was still some distance to go, however, and he seemed disinclined to speak, so Nell passed the time listening to her niece crooning nonsense to the tiny bundle of fur in her lap.

Once they reached Number Twenty-seven, Huntley paused only long enough to escort them safely inside before taking his departure. Nell left her niece to the happy task of explaining to Pavingham that she would require a bowl of warm milk and perhaps some minced beef for her charge, while she hastened upstairs to warn Lady Agnes about the newest arrival to the house. Amazingly, her ladyship seemed not the least dismayed.

''Whatever will make dearest Aurora happy. I am persuaded that it must be a very nice kitten. I shall be interested to make its acquaintance. Now do, Nell, hand me that tambour frame. I'm of a mind to work some petit point, I believe.''

"Of course, Mama," Nell replied, concealing astonishment. Clearly, Lady Agnes no longer feared that her granddaughter would set them all in an uproar. "Shall I get you anything else?''

"No, no, dear. You run along and take off your pelisse. You will catch cold if you let yourself get too warm. You may come back once you have tidied yourself.''

Accordingly, Nell repaired to her own bedchamber where she doffed her velvet pelisse and decided to change her walking dress as well. Without bothering to ring for Madge, she made a rapid search of her wardrobe and decided in favor of a simple moss-green frock with puffed sleeves that tied at the elbow with narrow yellow satin ribbons. While she changed her clothes, she thought back over the afternoon and wondered what the future would bring.

Rory had seemed perfectly content to wander by herself, and she had been greatly excited over the kitten. But she still expected everything to go her own way, so if Huntley had no intention of lending them his escort on a regular basis, how on earth was Nell to keep her niece in line? She would have to embroider the fact of their betrothal on every gown the chit owned! Undoubtedly, Crossways would have arranged for a notice in the London papers, but there had been none in the Brighton *Herald*, and she did not think she ought to arrange for one herself. She decided she would simply have to have a straightforward discussion with her niece, in hopes of avoiding some of the worst of the problems that no doubt lay ahead.

VI

Despite Nell's good intentions, there seemed to be little time for a heart-to-heart chat with her niece. If she hadn't known the thought to be a ridiculous one, she might even have suspected Rory of attempting to evade just such a confrontation. To be sure, they both had a number of things to occupy their time. Mr. Wade came to call upon them Saturday afternoon and agreed that invitations to the first assembly at the Castle Inn would be delivered into their hands no later than Monday afternoon.

He stayed no longer than the requisite twenty minutes, of course, but his rival from the Old Ship, Mr. Hicks, was announced by Pavingham before Mr. Wade's footsteps had faded out of hearing. Rory thought them both quaint little men, if a bit more puffed up in their own esteem than they had any call to be.

"Very true, in these days of relaxed manners, my dear," observed her grandmother, who had been present during both interviews. "But Mr. Wade—or Captain Wade, as he was known to us then—once held quite an important position here. 'Tis the same position he holds now, of course," she added vaguely, "but 'twas of vast importance then."

She went on to explain that Mr. Wade had been a fixture in Brighton for nearly thirty years. "At first he officiated in Bath, too, alternating his time between the two towns. Only there was a dreadful scandal in Bath, so his services came to an abrupt end there."

"Mama told me about that," Rory admitted. "He read aloud some love letters a lady wrote to him. Mama said the whole town was angry with him. She had that from Cousin

69

Selina in Bath after she wrote to tell her I'd be making my come-out here.''

"No doubt. I had the tale from Selina myself some years ago. We were both quite young at the time it all happened, of course."

"They say the housemaids in Bath were too indignant even to make his bed," Nell put in with a smile. "And I must confess, Mama, I have always thought him a disgusting little man myself."

Lady Agnes agreed that Mr. Wade had never been what one might call truly popular in Brighton. "Your papa was used to say he neglected his duties for the gaming tables. I know nothing of such matters myself, however."

"Well, he still enjoyed a good deal of power the year I came out," Nell said. "Why, even theatrical performances were allowed only on evenings convenient to his plans. They were certainly never allowed on Monday or Thursday evenings as they are now."

"There have been other changes, too, however," Lady Agnes said with a sigh. "To be sure, there are a good many more private parties now, but Mrs. Calvert was telling me only the other day that the public ball at the Old Ship on Thursday last—the first of the Season, don't you know—was quite deplorable. She would have it that all the rabble was there. City beaux and cits' wives, she said, dared to mingle with true gentry and the nobility. I make no doubt the assemblies there will soon become *mauvais ton*, and I am not at all certain, Nell, that you would be well advised to take Aurora. I have heard nothing against the assemblies at the Castle, for of course, Monday's is the first. But in these modern times, with so many foreign elements about, one never knows what to expect next."

"Never mind, Mama. I shall endeavor to take good care of her." It was an opportunity for that conversation, Nell thought then. But she could not bring herself to take Rory away to the privacy of her own bedchamber. Lady Agnes would surely demand to know the reason, which would prove awkward to explain, and it was possible that more people would come to call upon them, too.

Indeed, Lord Huntley was shown into the drawing room not ten minutes later. Rory greeted him politely but seemed to have little to say to him, so it fell to Nell and Lady Agnes to maintain the flow of conversation. This task proved simple enough, however, once Lady Agnes thought to ask his lordship how he had been occupying the years since she had last clapped eyes upon him.

"For as I recall it, my lord, you went out of town not three days before my poor husband's collapse, did you not?"

"As to that, my lady, I cannot say, as I was unaware of your tragedy until some months later. I was, however, called away very suddenly."

"Not a death in your own family, I trust, sir."

"Unfortunately, ma'am. My father, as it happens, passed to his reward quite as unexpectedly as Mr. Lindale passed to his. He was—again like Mr. Lindale—quite a young man."

"Mr. Lindale was only forty-six," she replied, reaching for her vinaigrette.

His lordship eyed that gesture with undisguised alarm and said hastily that he had subsequently joined the Army. The vinaigrette hovered as her ladyship paused, replying that she had not taken him for a military man.

"Nor I, sir," Nell put in, watching his rapidly changing expressions with amusement.

He glanced at her briefly, then rather pointedly gave his full attention to Lady Agnes. "A military career seemed better than hanging on my brother's sleeve," he said, "but I stayed only six years. I wasn't much cut out for campaigning, though I served in a Hussar regiment on the Continent for several years before a bayonet thrust to the shoulder got me sent home just before Amiens. Subsequently, I transferred to the Tenth, which by then had been ordered to Manchester, supposedly for training. By the time hostilities resumed, my brother had died and I'd sold out. I confess, I am not precisely sorry to have done so."

"Your brother, as well," said Lady Agnes weakly, waving the vinaigrette under her dainty nose. "Poor, wretched lad. You have suffered exactly as my dearest Nell has suffered, have you not?"

Huntley was certainly looking rather wretched, and although he glanced helplessly at Nell, he managed to keep a wary eye on the vinaigrette. "Have you suffered so much then, Miss Lindale?"

"Indeed, oh, indeed she has," replied Lady Agnes in lachrymose tones. "You'll scarce credit it, sir, and I could not have been more sorely provoked, I promise you. But we suffered six of them in as many years.''

"What? Not deaths!" Huntley sat up straighter in his chair, then looked more directly at Nell, who was having difficulty retaining her composure. Thankfully, he addressed his next words to her mother. "You are quite right, my lady. 'Tis a difficult fact to credit."

"Nevertheless, 'tis the very truth, sir. Six of them, and very inconsiderate I thought them at the time, I can tell you. For what was my poor Nell to do when she must positively *live* in black crape? 'Twas monstrous unfair. As though Fate herself thrust my poor darling onto the shelf."

"On the shelf? How absurd! Why, Miss Lindale is quite as beautiful as ever and seems to have developed a good deal of character into the bargain. She is scarcely at her last prayers."

Nell turned quite pink at these unexpected compliments, but fortunately there was no need for her to reply to them.

"Oh, but she is! Or, at least, if she is not at her last prayers, no one can deny that she is beyond her first youth." The vinaigrette paused directly under the little nose, and to Huntley's all too evident discomfort, a lacy handkerchief appeared in her ladyship's delicate hand. "What else," she demanded mournfully, "could one expect, my lord, when she is all of five-and-twenty and insists upon behaving like a spinster woman? Besides, the eligible men hereabouts are not seeking mature young women of character. They are looking about for youthful beauties whose character they might mold to suit themselves."

This statement being clearly unanswerable, Nell took pity on his lordship and spoke up in her own defense. "Pray, Mama, do not speak as if you expect poor Huntley to mend matters. You will at the very least unman him. What's done is done and cannot be mended, and 'tis just as well, I'm thinking. For if I was not so clearly upon the shelf, who, pray tell, would take dear Rory out and about? We are already agreed, are we not, that it would not suit your delicate constitution to do so."

"Oh my, no!" Lady Agnes replied hastily before turning melting eyes toward Huntley. "For you must know, my lord, that the least little exertion oversets me. 'Tis my poor nerves. Ever since my dearest Lindale passed on, God rest him, I have not seemed to have the energies of my earlier days.

Why, the smallest activity—even a mere afternoon spent playing at silver loo—sends me to my bed prostrated for quite three days' time.''

"Amazing, ma'am. And you still so young and beautiful.''

"Indeed, sir,'' she returned, smiling without a blush, as both vinaigrette and handkerchief came to rest in her lap. "I am still quite young enough to enjoy life, I suppose, if it were not for the dreadful burden of my weakened constitution.''

"I understand your plight, ma'am. My own dear mother suffers from much the same malady, but she has suffered,'' he added with the wry twist of lips that was rapidly becoming so familiar to Nell, "for many, many years—even before my father's untimely death.''

"Poor creature. How very sad for her. Although,'' she added thoughtfully, "I daresay her form of the malady, while longer-lived, is not quite so acute as my own. Doctor Penworthy, after grievous expense, I might add— Nell, do you know his last bill came to more than three guineas? Well, at any rate,'' she continued rapidly as though she feared Nell might actually trouble herself to respond, "he told me mine is quite a unique case. And you must know he has treated a good many nerves, sir. But he gave me to understand that mine was quite the worst case he has ever seen.''

"Indeed,'' Huntley responded, coloring the one word with a well feigned display of deep interest. Nell was pleased to note that he did not make the fatal error of attempting to defend the relative severity of his mama's ailments against those of Lady Agnes. From what she had seen so far, he could not hope to win such a debate.

She glanced over at Rory, who was seated quite at her ease in a chair slightly removed from the others. She appeared to be gazing intently out the window, as if concentrating upon some fascinating view. But since Nell's own experience gave her to know that there could be nothing out there worthy of such rapt attention, she deduced that her niece was daydreaming. Deciding not to disturb her, she turned her attention once more to the others.

Lady Agnes had taken the opportunity to expand upon the various disadvantages of being cursed with a delicate constitution, and Huntley bore with it for some minutes longer before making deft excuses and taking his departure. The three ladies sat quietly for a moment or two before Rory stirred in her chair, thus drawing her grandmother's notice.

"You were very quiet during his lordship's visit, dearest," that lady observed. "I hope you did not take a chill during your visit to the esplanade."

"Oh, no, I'm perfectly well, thank you, Grandmama. I was merely thinking about Ulysses. Did you notice that Huntley did not so much as inquire after the state of his health?"

"Why on earth should his lordship be expected to inquire after a man who has been dead these many centuries?" Lady Agnes asked, perplexed. "If indeed," she added conscientiously, "he ever lived at all. I know there was a book about him, for your papa, Nell, had it in his library and tried to explain to me once about the gentleman's travels. I expect it was his Grand Tour, you know, although I confess, I never truly understood whether the gentleman was real or only one of those very confusing Greek myths. Nell will put us right, I expect."

Nell chuckled. "He was the mythical King of Ithaca, Mama. The Greeks actually called him Odysseus, I believe. But 'tis of little consequence, since I am persuaded that Rory was making reference to her kitten, were you not, my dear?"

Rory had been staring at her grandmother with an expression of near awe, but Nell's words recalled her to her senses.

"Indeed I was. How could he be so heartless as to behave as if Ulysses doesn't exist?"

"What a very odd name for a kitten, to be sure," commented her ladyship. "Are you perfectly certain you wouldn't prefer something simpler, my dear? Such as Fluffy or Buttons or——"

"No, for I am confident that his name suits him better than any of those would do," insisted her granddaughter. "I daresay he had a good many adventures and did a vast amount of traveling before ever he came up against that sea wall. At the very least, he deserves Huntley's respect for his efforts. You don't think," she added, regarding her aunt with a small frown, "that Huntley can have forgotten about him, do you?"

Nell thought that was precisely what had happened, but she could conceive of no good purpose to be served by sharing that opinion with her niece. Nor could she think of any good reason to point out the unlikelihood of a three-week-old kitten's having had a vast number of adventures. Consequently, she merely smiled and told Rory not to be such a goose.

"I daresay Huntley simply assumes that Ulysses, having found a kind mistress and a good home, is faring very well. I expect," she added, when the frown did not dissipate, "that he is not profoundly interested in cats."

"Well, he'd best take an interest in Ulysses," Rory declared militantly, "for he shall be living at Huntley Green with us, you know. In the house," she added in a tone that brooked no argument.

"I haven't the slightest doubt of it," Nell replied, having no wish whatsoever to debate the matter. Since Rory appeared only too willing to continue the discussion, Kit's arrival on the scene at that moment was greeted by his sister with unfeigned pleasure and even a touch of relief.

He was looking very dashing in a coat of bottle-green over biscuit-colored pantaloons. His hair had been brushed forward into tapering locks, and Nell had no doubt as to the identity of his model for the new style. Evidently Rory also recognized the source.

"Never tell us you are attempting to ape Huntley's looks! Do you mean to appear old before you must?"

"Old! I'll have you know, Miss Wisdom, that your Lord Huntley dresses in bang-up style. A fellow could do a deal worse than to imitate him. Why, he's as natty as Brummell, and you should be grateful. At his age, he might well have chosen to dress more like Sir Henry and worn a wig!"

"He is not a Methuselah, for pity's sake!"

"Kit, I protest!" his mama exclaimed over Nell's indignant outburst. "You should not speak so of dear Sir Henry. He is very good to you—indeed, to us all."

"To be sure, Mama," her son replied with a grimace of distaste. "You have no occasion to listen to his endless jobations. He read me a lecture only last night. Said I was drawing the bustle too tightly, only because I chanced to find myself temporarily distressed and asked him to disburse a trifling sum to my tailor."

"But your allowance is more than generous!"

"You may think so, ma'am, with your paltry notions of generosity," Kit retorted, his voice taking on tones of a rising temper, "but it scarcely covers the half of what anyone else of my acquaintance spends on the barest necessities. Not that

I wouldn't have paid Holton. I truly meant to do so. But that was before . . ." He broke off, coloring slightly, then continued airily, "Before something of greater importance intervened."

"A cockfight or a card game?" asked his sister with wide-eyed interest. He glared at her, but his attention was claimed again by his mother before he was required to answer her.

"I should think it would behoove you, Kit, to pay your tailor what is owed him before you hand over your money to a friend in payment of some stupid wager."

"Good God, Mama, a man must pay his gaming debts immediately or he can scarcely call himself a gentleman. Holton will wait. He is a mere tailor, after all. Even Brummell does not worry over his tailor's bills. He merely orders a new coat, and, by Jove, if Sir Henry don't come across with the juice, I daresay that is precisely what I shall do, myself."

"Kit, no! Sir Henry would be vastly displeased."

"And rightly so," agreed Rory, putting her oar in with uncivil relish. "Why, even I have heard of Mr. Brummell, while I dare say no one outside of Brighton has ever heard of you, Uncle Kit. Mr. Brummell must ever do his tailor credit—and his bootmaker and hatter as well, no doubt—but what good you can do your poor Holton, other than seeing to his eventual starvation, as well as that of his wife and no doubt fifteen or so children, I can——"

"Enough, Rory," Nell said, laughingly calling a halt to the enthusiastic spate of words when her brother's complexion threatened to become choleric. "Not but what she hasn't made a point, Kit," she added, quite unable to resist making at least that much of a statement herself. However, when he appeared likely to lose his temper altogether as a result of this final straw, she hastily asked if he meant to stay to supper.

He glared at Rory, opening his mouth as if he meant to present them all with a few well-chosen words, but Nell's question stopped him. He favored her with a long look, then let out a sigh. But he still looked grim, and his answer came more as a dare than as a mere point of information.

"I do. And what's more, I've invited Harry to dine with us, as well. There can be no objection to that, I hope."

"Of course not," Nell returned quietly, but Lady Agnes looked doubtful.

"I trust you sent word to Cook, Kit. You would not wish her to lay a meager table simply for want of a bit of warning.

It will add to the week's expenses, of course, but I promise you, I shan't regard it.''

It was just as well for all their peace that she added the rider, since Kit had looked to be momentarily upon the verge of an apoplectic seizure when she mentioned the extra cost.

Despite the unpromising introduction, supper itself passed well enough. Both young gentlemen were on their best behavior, and Rory declined to bait her uncle. Nell realized that the reason for this abstention was the fact that Harry Seton had taken one look at his friend's niece and tacitly declared himself her slave for life. The knowledge did little to alleviate her worries about the near future, and when she realized that Rory was flirting quite outrageously with the impressionable Harry, she had to repress a strong desire to box her niece's ears on the spot. Instead, she quite made up her mind to discuss the matter with her just as soon as the young gentlemen took their departure, which she was certain they would do immediately upon finishing their after-dinner port. Thus, it was with some dismay that she greeted Harry's announcement that for the ladies to leave them to their own devices was an antiquated notion not worth adhering to, and that he, for one, meant to carry his port straight into the drawing room so as not to have Kit's sole company foisted upon him along with the resultant, inevitable boredom. Rory grinned at him, but Kit seemed quite as disgusted as his sister.

"I say, Harry, we dashed well promised to call in at . . . that is, surely you remember we have an appointment. You will not wish to keep the others waiting.''

"Fiddle,'' replied Harry, looking quite as astonished as Kit did to hear himself using such a word. He recovered rapidly, however. "I daresay no one expected us to show before midnight. If we are there by eleven, we shall be betimes. I've a mind to teach your young niece here the finer points of piquet. Or,'' he added diplomatically, when Kit glowered, "perhaps we might play whist instead, if your sister will oblige us by taking a hand.''

Nell declined, so they finally agreed to play three-handed cassino instead. She left them dealing out the cards and arguing amiably over whether it was a children's game or one fit only for expert cardplayers, and went to fetch her book and Lady Agnes's needlework. Time enough later to lecture her errant charge.

The game grew steadily more lively and boisterous, however, and by the time Lady Agnes pointed out that dear Rory would never arise in time to attend chapel services, as one knew she meant to do, if she did not retire to her bed at a seemly hour, both young gentlemen seemed to have forgotten all thought of a prior engagement. The teatray had come and gone again, and the hour was advanced well past eleven. Nonetheless, when Rory agreed promptly that it was indeed past her bedtime, the others announced that it was time and more that they joined their friends. Lady Agnes's weak protest that Kit, too, required some sleep, was ignored entirely, and both gentlemen departed immediately.

"I am tired, Grandmama, so I will go straight to bed, if you will both excuse me," Rory said, stifling a yawn.

"Of course, my dear. I mean to go up myself. 'Tis fatal to one of my delicate constitution to keep late hours. I cannot think how I became so engrossed in my fancywork, for usually, you know, I am fast asleep long before now."

"I'm sorry if we kept you up, ma'am."

"No such thing. Nell was here, so I might just as well have gone to bed had the thought occurred. Don't bother your head, my child. I daresay I shall do well enough."

Nell listened to this exchange with well-concealed amusement, knowing perfectly well that Lady Agnes kept whatever hours suited her. That that often meant staying up reading or working her petit point until well past midnight was a well-kept secret, however. But since her ladyship was quick to assert that she knew she could not sleep if she tried, even Nell forebore to tease her. Lady Agnes's delicate constitution, while serving as an excellent excuse whenever she wished to avoid any distasteful duty, rarely interfered with her pleasure.

Rory moved toward the door, but Nell spoke before she reached it. "I should like to have a word with you, dear, if you don't mind. I shall come to your bedchamber directly."

"Oh, I should like a comfortable coze above all things, *dear* Aunt Nell. But as it happens, I have the headache. Only a trifling thing, I promise you, so you needn't worry about me, but couldn't we talk just as well tomorrow?"

Nell agreed, although she suspected her niece of laying the sugar on a bit thickly. The next day was Sunday, and they had no pressing plans. Surely there would be a time to have a serious talk.

By the time they had attended services at the Chapel Royal and had entertained no fewer than three afternoon callers, including Mr. Seton, it began to seem as though Sunday would follow the same pattern as Saturday. Nell felt her temper rising, and did not know whether it was out of frustration at her seeming inability to corner her niece or simply because Lord Huntley had been so careless as to fail to number among their afternoon callers. The man simply had to be brought to a stronger sense of his duty toward his intended wife!

Her opportunity to speak to Rory did not occur until the supper table had been cleared and Kit had announced his intention of meeting Harry Seton for a quiet game or two of piquet. Once he had gone, Rory said something about speaking to Jeremy with regard to Ulysses' supper, and moved toward the doorway, but before she could escape, if indeed that had been her intent, she was stopped in her tracks by her aunt's voice, sharper than she had yet heard it.

"One moment, my dear."

Rory turned, her expression one of innocent curiosity. "Yes, Aunt Nell?"

"Once you have dealt with the matter of Ulysses' supper, I desire that you shall attend me in my sitting room."

"Of course, ma'am. I had meant to see about—"

"As soon as you have seen to Ulysses, Rory. I shall be waiting." Nell's tone brooked no further delay.

"Yes, ma'am."

Rory fled, and Lady Agnes turned a look of distress upon her daughter. "Dear me, Nell, but you sound nearly cross. What can poor Rory have done in order to deserve a scolding?"

Nell's features relaxed into a rueful smile. "Did I sound as if I mean to scold her?" Lady Agnes nodded. "Well, perhaps I do at that. Have you listened to her, Mama? She speaks only of her own pleasures and seems to have no regard at all for the fact that she is betrothed to Lord Huntley. And last night she behaved abominably."

"I thought her a trifle high-spirited, perhaps," her ladyship acknowledged feebly. "However, I daresy 'tis merely her youth makes her behave so."

"Stuff," Nell retorted. "Clarissa and Crossways have spoiled that child to death, and she has not learned to behave like a well-bred lady should behave. 'Twas not mere high spirits that caused her to flirt so outrageously with Harry Seton, and surely you cannot wish her to encourage a friendship with that rattle!''

"Well, no, but truly, Nell, it is most unlike you to be so strict. Do you not think that if Huntley were to pay her a bit more attention, Rory might heed his claims more willingly?''

"Of course I do. You will get no argument on that head, ma'am. I intend to speak to him on that very subject before *he* is much older, too.'' With that, Nell got up and went to deal with her niece, scarcely noting her mother's astonished expression.

Rory entered the small sitting room off Nell's bedchamber a few moments later looking wary. She greeted her aunt calmly enough, however, and asked what she had done to vex her.

"You haven't vexed me precisely, dear," Nell answered, striving to sound fair-minded at the very least. " 'Tis merely that I think you do not realize how very easy it is in polite society for a young girl to step beyond the line of being pleasing.''

"I have gone beyond it?''

"Not yet, perhaps. Not really. Although I could not like your manner with Mr. Seton. You were much too forward, I fear, and might easily have caused him to believe you were encouraging his attentions.''

"But I was encouraging them. I like him.''

"That has nothing to do with anything, my dear. You are betrothed to Huntley, you know, and therefore must not encourage others to pay court to you.''

"Oh, Aunt Nell, I never thought you would be so fusty. What harm is there in a simple flirtation? I came to Brighton to find pleasure, and so far I have spent most of my time in the company of persons a good deal older than myself and have done nothing exciting at all. Mr. Seton is, at least, near to my own age, and I thought him perfectly charming.''

"No doubt," said Nell dryly, "but I daresay his lordship would scarcely approve such a connection.''

"Well, he's got nothing to say to it!''

"Nothing to say to it!''

"Of course not. He promised, after all, that I should have

all the fun of a proper come-out, and I mean to do so. I doubt he will interfere, and I shall take it most unkindly if you do, for you are quite my favorite aunt and would be even if I had more aunts, and it is most unfair to expect me to comport myself as if I was already a prisoner of Huntley Green.''

Nell did what she could to bring her niece to an understanding of the difference between enjoying parties and balls, and behaving in a manner destined to bring shame upon them all, but it could not be said that she enjoyed any very great success in the matter. By the time she dismissed the Lady Aurora to her bedchamber, Nell was exhausted and looked forward to the Castle Inn's assembly, scheduled for the morrow, with nothing less than a feeling of acute trepidation.

VII

Viewed from the outside, the Castle Ballroom, directly across Castle Square from the Marine Pavilion seemed to be nothing more than a tall, rather ordinary red-brick building with arched windows. The interior, however, expressed all the grace and elegance that the architect, Mr. Crundon, had plagiarized—as was his custom—from such masters as Robert Adam and Henry Holland. There were actually four rooms, the principal ones being the ballroom itself and a card room.

The ballroom's dimensions much impressed Rory, who had seen nothing larger than the assembly rooms at Tunbridge Wells, for the elegant room was eighty feet long, forty feet wide, and forty feet high. Recesses at either end and along one side were framed by the sort of columns Adam favored, with capitals like plain inverted bells with single rows of acanthus leaves, and the walls were decorated with plaster reliefs in panels and medallions, delicate Adamesque moldings, and scroll ornaments. Facing each other above the frieze from opposite ends of the room were elaborate but nonetheless commonplace portraits of Dawn and Night, while the ceiling, a shallow arched vault, was a direct copy of Henry Holland's design for the subscription room at Brook's Club in London.

Neither Nell nor her charge had any reason to despise such details, of course, and it was their opinion—as well as that of nearly everyone else in Brighton—that the Castle Ballroom was most elegantly appointed.

Nell had not attended an assembly there since the year of her own come-out, and her first impression of the place, from the anteroom as a haughty footman stepped forward to take their wraps, was that her mother's friend Mrs. Calvert had had the right of it. The place, besides being much more crowded than she remembered, seemed to contain a vast cross-section of society among the guests.

"Aunt Nell, look at those peculiar women!"

Following the direction of Rory's astonished gaze toward a group passing through to the ballroom, Nell hid a smile. At least the two women drawing her niece's attention were not cits' wives. The first, an enormously fat lady with a vast, undulating bosom, wore an odd, green-striped garment that more nearly resembled a circus tent than an evening gown. Her squat little companion, though wearing a blue gown that was nothing out of the ordinary, had rendered herself quite as much a figure of fun by wearing an inordinate amount of glittering jewelry, including a multitude of bracelets on each of her plump arms, rings that flashed from every finger, plus any number of diamonds and watches pinned to her person.

"The larger of the two," Nell said diplomatically, in a discreet tone, "is Lady Pomfret. I do not know her scintillating friend."

Rory giggled and shook her head, but beyond glancing complacently down at her own slim, muslin-clad self and wondering in a low voice if Lady Pomfret meant to astonish the company by dancing, she soon lost interest in the pair, though she continued to cast curious glances hither and yon.

As she preceded Nell into the ballroom, her gaze came suddenly to rest upon a pair of broad, blue-and-gold draped shoulders. Her attention riveted and she actually came to a halt, causing Nell to remind her that there were others behind them and that if they meant to find chairs for themselves along the far wall, it would be best if she kept moving.

"Oh, yes, of course," Rory answered vaguely, narrowing her eyes. "Aunt Nell, do you see that gentleman ahead of us in the Hussar uniform?"

Since a great number of the gentlemen present were wearing if not the scarlet uniform of the King's Dragoons then the blue and gold of the Prince's Own Hussars, Nell had all she could do not to laugh at such an absurd question. She managed to preserve the gravity of her countenance, however, and merely requested that her niece indulge her by being more precise in her description.

"The one with the shoulders," replied Rory helpfully.

"Rory, they all of them have shoulders!"

"Not like his," declared her niece flatly. "I do like a man

with decent shoulders, don't you, Aunt Nell? 'Tis one of Huntley's few attributes, I think. But, Aunt Nell, I am persuaded—indeed, I am nearly certain—that that is the same extraordinarily handsome young man we met in Donaldson's on Friday.''

"We did *not* meet him, Rory, and I utterly forbid you to seek him out or in any way to call his attention to yourself," Nell said hastily, careful to keep her own voice down. "Do you understand me, young lady?"

"But I want to meet him!"

"Then we must try to discover—discreetly, mind you—if we enjoy any mutual acquaintance. But that is all I will allow, and you would do very well to mind me."

"Very well, ma'am."

The mournful tone did little to relieve Nell's mind. With a sigh she thought—and not for the first time—that it would be a deal easier to prevent Rory's doing something utterly shocking if they had a proper male escort for the evening. To be sure, she had taken courage in hand and had made a strong attempt to persuade Kit that he would find the assembly an amusing pastime. But he had merely laughed at her, reminding her that Rory was her responsibility and recommending with a sad want of civility that she acquire the services of a strict governess if she truly meant to keep the chit out of mischief.

Fearing that Rory would persist in her determination to make the young officer's acquaintance, Nell did what she could to prevent her from going beyond the line by introducing her to everyone she knew, including several stout matrons who could be trusted to know nearly everyone who *was* anyone. She could not feel, however, that the younger girl had been much impressed by the advice that she cast her bread upon the waters and hope that eventually someone who knew him would present the young Hussar as a desirable partner. Indeed, Nell placed little dependence upon her niece's patience and was therefore not so surprised as she might have been when, at the end of the second set of country dances, Rory's innate grace seemed to desert her and she stumbled, falling heavily against a young man who had not been part of her set but who seemed, in fact, to be wending his way toward the exit. Nor was she surprised that the young man was clad in blue and gold, nor by the fact that he possessed a pair of shoulders magnificent enough to have rivaled Huntley's.

Rory's partner, a shy young sprig who had already shown distinct signs of being besotted, stepped forward anxiously to assist her, but Rory clung—quite unnecessarily in her aunt's opinion—to the man she had fallen against. He had reacted quickly enough to keep her from falling to the floor and seemed willing now to set her on her feet again, but Rory appeared to be quite unable to rest any weight upon her right foot. She spoke to the young officer, ignoring her own partner shamelessly, and a few moments later Nell watched with a jaundiced eye as her niece approached, limping, but supported on either side by the two gentlemen. Rory practically quivered with pent-up mischief, the young sprig looked resigned, and the officer shot Nell an apologetic look that nearly caused her to shake her head in a gesture of shared understanding.

He was tall, very likely taller than Huntley, she thought, watching him. His hair, coarsely textured and medium brown in color, was tied back in the regulation pigtail, and he sported the bushy sidewhiskers and thickly curling mustache generally preferred by Hussar officers. His features were regular, and the lines at the sides of his dark brown, heavily-lidded eyes seemed to suggest both an outdoor life and a habit of laughter. He was a nice looking young man, Nell decided, although in her opinion he looked pretty much like any other Hussar officer, and she could not imagine for a moment why Rory should fancy him to be better looking than his lordship.

"Aunt Nell, you are cursed with a clumsy niece," Rory said cheerfully after her two aides had helped her to the gilt, harp-backed chair next to Nell's and the young sprig had taken his reluctant departure. "I have twisted my ankle and, in the process, nearly knocked poor Major Talcott off his feet. Oh, this is Major Gideon Talcott, ma'am," she added as an afterthought. "And this is my aunt, sir, Miss Lindale."

"At your service, Miss Lindale." His voice was pleasant, and his bow was polished. Nell nodded but was given little opportunity to speak.

"He *is* the same gentleman we saw at Donaldson's, Aunt Nell, and he remembered me—that is, us—as well, for he called me by name when he apologized for his clumsiness, and when I asked how he knew who I was, he admitted he had looked in the visitors' book after we had departed." She cast a roguish look at her by now acutely uncomfortable companion, which made Nell long to shake her. "Was that not naughty of him, ma'am?"

" 'Tis not an uncommon practice, however," Nell said evenly. "I am persuaded that my niece will do very nicely now, sir. Thank you for assisting her."

" 'Twas the least I could do after nearly mowing her ladyship down in my path," he replied gallantly, making no effort to accept Nell's broad hint.

Rory, her right foot daintily extended, had taken the brief moment to inspect it, turning it first one way, then the other. She looked up in response to Talcott's words and chuckled disarmingly.

"You are most kind, sir, but you know perfectly well that that is not what transpired at all. 'Twas I who fell against you. If you were not so strong—"

"Rory, please!" Nell expostulated under her breath.

"But he *is* strong, and he saved me from a fall and very likely from being trodden upon, as well, so why should I not speak of it?"

Major Talcott's eyes twinkled, and his expression as much as dared Nell to answer as he no doubt believed she would have liked to answer. Instead, Nell smiled at him, albeit weakly, and said, "We are indeed in your debt, sir. Rory, is your ankle swelling?" She could see perfectly well for herself that it was doing no such thing, but she was curious to know how the minx would respond.

Rory flexed her foot experimentally, then directed a limpid gaze at her aunt and replied, "Do you know, I think I must be very lucky, for it does not hurt me in the slightest now."

"We must all be thankful for that," returned her aunt dryly, shooting a darkling look at her. Rory avoided her gaze.

"Indeed, I am persuaded I need not miss a single set." She gazed speculatively at Major Talcott from under her dark lashes.

"Don't be foolish," Nell said briskly, restraining an increasing urge to throttle her niece. "Major Talcott would be the first to warn you to rest your foot, my dear. You must resign yourself to sitting out at least one dance."

Rory looked mutinous, but providentially the major suggested that she might like a glass of orgeat while she rested. She agreed happily and watched his retreating form with an expression that, in her aunt's opinion, could be best described as nauseating.

"You will have a good deal to answer for when we have a private moment, my child," Nell said quietly.

Rory turned to her, wide-eyed. "But, Aunt Nell, I could scarcely help fall——" Nell's patent disbelief caused her to break off and look down at her hands. She began to pick with one at the fingernails of the other, speaking again only after a long moment. "Well, I am sorry, then, if I have vexed you, but I was afraid he meant to leave, and I knew it would take days to arrange a proper introduction even if we did manage to find someone who knows him."

Nell sighed. "Do you do things to suit only your own pleasure, my dear?" Rory looked at her, but there was nothing in her expression to indicate the slightest understanding of Nell's feelings. A moment later Major Talcott reappeared with her orgeat, and as soon as the orchestra struck up for a Scottish reel, he obeyed her unspoken command by requesting her hand for the dance.

When they had gone, Nell looked about her, trying to see if she could discover anyone who might have taken notice of Rory's deplorable tactics. Thankfully, she saw no one who might have been expected to pay them any heed. A fashionably attired young man strolled up to her chair just then to ask her to honor him with a dance. She refused politely just as she had been doing all the evening. In point of fact, the number of offers she had received quite surprised her. She had known that her gown of bronze watered-silk became her well enough, and the new beribboned hairstyle, à la Aphrodite, was perfectly suited to her long chestnut hair. But she had not expected to be such a success. Had she been so inclined, she would not have needed to sit out a single dance. But of course it would be unthinkable when her charge required her constant attention.

Stifling a small sigh, Nell scarcely realized when her toes began to tap in time to the reel, noticing only when the sudden ceasing of the music caught her with toes raised. Color rushed to her face as she glanced self-consciously about to see if anyone had been watching. Surprisingly, every head seemed to the turned toward the entrance, where there seemed to be a great stirring of activity.

Some young girls off to her right were actually climbing

onto benches in order to see better, a clear example of a lowered standard of behavior. Surely, no young lady would have dared make such a vulgar display of herself in bygone Seasons! They were muttering now among themselves, and Nell strained her ears to hear what they were saying. Someone mentioned his highness, and someone else mentioned Norfolk, which was enough to inform her that the Prince of Wales and the Duke of Norfolk had chosen to honor the assembly with their presence. She looked around for Rory, devoutly hoping that she would not find her among the girls on the benches, and was nearly startled out of her skin by a familiar voice at her side.

"Lost her ladyship already, have you?"

"Huntley! By all that's holy, my lord, do you wish to frighten me silly?"

"It was not my intention," he replied with one of his more enigmatic smiles. "I am a victim of circumstances and decided to seek compatible company."

"Victim of circumstances?"

"Indeed. I have dined at the Pavilion and was unable—at such short notice, you know—to think of a reason not to accompany Prinny and his grace when they took it into their heads to come here. They are very drunk, although Norfolk doesn't show it, of course. Man has a head like an ox."

"The prince does not carry his liquor so well," Nell said wisely, thinking Huntley himself was no doubt a little worse for drink if he had been dining at the Pavilion. "I collect there was a fair amount of wine at the table."

"Of course, since Maria was not present," he replied. Nell nodded, knowing as well as anyone in Brighton that Mrs. Fitzherbert kept a tight rein on his highness's drinking. "Ought to warn you," Huntley added with a sidelong look at her. "He wants to meet my intended. What have you done with her?"

"I have done nothing with her," Nell replied indignantly. "Not, mind you, that I have not been sorely tempted."

Favoring her with a quick grin of comprehension, he sat down, casually crossing one long leg over the other. He was attired in the evening garb made popular by Mr. Brummell—dark coat, black knee-breeches, white waistcoat and stockings, and black shoes. His watchchain sported a single gold fob, and he wore a diamond stickpin in his intricately tied, well-starched neckcloth. Nell thought he looked particularly elegant. When he turned to face her, she thought she could detect a glint of sympathy in deep-set hazel eyes.

"You've encountered difficulties? Where is she?"

"Dancing, of course," Nell replied. "And I said nothing of difficulties, nor," she added contradictorily, "is this the proper place to discuss them."

"But you would like to discuss them at a more suitable time and place?"

"I would, sir. I don't know how you can expect me to—to. . . ."

"To keep the baggage in line?" he suggested helpfully.

She glared at him, but the teasing twinkle in the hazel eyes defeated her, and she surprised him by chuckling.

"That's better," he said.

"Well, it is no matter for jesting, my lord. I don't know how you came to make me laugh, because Rory is likely to land us all in the basket with her outrageous behavior."

"I admit the possibility, and I am sorry if I seem to have deposited my burdens in your lap, but you are quite right in that we cannot discuss the matter now, for here she comes. Who is that splendid fellow at her side?"

"He would be arm in arm with her if his principles were not rather better than hers, my lord," Nell said tartly.

"I'm glad you manage to provide her with principled partners, at least. By the look of this company, it cannot be an easy task."

"Your sentiments, though gratifying, are of little consequence," Nell replied, lowering her voice as the others drew nearer. "I did not present him to her."

"Then who . . ." The thick brows knitted together when Nell shot him a speaking look. "Ah, I see. The chit's manners want correcting, do they? Well, that *is* something I can attend to."

Before Nell could comment, the others were upon them and Rory was making the introductions, her manners as polished as anyone might wish. A moment later, Major Talcott took himself off, and Huntley sternly informed his intended that he meant to dance with her. She quickly mentioned her dance card, whereupon he countered by submitting that, as yet, no partner had appeared to claim her. Left with no further argument she went off with him, and Nell braced herself for fireworks.

She was not surprised to note that, instead of joining one of the sets now forming for a cotillion, Huntley guided his reluctant partner inexorably toward one of the recesses at the end of the room. They did not return until the dance was nearly over, and when they did, Rory's chin was up, her lips were pressed together in a straight, narrow line, and her eyes were mere slits of resentment in her lovely face. Huntley, just behind her, looked decidedly grim.

Nell let out a long sigh but did not attempt to speak to either of them, and it was not until the approach of a scarlet coat that Rory showed signs of reviving. Huntley frowned, but when Nell greeted the young man warmly and introduced him as the son of one of her mother's oldest and dearest friends, his lordship relaxed noticeably, and Rory promptly accepted the forthcoming invitation to take part in the contradanse.

"I can see that you have your work cut out for you," Huntley said when they had gone.

Nell looked at him searchingly, wondering if he was offering deliberate provocation. "I should say, rather, sir, that you have yours cut out for you."

"Not for several months yet, thank God," he replied.

"My good sir, surely you do not expect me to have much effect upon a character that has been seventeen years in the making. Not without a good deal of help, at any rate."

He smiled. "Do you mean to infer, Nell, that you could make the necessary changes if you had help?"

"Well, I should certainly make a push to try," she retorted. "But so long as she encourages the attentions of every rattle in Brighton, and so long as you deny us your escort—which would at least *show* them that she is spoken for—there is not a great deal I can do beyond praying that she will come to no great harm."

"Does she truly encourage rattles?" Huntley asked as if he were truly interested.

"She encourages anything in pants, my lord, particularly if they are uniform pants!"

"My poor Nell." She looked at him in astonishment, but he was not attending to her. Instead, his eyes were focused upon a point behind her, and they narrowed as he got to his feet and held out his hand as if to assist her to hers. "I am sorry for this," he said quietly. "Good evening, your highness. May I have the honor to present Miss Lindale."

Nell turned quickly and dropped a curtsy to the prince, who hung on the arm of his friend the Duke of Norfolk. "Your highness."

The Prince of Wales extended a hand and drew her to her feet. He seemed to look her over, she thought, much as if she had been a filly presented for his inspection. "Pleasure, Miss Lindale. D'ya know Norfolk?" His words were greatly slurred.

She curtsied again, and Norfolk nodded, then clapped Huntley on the shoulder. "This the one, man?"

"No, sir. Lady Aurora is dancing. Miss Lindale is her aunt."

"Wish I had an aunt looked like that," muttered an unidentified voice behind the prince.

He laughed loudly. "Damme, so do I! Mine are all Friday-faced shrews, damme if they aren't."

"His highness," said Norfolk to Huntley, "was just telling us one of his tales, my lord. Do continue, sir. Huntley's lass will be here by the time you have done."

"But I already began," the prince protested, "and now I shall have to begin again, for Huntley and Miss Lindale do not know the beginning."

"I should like to hear your tale, sir," Nell said before Huntley could speak. "I have heard that you are a fine storyteller."

He looked pleased, but she heard Huntley let out a small sigh beside her and wondered if she had somehow managed to incur his displeasure.

"Fact is, Miss Lindale, no one tells a better tale," stated the prince, not one for false modesty. "As I told Norfolk here, I was out one day with my harriers, and we found a hare, but the scent was catching and uncertain, so we could go no continuous pace at all. There was a butcher out, damme, if there wasn't, a great huge fellow, fifteen stone, six-feet-two-inches without his shoes—the bully of all Brighton. He overrode my hounds several times, though I spoke to him to hold hard. At last, damme, ma'am, he rode slap over my favorite bitch, Ruby. I could stand it no longer, but jumping off my horse, said, 'Get down, you damned rascal, and pull off your coat. None shall interfere with us, but you or I shall go back to Brighton more dead than alive.' Damme, ma'am,

I threw off my coat, and the big ruffian, nothing loth, did the same by his. By God, ma'am, we fought for an hour and twenty minutes! My hunting field formed a ring around us, no one interfering, and at the end of it the big bully butcher of Brighton was carried away senseless, while I had hardly a scratch." Having brought his tale to its triumphant conclusion, the prince turned to Norfolk. "Damme, man, you remember it!"

Norfolk nodded obligingly, then gestured toward the dance floor. "And as I predicted, sir, I believe this must be Huntley's lady approaching us now. A diamond of the first water, my lord. I congratulate you."

"Thank you, your grace." Huntley turned as Rory approached with her partner. "My lady, here is a treat for you. Highness, may I have the honor to present the Lady Aurora Crossways."

Nell was glad she had not had to comment on the prince's tale. She watched as the introductions were made, noting that the prince seemed to go out of his way to be charming. She might wish that his language were a little more circumspect, but she could not fault his manners otherwise. Nonetheless, the tale had puzzled her, and when the royal party had melted back into the throng and Rory's next partner had come to claim her, she turned to Huntley, a small frown wrinkling the space between her straight, narrow brows.

He smiled down at her. "That was not so bad as it might have been. Why the frown, Nell?"

" 'Tis the bully butcher of Brighton, sir. Surely, such an incident could not long have remained secret, but I never heard so much as a whisper about it."

"Not all of Prinny's tales have much foundation in fact, I'm afraid."

"Do you meant to say he tells lies?" Nell was shocked. It was a side of the prince she had been unaware of, if indeed it was a side of him at all.

Huntley paused, giving the matter serious consideration. "I do not know that I would call it anything so serious as that," he said at last. "It only occurs—that I know of, at least—when he is telling his stories. And it does not happen so much, I am told, when Maria is present. She is able to curb his tongue. But it is more as if he loses himself in his imagination. I think he honestly believes the things he talks about actually occurred.''

Nell's eyes widened. "You speak as though the man is mad, sir. He is Prince of Wales!''

He smiled. "That factor does not preclude madness, my dear. Indeed, as everyone knows, the family is riddled with insanity. It would be no odd thing for him to follow the example set by his father, though Prinny's is not an extreme case at the moment. Maria Fitzherbert exerts an excellent influence. We must hope for the best.''

"Indeed, sir, we must," Nell said slowly, turning over the astonishing information in her mind.

"There is another set forming," he said. "Will you do me the honor, ma'am?"

"I do not dance, sir," she replied absently, still thinking of the prince.

"Nonsense. You are not an invalid. Come." His hand at her elbow brought her out of her brown study. She looked at him in confusion.

"I am here as a chaperon, sir. 'Tis not seemly.''

"Fiddle. Do you think for one moment that Lady Crossways would sit idle had she brought Aurora to this affair?''

The question was unanswerable, but still Nell hesitated. "It has been eight years, my lord. I shall not even know the steps.''

"Don't give that another thought. Just follow my lead and watch the other ladies. I'll see you through. Besides, if you're worried about presenting a scene for gawkers, you needn't be. No one will give you a glance with such a spectacle to amuse them as that quaking obesity in green stripes yonder.'' Nell glanced toward the set he indicated and saw Lady Pomfret, in all her undulating glory, throwing heart and soul into the patterns. "With such an example of courage as that to guide you, my dear," Huntley said provocatively, "surely you will not be so timid as to refuse my humble invitation.''

Her eyes twinkled. "As you say, my lord. If you dare to risk it, who am I to quibble?''

Half an hour later Huntley suggested and, much to Rory's patent disgust, Nell concurred that it would be as well not to wait until after the late supper had been served to take their departure since the morrow, being the prince's birthday, would be an exceptionally busy day.

"But I am promised for the supper," Rory protested.

"Then you must excuse yourself to your partner," Huntley replied evenly. "In fact, I shall endeavor to perform that office for you, if you will be so good as to point him out to me."

"I-I don't see him just at the moment," Rory said falteringly. The color in her cheeks had heightened, too, and Nell thought for a moment that she might have prevaricated in order to remain at the assembly. Huntley's quick frown returned.

"Perhaps I know him. What is his name?"

Rory looked more uncomfortable than ever, but she took a deep breath and, managing a look that was half defiant, half fearful, said, " 'Tis Major Talcott. And it is of no use to look like that, Huntley, because I promised him before ever you spoke to me. And I keep my promises," she added rashly.

"Then I wish that you will promise me that you will contrive to behave more in the manner expected of a lady of quality," Huntley retorted. He chose to ignore the glare directed at him from the golden eyes, and turned to Nell. "Take her to collect her wrap, if you please, while I endeavor to find the good major. Will your coach be waiting?"

"Yes, although I expect I shall have to send a linkboy to wake up my driver. Poor Trilby is getting on in years and does not stay awake so easily as he did in his younger days. Do you come with us?"

"I do. 'Tis only a short stroll from your house to mine, after all."

"Well, you needn't walk, sir, for Trilby will have to drive round to the stable, and in order to reach it, he can as easily go by way of the Marine Parade as by Edward Street, you know." He nodded, then left to discover the whereabouts of Major Talcott, and Nell turned to her niece. "Come along, dear. Sulking will accomplish nothing, you know."

"Well, I think Huntley is by far the greatest beast in nature," Rory said roundly. "I cannot think what it will be like to be married to such a man as that. Very likely I shall suffer untold brutality, and no one will care a jot, either!"

Instead of replying to this outpouring as it deserved, Nell merely muttered in vague agreement, thus causing her offended niece to stare at her in bewilderment. But Nell felt none of the irritation one might have expected her to feel. In its place she felt a stirring of sadness.

VIII

The morning of the Prince of Wales's birthday dawned with a pandemonium of church bells ringing in celebration throughout the town. As a result of the noise, if not the bright sunshine pouring through bedchamber windows once the servants had opened the curtains, the Lindale household was up and about some time before its members were normally accustomed to begin their days.

Rory announced upon entering the breakfast parlor that she found the whole business greatly exciting. "There is nothing like this in Kent," she said happily. "Not even in Tunbridge Wells."

Her uncle glowered, the puffiness around his eyes having already indicated to his observant sister that he was a bit the worse for a late evening. "My compliments to Tunbridge Wells," he grunted. "I'd no notion the place was so civilized. How long," he added, wincing, "do they mean to continue that din?"

"Have you a headache, dearest?" inquired Lady Agnes solicitously from the foot of the oval table. "Shall I ring for my maid to fetch you some hartshorn and water?"

Her son's expression indicated incipient nausea.

"Perhaps some minced rhubarb would be more in keeping with his needs, Mama," Nell suggested, her eyes atwinkle. "He appears to me to require something to settle his stomach. Or perhaps he is feverish," she went on, stretching out a hand to feel his brow, "in which case he will best be served by a dose of Dr. James's Powders."

"*Will* you be quiet," pleaded her brother in exasperated tones.

Rory, taking her seat opposite Nell, chuckled at his obvious distress. "I do believe poor Uncle Kit is bilious," she said in sugar-sweet, mock commiseration. There was no sign this morning of the sulky child Nell had unsympathetically packed off to bed the previous evening. Dressed becomingly now in green-sprigged muslin with a narrow pink sash and matching leather sandals, she presented a picture of demure maidenhood that made it difficult to remember her less endearing moods.

Nell smiled at her but spoke to the hovering footman. "Bring Mr. Lindale some more hot coffee, please, Jeremy. Lashings of it, I should think. Blue ruin, Kit?"

"You've a tongue too long for your teeth, my girl."

"What is blue ruin?" asked Rory innocently.

"Nothing you need know about, chit," snapped her uncle.

"Gin," explained Nell, still smiling. "They call it blue ruin because of the effect is has on the imbiber. Actually, the term usually refers to bad gin."

"Kit, you don't drink that awful stuff, do you?" asked his mother anxiously. "I am persuaded 'tis a frightful waste of money, besides doing dreadful things to the state of your health."

Shooting a glare at his sister that, in earlier days, would have warned her to search between her sheets before retiring, he replied irritably, "I am well enough, ma'am. Just blue-deviled. The noise of those blasted bells is enough to drive a fellow mad."

"Well, they will stop in another fifteen minutes," Nell said soothingly after looking at the little watch pinned to the bodice of her light green walking dress. "Do you mean to accompany us?"

Gruffly, Kit agreed that he might just as well, since there was not likely to be any other way to amuse oneself until the celebrations were over and done. But he warned that he would more than likely leave them to join his cronies once they had reached the field outside of town where most of the festivities would take place.

"Well, if you mean to ride with us, we shall have to take the barouche," his mama said with a tiny frown. "The landaulet won't hold us all."

"What? Don't tell me you mean to go with us, Mama?" Kit seemed to forget his own troubles at this astonishing news.

"Well, yes, I have decided to attempt it. Sir Henry reminded me that I might just sit quietly in the carriage, you know, and still watch most of the fun. You needn't think I shall expect any of you to bear me company, however," she added, her words causing her granddaughter's falling expression to lighten again. "Sir Henry has graciously engaged himself to perform that task and thus to prevent my becoming bored with my own company."

"Oh, Lord," Kit moaned. "That's torn it, then. I shall certainly look for my friends. I may even have my horse saddled."

Nell chuckled. "A nice trot to the other side of town ought to put you in prime twig. All that bouncing and jolting, and——"

"Enough," groaned her sorely-tried brother. "I'll ride in the carriage, but if that crusty old reprobate begins preaching, I'll not be held responsible for the consequences."

"Well, I don't think it is at all kind of you to call a nice old gentleman like Sir Henry an old reprobate," Rory said sweetly.

Kit turned pointedly to his sister. "Does Huntley mean to join us on this little expedition?"

She grinned at him. "I invited him to share our picnic later, and he has engaged to escort Rory and me to the ball at the Pavilion tonight, but I doubt we shall see much of him this morning. I believe he mentioned that he is expected to accompany the prince's party."

Rory did not look particularly overjoyed at the news that Huntley would be joining them. Her expression was rather one of resignation. Nell felt a stirring of pity.

She had no doubt that his lordship would make her niece an excellent husband, but it was unfortunate that Rory was so young. Arranged marriages were still customary, of course, and there could be no doubt that it would be wiser to allow her parents to choose a husband than to allow someone as flighty as Rory to choose her own. Why, by her own account, she was prone to fall in and out of love as quickly as a cat might lick her ear. The previous night it had been Major Talcott, two nights before that, Harry Seton, and before that a groom and a drawing master!

Still and all, Nell thought, watching her, it was a shame she was to be married so quickly and with so little experience of the world. Of course, she did not doubt for a moment that

Rory would see more of London, at least, than Huntley seemed to anticipate. He would be as putty in her hands once she learned how to manage him, his brief show of authority at the Castle assembly notwithstanding. That had accomplished nothing other than to set up her back. Certainly, he would have to discover some better means of dealing with her than mere harsh words. And considering how easily his mother and sister seemed to govern the man——

"*Nell!*" She looked up, startled, to see her brother standing impatiently by his chair. "Mama asked how soon you wish to depart. Sir Henry will arrive at ten, so I expect you will want to leave the house *immediately* thereafter."

She grinned at him, but agreed willingly enough to be ready to depart the moment Sir Henry should arrive.

The old gentleman was prompt, as was his habit, and they were soon squeezed into the Lindale barouche and on their way to the festivities. Rory exclaimed at the sight of the gaily waving banners that festooned nearly every lamppost and building along the way. Adding to the festival atmosphere was a military band playing a lively tune on the Steyne as they passed by, and by the time they reached the edge of town, their carriage had joined a host of vehicles of every description, crowded with laughing, chattering townspeople. The royal party was already in place when they arrived at the field.

"Look!" exclaimed Kit, "Mrs. Fitz is here." Nell looked past him and out the window to see that Mrs. Fitzherbert was indeed at the prince's side.

"She must have arrived late last night in order to surprise him," she said with a chuckle, "and I daresay the fact that she was waiting to greet him was all that dragged him from his bed, for after seeing his condition last night, I'd wager that his head is a match for yours this morning, Kit."

"Where?" demanded Rory, who was squeezed in between them in order that Lady Agnes and Sir Henry might share the rear seat in comfort.

"Where is what?" asked Kit.

"Mrs. Fitzherbert. I have never seen her." She twisted around and leaned across him in an attempt to see the famous lady.

"Next to his highness, of course."

"But there is no female near him except that fat old woman," she protested.

"That is Mrs. Fitzherbert."

"But she is old!"

"In point of fact," Kit explained, "she is merely five years older than the prince, who is today celebrating his forty-fourth birthday."

"Age has not been kind to her," Lady Agnes observed, "but I think she has a charming countenance."

"Her mouth is ugly, and her false teeth don't fit properly," Kit disagreed.

"But even you must agree that her other features are still very good," Nell said, "and her manners are very good-humored."

"She is very fat," Rory said flatly. "Not so fat as that dreadful Lady Pomfret who made such a spectacle of herself at the assembly last night, but then Lady Pomfret is not so old. And she had the good sense," she added, settling back in her seat, "*not* to wear a gown cut so low as to display most of her bosom."

"Aurora!"

"Well, only look for yourself, Grandmama. I daresay, if she so much as coughs, the whole thing will spill right out."

"But you should never discuss such matters in the presence of gentlemen, my dear," complained her ladyship in failing accents. Sir Henry, dapper in a gray coat and cherry-striped waistcoat, his long gray curls confined at the nape of his neck with a narrow, black ribbon, had appeared to be dozing in his corner. However, he proved now that he was sufficiently alert by handing Lady Agnes her crystal vinaigrette, which he had carried in his waistcoat pocket. She smiled her thanks.

Rory was unrepentant. "I daresay my chatter does not scandalize Sir Henry," she said, grinning impishly at him.

Sir Henry sat up a little straighter and smoothed his neckcloth. "Not at all, my dear child. Mere youthful high spirits, Lady Agnes. I promise you I shall not regard it."

She patted his hand, but Kit could be heard to mutter a suggestion, just as the barouche was drawing to a halt, that his niece should try for a little conduct. Nell had small hope, however, that this very excellent advice would be much heeded.

The day was already turning warm. Even the breeze blowing across from the cliffs was a balmy one, and as the younger members of the Lindale party descended from the carriage, it was clear to them that the merrymakers were prepared to enjoy themselves.

The late morning and early afternoon were filled with such activities as jackass-racing, girls' footraces, and sack races for men, as well as other amusing diversions. Meanwhile, a whole ox was being roasted on the green and, once the signal was given, the men, women, and children pushed and jostled each other to get pieces of meat that were often burning hot cut off the carcase with a broadsword, while hogsheads of beer were set about so that people might help themselves.

Kit had promptly taken himself off, leaving his sister and niece to their own devices. At first, Nell did not mind a bit. The atmosphere was contagious. Her charge was excited and keenly enthusiastic, even to the point of bewailing the fact that she had not been warned to wear more sensible shoes.

"For then I might have entered the footrace, Aunt Nell. I am a very fast runner, so I daresay I might easily have won the gown they are offering as first prize."

"It is not customary for gently-bred young women to enter the contests," Nell said diplomatically. "That gown is meant to be won by some girl who could ill afford to purchase it for herself."

Rory accepted the explanation but joined the rest of the spectators in shrieking encouragement to her chosen favorites. It was not long before the constant din and surge of humanity around her gave Nell a headache, and she began to think rather longingly of her mother's carriage. It had been drawn up on a low hill near enough for Lady Agnes to see what she wanted to see, yet far enough back to escape the worst of the din. And one would not be continually pushed and prodded.

By the beginning of the third contest, the crowds had thickened, making Nell wonder where her brother and his friends had taken themselves, for she had to admit she would have felt the better for their company. Once a burly towns-man had actually clapped her on the shoulder and demanded to know what she thought of it all. He was perfectly harmless, she reassured herself, wondering at the same time what had become of Rory, who seemed to have been swallowed up by the crowd. The beer barrels had been tapped, and many of the men who had quenched their thirst more than once already might not be so harmless as the burly townsman. She won-dered if it might not be the wisest course to insist that her niece accompany her back to the carriage. Where was Rory, anyway?

It was fifteen minutes before she found her, and by then Nell was nearly in a panic. She had decided it would be best to remain where she was and to let the girl find her; however, she breathed a sigh of relief when Rory simply appeared through the crowd. The younger girl did not look at all distressed but merely laughed and said, "There, I knew I should find you!"

"Where have you been?" Anxiety sharpened Nell's voice, and the tone brought a little frown to Rory's lovely countenance. She reached up to straighten her hat, which had been knocked off its pins by a tall, rather wide gentleman.

"Goodness, were you worried? I am ever so sorry, but I only just realized we'd got separated. I simply kept stepping to one side to let people pass, you know, and I suppose I must have stepped the same way every time. As soon as the race was done, of course, I realized it was not you beside me at all, so I pushed my way through the people till I found you. I knew you would wait for me. Please say you are not vexed, ma'am."

The coaxing tone and pleading expression did much to restore Nell's spirits. She even agreed that they might remain to watch just one more race. Then, because the one following that one was the men's sack race, which promised to be particularly amusing, she agreed to remain for that one, too, and soon found herself laughing right along with the rest of the onlookers at the ludicrous positions the contestants seemed to get themselves into. When it was over, she had to pull her handkerchief from her reticule in order to wipe away the tears of laughter streaming down her face. But even as she mopped her cheeks, she realized that Rory had disappeared once more.

"Drat the girl!" Nell muttered, choosing from her brother's vocabulary in order to vent her feelings more satisfactorily. She looked around, more in vexation than anxiety this time. The crowd seemed at first to be breaking up, but then she realized they were all moving in much the same direction. The races were over. The smell of roasting beef drifted on the gentle breeze, telling her even before word moved swiftly through the crowd, that the ox was done to a turn.

Still no sign of Rory. Catching sight of the royal party

moving toward the gaily decorated tents erected for their comfort, she saw the prince, Mrs. Fitzherbert, the royal dukes, as well as Norfolk, Marlborough, and several other less august persons, but there was no sign of Huntley. Anxiously now, she began searching the faces in the crowd, hoping to find Rory before Huntley came in search of them both. It would certainly do her credit little good if he were again to think she had misplaced his intended bride.

"Aunt Nell, Aunt Nell, behind you!" Rory's crystal voice floated clearly above the even rumble of the crowd. Nell turned, but her sense of profound relief was short-lived when she saw that her niece was being escorted by Major Talcott and another young Hussar officer. "Look whom I have found, Aunt Nell."

Nell managed to achieve the semblance of a smile, and Talcott grinned cheerfully back at her. "Good day to you, Miss Lindale. May I present Lieutenant Lord Hubert Coltrain, who is a good friend of mine."

"How do you do, my lord," Nell replied politely. "Rory, where have you been?"

"Oh dear, did you think I'd got lost again? It was no such thing, I assure you," her ladyship replied earnestly. " 'Twas merely that I saw Major Talcott—he is so tall, you know, that he is rather conspicuous even in a crowd—and I decided to invite him to join our picnic. And Lieutenant Coltrain—or must I say Lord Hubert? One never knows. Anyway, he was there, too, and I was persuaded there would be quite enough food to share with both."

"My friends call me Bounce," Lord Hubert Coltrain informed them in confiding tones. Shorter than the major, he was a rather plump young man with an open face and eyes that reminded Nell of a friendly puppy, but his expression showed a touch of anxiety just then. "I trust, ma'am," he said, "that we do not intrude."

Nell had stifled an irritated sigh at the news of Rory's impetuosity, but she was too well-bred to show her annoyance before the two young men. There was nothing to be done but to assure them with as much warmth as she could muster that they would be welcome to join the Lindale picnic. And whatever her feelings about her niece's improper behavior, she had to admit—to herself if to no one else—that making her way through the crowd was much more comfortably accomplished with a masculine escort than without one. A moment later, when she saw Huntley approaching them, she was no longer so certain of that comfort.

His greeting was warm enough, and he did not seem particularly displeased to see their military escort. He even seemed to know Coltrain, and shook hands with him before drawing Nell back a little to walk behind the others.

"Should you not be walking with Rory?" she asked.

"What, and deprive her gallant swains of her company?"

"I don't believe Talcott even knows she is betrothed, sir. I doubt she would tell him."

"He knows. I told him myself last night."

"Oh." She digested this information, watching the trio ahead. Rory looked up at the major just then and her eyes fairly sparkled with pleasure as she laughed at something he had said. He grinned back at her. "I don't think he means to let it make any difference, my lord," Nell said. "Surely, he doesn't behave like a man who has been warned away."

"Oh, he will behave well enough. His career means a great deal to him, and I daresay he'd do nothing to jeopardize it. I don't mind a friendship between them, so long as they both realize the relationship can go no further. I shall depend upon you, of course, to see that the young lady don't disgrace herself."

"I am beginning to feel very much imposed upon, my lord," Nell replied tartly. "I'll have you know that when I lost sight of her not long ago, I nearly panicked. Not for fear of what harm might come to her, mind you, but for fear of your reaction if I'd lost her. You simply must take some of the responsibility unto yourself."

"Poor Nell."

She glanced up to find him grinning at her, his eyes atwinkle. How could she have thought for a single moment, she wondered, that he'd lost his sense of humor and could only be cynical? The grin was an infectious one, and she found herself returning it, her brief annoyance all but forgotten. A heavy-set woman, hurrying to get in line for the roast ox, bumped into her, making her stumble slightly, and Huntley quickly placed a hand under her elbow to steady her. He did not take it away again once she had recovered.

Nell looked up again. "Thank you, my lord, but I am perfectly steady again, you know."

"This is a dangerous mob. I might not be so quick the next time."

"Mob, my lord?"

"Dangerous mob," he repeated firmly.

Nell said no more. His hand was actually very light, at times not even touching her. But she knew it was there, and when it did touch her it seemed to send little sparks pulsing up her arm and all through the rest of her. It was only that she was unaccustomed to such chivalry, of course, she told herself. It was merely a case of nerves. That plus the fact that she was relieved to know she had not incurred his displeasure.

Neither Talcott nor Coltrain showed the slightest sign of discomfort at Huntley's presence, and Rory seemed to be in her element, flirting indiscriminately with all three and with Sir Henry as well. She helped Nell to set out the food for the picnic, while the gentlemen assisted Lady Agnes to a thick quilt that had been spread for her comfort in the shade beneath a group of poplar trees.

No sooner had the food been set out than Kit appeared with Harry Seton and another young man, who was tall and as thin as a bean pole, with narrow gray eyes and a long, thin nose. His skin-tight green coat and yellow pantaloons gave him the appearance of a comic matchstick doll, and he wore a mauve-and-cream spotted Belcher kerchief tied around his neck, as well as a striped waistcoat of matching colors. Kit introduced him as the Honorable Timothy Tree, but if his attire was odd enough to draw public attention, it was his hairstyle that caused Nell to forget her polished manners and to stare with the others. His dark hair was arranged in tight little curls à la Caesar that fell in love-locks over his brow and around his ears. Moreover, he carried himself with such pomp as to make her think him a veritable cockscomb. And on the strut at that, she told herself wickedly.

"Ain't Timmy a pretty fellow?" Kit asked the group in general. "Puts the rest of us chaps in the shade, don't you know." The Honorable Timothy blushed to his love-locks, but other than that he seemed to take his friend's roasting in good spirit. Rory announced that the meal was quite ready, and everyone fell to.

There was plenty of food and wine, and even Lady Agnes declared the picnic a huge success. Dabbing daintily at her lips with her serviette, she declared her intention of staying right where she was to rest and let her lunch settle.

"Take a catnap, more like," teased Kit, with a chuckle. "You'll miss the sailing races, Mama."

"Kit, for the love of goodness, I have only just finished a meal. Have pity," his mama begged him. "You know perfectly well that sailing vessels or indeed any boats make me quite dizzy."

"Not if you merely watch them from the cliffs, Mama."

"Always," she replied.

"Well, Harry and Tim and I mean to watch them. We know of an excellent place where one's view of the entire race will be unobstructed."

"Oh, do let's go with them!" Rory exclaimed, looking excitedly at Talcott and Coltrain.

Major Talcott shook his head. "It would surely be our pleasure to escort you and Miss Lindale, my lady, but there is a grand review scheduled for later this afternoon, so although I regret the necessity, we must take our departure in just a few moments to join our regiment. I hope you will come to watch the review."

"Oh, we will! I promise you we will. Won't we, Aunt Nell?"

"We must wait to discover Mama's wishes, Rory dear," Nell said quietly. "You would not wish her to become overly tired."

"Oh, no, of course not," the younger girl replied, her disappointment clear. Then her expression lightened. "However, I daresay when I tell her how very much I am longing to watch a grand review, she will agree to stay. She will not wish to spoil my pleasure, you know."

Huntley, who had been assisting the others in replacing the picnic supplies, approached the group in time to overhear Rory's last remarks. Nell noted with some misgiving that his brows had knitted together ominously. "I am sure," he said now, his tone rather sharp, "we must all see to it that Lady Agnes does not place more importance upon your pleasure than upon her own continued good health."

Rory looked up at him in quick protest, her gaze clashing with his. But it was she who looked away first, muttering that she was certain no one meant to endanger Grandmama's health.

Talcott chuckled, bringing the golden gaze to bear accusingly upon himself. "You behave yourself, lass," he ordered, unimpressed. "When you frown like that, it makes you look more like the witch of Endor than your Grandmama's golden angel."

Rory's lips twitched. Then laughter bubbled up again. "You do say the most outrageous things, sir." She turned back to Huntley. "I beg your pardon, my lord. I behaved childishly. Aunt Nell," she went on, holding out her hand, "do say you will forgive my thoughtlessness once more."

Nell had been thinking that the major's manners were quite as deplorable as her niece's, but at this turn of affairs she found herself regarding him with dawning respect. How easily he had banished the sulks. Here again was the endearing and disarming golden girl. Nell gave the hand that had been pressed into her own a firm squeeze and assured her niece that there was nothing to forgive. The two officers took their leave only a few moments later.

Rory looked at Nell. "I do want to see the sailing races, ma'am. Shall we accompany Kit and the others?"

"Oh, Rory, really," Nell protested. "There will be such a crush along the cliffside. I am sure we shall see enough of it if we but drive home with Mama along the esplanade and the Marine Parade."

Rory's face fell immediately, and a diffident voice sounded behind Nell. "There will be no crush where we'll be, ma'am." Seton's words banished the woebegone look as though by magic.

"Oh, Mr. Seton, do say we may come with you!"

"Don't be daft, Harry," Kit said. "There won't be room for all of us."

"Fact is, Miss Lindale," Harry said politely, ignoring him, "that my sister and her husband have taken a sitting room on the top floor of the Belle Vue Hotel for the day. We shall be able to view the entire race from there and in deuced elegant comfort, at that."

"But surely, Mr. Seton, your sister and her husband, obliging though I know them to be, cannot have expected you to bring such a large party as this. Why, you would be adding at least three persons, you know."

"Three!" He glanced at Nell and at Huntley, then recollected himself. "To be sure, ma'am. Just go. All welcome.

M' sister won't mind a bit. Assure you!'' He doffed his curly-brimmed hat to emphasize his point.

"Well, I am persuaded you mean it for the best . . .'' Nell began doubtfully.

"Let her go.''

She looked up at Huntley, her eyes wide. "Sir?''

"I said, let her go.''

"But——''

"Don't argue, Nell. See here, Lindale,'' he went on, raising his voice to reach Kit's ears, "you'll look after Aurora, won't you?''

"I . . .'' Kit looked dubious. "I expect so, sir. Don't you mean to come along, Nell?''

"Well, of course——''

"No, she doesn't,'' Huntley interrupted. "Your sister is suffering from the headache, as you could see for yourself if you would but take the trouble, so you may attend to your niece for a spell. We will meet you on the esplanade after the races, so that you will not need to see Aurora home again. I quite realize such a necessity might well interfere with your plans for the evening.''

"Well, that would make a difference, sir, but I'm not much of a dab——''

"Stubble it, Kit,'' Harry Seton interrupted quickly. "Lady Aurora wants to see the races. We'll help you look after her. M' sister will help you. Her husband—you know Tom, a fine fellow—daresay he'll help you, too.''

"Lord, Harry, don't run on like a fiddlestick!'' Kit snapped. "We'll take the chit if you're so dashed set on it.''

"Does that mean I may go with them, Aunt Nell?'' Rory demanded.

Nell looked doubtfully at Huntley. He nodded, a little smile playing upon his lips. "I suppose you may, dear. Kit,'' she added quietly, "I must place my dependence upon you.''

"I didn't ask for the charge,'' he grumbled.

"Nevertheless, Kit. . . .''

He gazed at her. "Oh, very well. Come along, then, my girl, and mind you don't land us all in the basket.''

Filled with misgivings, Nell watched them go, then turned to Huntley. "I hope we may not both be sorry for this, my lord. I must tell you—though, of course, I could say nothing before—that Mr. Seton's sister Mary is as young and flighty as Rory herself and not at all to be trusted. I have met her husband only once, and he is much like Harry, I fear. Can we truly place any dependence upon them to make sure Rory does nothing foolish?''

''We shall rely upon Lindale,'' his lordship said, smiling at her. ''You said last night that you desired an opportunity for private speech with me. The crowds have thinned out now, and a quiet walk will no doubt do much to ease your headache. Shall we leave your mother and Sir Henry to enjoy a bit of solitude?''

Sir Henry snored just then, and a gurgle of laughter escaped Nell's lips. ''I only hope he does not wake Mama,'' she said, still chuckling.

IX

"How did you guess I had the headache, sir?" Nell asked him after they had been walking for some moments in silence.

"You get tiny lines between your eyebrows and at the corners of your eyes," he replied. "I remembered the signs, that's all."

She digested his words slowly, then looked up at him with a teasing smile. " 'Tis not very chivalrous of you, sir, to call attention to the lines in a lady's face."

"Are you offended, Nell?" He looked down, his gaze seeming to catch and even to search her own for a brief moment before she looked away. "I thought not. It was an excellent picnic," he added.

"Yes," she agreed, grateful for the change of subject. "Cook prides herself on such cold collations as that. I particularly like her fried chicken. There is some spice or other that she uses that——"

"All right, Nell, take a damper."

"You brought up the subject," she pointed out. "I was merely doing my possible to pursue it."

"The devil you were. You are not usually so diffident, my dear. In general, I have found you to be refreshingly direct. What did you wish to say to me?"

He was right about her lack of diffidence. Nell had not previously thought she had retained a diffident bone in her body. In the old days, to be sure, she had been shy upon meeting new people, and had found it to be extraordinarily difficult to indulge in the general sort of small talk that was so common at social affairs. But even then, within the ranks of her own family and friends, she had not been averse to speaking her mind. In fact, she had often thought that perhaps it had been her more assertive habits rather than her shyness that had kept her from finding a suitable husband during her first and only Season.

She realized that Huntley was patiently awaiting her response, and tried to think how to answer him. Though she believed they were in a way to regaining their old footing, she did not wish him to think she was daring to criticize his behavior, nor—remembering his comments about his sister—did she want him to think she had grown overly assertive. For although she had not before believed him to be a man easily intimidated by others, he had said he was, and she had seen for herself his reaction to Lady Agnes's gentle vinaigrette.

"I believe," she said at last, slowly, "that I have made my opinions clear, my lord."

"Cut the formality, Nell. It is unnecessary. Do you refer to your wish that I should lend my escort whenever you and Aurora accept an invitation for an evening's pleasure?"

She nodded. "Oh, not every invitation, my lor—— Sorry," she interjected quickly when he shot her a pained look from under his heavy brows. "I do realize that you have obligations of your own, and neither Rory nor I would expect you to be continually dancing attendance upon us. Even a husband would not do so much as that. But I do think you ought to make your claims more evident than you have been making them, lest her behavior and your lack of interest serve to inform others that she is free to accept their advances."

"You think I should be with her now, do you not?" Her silence answered him, and he sighed. "I confess that after an hour or so I begin to find the company of Rory and her young friends a trifle tedious. 'Tis no doubt due to my advancing years."

Laughing, Nell shook her head at him. "Really, sir, there is nothing at all advanced about your age. One look at Sir Henry ought to reassure you on that score." But then she turned serious again. "Do you not fear that perhaps you will find Rory tiresome as a bride?"

He shrugged. "It is a possibility, I daresay, but it is a condition that must, in the nature of things, be leavened by time. At all events, since the halls of Huntley Green are not likely to be found teeming with other members of the younger set, I shall have only Aurora to contend with. No doubt she will soon learn to conform peaceably to my wishes."

She stared at him, thinking in amazement that he seemed perfectly sincere. For the first time, Nell entertained some doubts about the possibility of Huntley's making a suitable husband for her niece. It was clear at any rate that if his future was not to be made entirely miserable, he must be brought to a better understanding of Rory's nature. And since no one else was likely to take the trouble to explain matters to him, Nell came to the uncomfortable conclusion that she must take that task upon herself. She straightened her shoulders and, laying a gentle hand upon his arm, drew him to a halt.

"Let us sit quietly beneath that tree yonder, my friend," she said quietly. "I think we must discuss this business more thoroughly."

Obediently, he followed her, and once they were seated on the grass beneath the tree, Nell searched her mind for a tactful way to begin. There were other people strolling about on the green, but none who gave them more than a passing glance. Huntley smiled at her.

"Well?"

"You must know that my niece has been greatly indulged all her life, sir," she began, still feeling her way.

"Indeed, and what is that to say to anything? Do you fear I shall deprive her of the little luxuries she is accustomed to? I assure you, I have no such intention. I do think her a trifle spoiled, however, and I have no intention of allowing her to rule the roast. Surely, you do not expect that of me."

"It is not merely that Rory is accustomed to luxuries, sir. She is also accustomed to getting her own way. I cannot believe you actually thought it a good notion to let her go off with those young rattles this afternoon. Yet you agreed to the scheme. It was not, believe me, a good precedent to set."

"I encouraged her to go because I wished to speak with you."

"You might have contrived to speak privately with me," she pointed out, "and still have kept her safely here with us."

"You contradict yourself, my girl."

"I am not your girl, and I wish you will stop taking such familiarities with me, sir. 'Tis most improper. And do not quibble," she added more tartly yet when he only smiled at her. "Rory might just as easily have remained with Mama and Sir Henry while we had our talk. You sent her off with Kit and the others because you did not wish to be subjected to a fit of the sullens, or worse. And if that is plain speaking, well I'm sorry for it, but I believe it to be the case."

"Do you truly think me incapable of dealing with a childish fit of the sullens?" His voice was gentle, but there was also a note in it that she could not identify.

"Yes, I do," she answered roundly. "Not when the fit is one of Rory's. You would scold her, sir, which merely serves to stir her resentment. She must be coaxed and jollied along and treated with gentleness. I had thought you would understand that, for you appeared always to be a patient man. But now you seem quick to exasperation, which can only serve you ill, sir."

He looked thoughtful for a moment before he spoke. "I am sorry if you think I am too quick to scold her, but to put the matter bluntly, ma'am, your niece displays a lamentable resistance to having her actions curtailed in any way, which is one of her less endearing characteristics and one that will have to change as she grows older. She cannot expect to continue to do as she pleases without regard for anyone else. Such behavior may have done well enough in her father's home. It will not be tolerated in mine."

"Oh dear," Nell said. "I do not envy you the months ahead."

"I daresay you fear tears and tantrums, do you not? I cannot deny the possibility, of course, but I am not an ogre. I do realize that Rory is very young. But you must have realized that her youth is an advantage. She has not yet become so set in her ways that she cannot change. One of the main reasons, in fact, that I have chosen to allow her a loose rein here in Brighton is that I wish her to see for herself that I mean her no harm. However, if my indulgence is going to be interpreted by others as a lack of interest, I quite agree that I must make a greater show of my presence. Now, what do you say to a stroll toward the esplanade? We shall excuse ourselves to your mama and Sir Henry, or to your coachman if they are not yet receiving visitors, and then I shall inform Laxton that I desire him to meet us later with my carriage."

Nell nodded and let him help her to her feet, even chuckling when he threatened to murder her if he had gotten grass stains on his cream-colored breeches. But her thoughts were moving in other directions.

Huntley honestly seemed to believe that with his guidance

Rory would simply mend her ways to suit his, but Nell, having seen for herself the results of a no-doubt severe tongue-lashing the previous evening, did not for a moment believe her niece would prove to be so malleable as his lordship expected. Rory only resented such interference in her pleasure. At this rate, and with nothing to prevent it, their marriage would surely prove to be a continual battleground. Nell decided she would consider the matter more deeply. Surely there must be a way to steer his lordship toward a more acceptable, less frustrating, method of dealing with Rory's volatile character.

Since they made no effort to hurry, the afternoon was waning, and the breeze blowing in across the cliffs was growing crisper by the time they reached the esplanade. There were still a good many persons strolling about on the lawn, but it was clear that the race was done, for several people were standing on the sea wall, a thing that certainly would not have been tolerated by the spectators lined up behind them while the race was in progress. Suddenly Nell gave a little cry of dismay and clutched at Huntley's arm.

"I see her," he replied grimly. "Come along." His pace increased to a speed that made it difficult for Nell to keep up with him, but she skipped and nearly ran at his side rather than begging him to slow down. The sight that had stiffened his pace was that of the Lady Aurora Crossways standing up with several others on the sea wall. Rory saw them approaching just then and waved, calling out their names.

"Merciful heavens, she will fall!" Nell exclaimed.

"Nonsense," he replied. "She will not be that lucky."

She could tell from the set of his jaw that he was angry, but she dared not warn him now to control his temper for fear of inciting it further. Besides, she would rather like to tear a strip from her niece, herself. As they drew nearer, she realized that things were worse than she had feared, for she had seen her brother and his friends. They were arm in arm below Rory on the flagway and appeared to be singing. Rory was waving her arms as if she were a conductor leading an orchestra.

"They must be tipsy," Nell said, annoyed. "Otherwise, surely they would make her get down from there. They must realize how dangerous it is."

"They are all castaway," Huntley growled.

"All? Surely, you don't mean Rory as well!" she protested, peering ahead to get a better look at her niece. Rory seemed only very gay. Her eyes sparkled and there was a great deal of color in her cheeks. Several hairpins seemed to have escaped her coif, and there were strands of golden hair blowing about her face, but she seemed energetic rather than tipsy. Nevertheless, when Nell looked up at Huntley, he nodded, not seeming to doubt for a moment that Rory had been imbibing something other than lemonade or orgeat.

They had reached the group by now, and Kit was the first of the gentlemen to see them. He grinned at his sister.

"Step right up, m'dear," he said cheerfully. "Dashed if you shan't join us in a rousing chorus. All right now, boys, with a fal lal lal—all together now!"

"Kit! Whatever are you about?"

"Now, don't be a dashed spoilsport, Nell. Sing!"

"Lindale!" Huntley's voice ripped across the intervening space.

Kit's eyes focused with difficulty on his lordship. "Sir?"

"I shall not attempt to discuss your perfidy with you here, young man, but I shall most certainly want a word in private with you later."

"I, too," Nell said, her own temper flaring as she watched her niece swaying atop the sea wall. It was clear enough now that Rory was not simply indulging high spirits. "Rory, come down from there at once!"

"Aunt Nell, you cannot imagine how high above the sea one is when one stands up here. Come up and see for yourself. 'Tis prodigious exciting!"

"Come down, Rory," Nell said, gritting her teeth.

"Well, I won't. 'Tis far too intoxicating to be so high up in the world. The air is wonderfully rarefied. You must try it . . . Oh, how dare you!" she demanded in sudden fury as Huntley reached up and lifted her unceremoniously to the pavement. Despite her struggles, he retained a firm hold on her and commanded Nell in grim tones to look about her for a team of dappled grays drawing a dark green landaulet with its wheels picked out in yellow.

"In front of the Bedford at the end nearest the Mansion," she said a moment later. "Oh, Philip, couldn't you release her? People are beginning to stare."

"Let them," he retorted harshly. A moment later, he bent

his head to whisper something in Rory's ear, and though she glared at him and seemed perilously near to tears, she ceased her violent struggles and allowed him to guide her past the others. Nell hurried along in their wake, ignoring the surprised inquiries from Kit's friends as to why they were taking themselves off in such a rush.

"Won't you join us for supper?" Harry Seton called after them. "'M' sister's ordered a bang-up spread, and there's still the odd bottle of champagne left, y'know. You're welcome. Lady Agnes and Sir Henry, too, if they've a mind."

Nell couldn't bring herself to reply at all, but she thought from the look of him that he was enjoying a state of inebriety far more advanced than Rory's, which made it fairly certain that he wouldn't remember her lack of manners any time beyond the next few moments, anyway.

Ahead of her, Huntley had managed to catch his driver's eye, and the dark green landaulet was moving slowly through the crowded street toward them. A few moments later, Rory was seated on the forward seat wrapped up in a warm blanket and glowering at her future husband while he addressed a few shattering home truths to her in tones that made Nell, an uncomfortable third party, fervently wish herself elsewhere. Once he had had his say, a tense silence enfolded them all, but since Nell, at least, kept expecting another explosion from one or the other of her two companions, the journey back to Upper Rock Gardens was scarcely a comfortable one.

Once they reached the house, Huntley stepped down from the carriage and stretched out a hand first to Nell and then to Rory. The younger girl seemed unnaturally subdued, which was not to be wondered at, Nell thought sympathetically, following her into the house. Huntley asked Jeremy, who opened the door to them, to send for her ladyship's maid.

"I'll go up with her," Nell said.

"No, I want to speak with you," he said quietly. "She will prefer to have her maid just now, I assure you."

"But I could take her up and then come back, my lord."

"No, Nell."

Rory's gaze drifted vaguely from one to the other. The high color was gone now, and her cheeks seemed pale, although her eyes had an odd sparkle and her pupils seemed overlarge. She still did not speak.

Sadie came hurrying to greet them, clucking her tongue at

her mistress's indisposition and saying Miss Lindale could just leave her to see she was all right. Rory no longer swayed when she walked. In fact, Nell thought she moved rather stiffly. She mentioned this observation to Huntley when they had adjourned to the small green saloon.

He chuckled. "She's simply determined to look as though she's perfectly all right, that's all. You should have seen what I used to look like when I'd come home and meet my father in the hall after a night out on the tiles. I walked like an animated poker. Must have given the old man more than the odd chuckle, I must say."

"Well, I don't think it's funny, sir. I don't for a moment believe she knew what she was about, and I think you were very harsh with her. Though, to be sure, she might have been seriously injured had she fallen from the wall, and I think it's a disgrace that those young men encouraged her to behave in such a fashion. But I hope you don't mean to scold me as well, for I warned you how it would be. Oh, I should have trusted my instincts and refused to allow her to go off with them! Only think of that Mary Seton, or whatever her name is now, letting her have champagne!"

"Lord, you don't think it was a mere glass or two of champagne, do you? If that young lady hasn't been trying her taste for gin, you may call me a Dutchman."

"Well, I shouldn't do anything so uncivil. But what makes you certain it was gin? I know Mr. Seton said they had champagne."

"I could smell the gin on her breath," he replied. "And if they had champagne before, I can tell you she didn't drink much of either one or she'd be very sick by now. I daresay she merely had a glass of the one and a few swallows, if that much, of the other. Foolish beyond permission, of course, and she deserved everything I said to her, but I'm sorry you had to witness such a scene, Nell." He paused, smiling down at her in a way that made her pulse beat a good deal faster. "The real culprit is that brother of yours, you know. He should have known better than to allow her to drink more than a very small glass of the wine."

"Indeed, and I shall have his head for this dreadful business," Nell agreed, but the words, uttered as they were while she was staring into his eyes, lacked force.

"Perhaps you had better wait until I have spoken with

him," his lordship said gently. "I shall endeavor to leave you a nibble or two." The sally made her chuckle, and he winked at her. "As for that baggage upstairs, give her some moments to recover her dignity before you go up, and if she is sleeping, so much the better. It has been a long day already, and there is still the ball at the Pavilion to be got through. And Nell?" He waited until she looked up at him again. "Don't think too badly of me for losing my temper. I daresay you are right, and she had no notion what would happen, but she will know better next time. The scold will not have harmed her in the slightest, and no doubt she will be feeling heartily ashamed of herself before long."

Nell did not expect any such proper feeling to manifest itself, but she had better sense than to say so at this juncture. Therefore, she merely agreed with him, adding that she had a thing or two she meant to say to Rory before the matter was laid to rest.

"Well, don't scold her too sternly," he said, grinning when she made a face at him, then turning serious again. "It is a pity she made a display of herself in public, but I daresay few if any of the onlookers know her by sight. It is not as if she disgraced herself at Almack's Assembly Rooms in London, after all. That would have ruined her." He stood up. "I shall leave you now and return at nine o'clock. She should be perfectly well recovered by that time."

Nell went with him into the hall and then went upstairs to discover that, as he had predicted, Rory was tucked up in bed and already asleep. "She's dreadfully tired, Miss Lindale," Sadie said in hushed tones. "I shouldn't be at all suprised if she was to sleep clear through to morning, poor lamb."

"Well, she is not to sleep so long, Sadie, and I depend upon you to see she is awake soon enough to have some tea and something to eat before she dresses for the ball."

"Oh, ma'am, I doubt my lady should go out tonight at all."

"The decision is not yours to make, however," Nell said firmly. "The responsibility for seeing that she awakens at a reasonable hour I do leave to you, however. And I shall expect you to obey me, Sadie. Is that perfectly clear?"

"Yes, ma'am." Flushing, young Sadie dropped a hasty curtsy, and Nell departed, satisfied that her charge would be up and dressed in time to leave for the ball when Huntley arrived. For a short time she had feared that Rory's foolhardiness would keep them from attending the ball altogether. And Nell had never seen the inside of the prince's Pavilion.

Mrs. Fitzherbert and the prince had been separated the year of Nell's come-out and were not reunited until some three years later. It was then that his highness had plunged into his startling new adventures in architecture. The chief of these, of course, was the magnificent royal stables, which had been finished only some weeks before. While the building of the stables was still in progress, however, it had occurred to the prince that with all the old and new friends who would be flocking around him and Mrs. Fitzherbert, the Pavilion itself would have to be enlarged. In consequence, he had asked Henry Holland to prepare some designs, and it had been feared by many of Brighton's worthy citizens that his highness would indulge his well-known penchant for oriental fantasy. Instead, he had finally decided to project two new wings in a classical style from the eastern facade, the northern one to form a dining room and the southern one a conservatory or drawing room.

The prince had not denied himself his fantasies, however, for the whole of the interior had been transformed and completely decorated in the Chinese style. Nell had heard a great deal about it from persons whose opinions as to its elegance and beauty differed widely, and she was most anxious to see the results for herself.

When the news reached her that evening that Huntley had arrived, she took a final hasty look at herself in the walnut-framed cheval glass, gave a twitch to her pale blue silk skirts to smooth the line at the curve of her hips, straightened the narrow, sapphire-colored bow just beneath her firm breasts, snatched up her velvet cloak, and hurried to her niece's room.

"Rory, are you ready to depart?" she asked as she pushed open the door. Then she stopped and stared at the radiant vision before her. The Lady Aurora was not wearing the sort of plain white muslin gown that was the garb ordained for the debutante. Instead, she had chosen a pale-yellow, low-cut silk that shimmered in the candlelight of her bedchamber and that clung seductively to every generous curve. It was a gown destined to set men's eyes popping, Nell thought, although since Rory was already betrothed, there was nothing really improper about it. If it was not quite what people might expect, it was still extraordinarily becoming to its wearer, and she could not help a small gasp of admiration. Rory turned to face her.

"Do you like it?" She smoothed the emerald sash and twisted her head to see if it fell properly in the back. Then, drawing on emerald elbow-length gloves, she waited confidently for her aunt's response.

"Oh, Rory, you look truly like a golden girl tonight!" Nell exclaimed. "It is an exquisite gown, and oh, my dear, if I had had your figure eight years ago, I might have named my destiny."

Pleasure glowed on Rory's lovely face, and she declared herself ready. The look in Huntley's eyes when he beheld them told Nell that he, too, was impressed with the younger girl's appearance. It occurred to her only then that she had said nothing to Rory about the afternoon's incident. She wondered if he would speak further of it, but he did not, and Rory herself seemed to have put the matter out of her mind entirely. The brief journey to the Pavilion was enlivened by her excited questions about what she would see there and Huntley's patient replies. Nell began to look forward with more enthusiasm than ever to the evening ahead.

The carriage arrived at last, passing through the lodge gates to draw up to the porch, where they descended to join the throng of merry guests making their way into the Pavilion itself. They followed the crowd through the entrance halls and a large gallery, then into a splendid salon and the famous Chinese gallery, which had been created by throwing the original dining room and library together into one enormous chamber. The walls were hung with very beautiful Chinese paper and the rest of the gallery had been painted and decorated in a corresponding style.

After greeting their beaming host, Huntley guided the ladies toward the music room, explaining that a good many of the furnishings had come from London when the Chinese Room at Carlton House had been dismantled. There were immense quantities of Chinese porcelain, chairs, stools, and sofas of bamboo, cabinets of Japanese lacquerwork, as well as other oriental decorations and curiosities of all kinds. There were even Chinese costumes and weapons, and everything was illuminated by brilliant Chinese lanterns hanging from the ceilings. It was as if, Nell confided to Huntley, his highness had sought to re-create the legendary land of Cathay that had been sought by explorers for so many hundreds of years.

"Do you like it?"

"I think it is enchanting," she said. "Don't you?"

"The oriental influence is a trifle overblown for my tastes," he confessed with a rueful twinkle. "I think Huntley Green would look a little odd tarted up with bamboo forests and scarlet peonies. And it would startle me to come upon an oriental fisherman fishing from a niche in one of my corridors."

Nell chuckled appreciatively, but Rory grimaced and announced that there was no need to spoil everyone else's pleasure just because he hadn't got a romantic bone in his body. Nell stared at her.

"Surely you realized that his lordship was funning!"

"Don't be a goose, Aunt Nell. You don't think for a minute that he *would* allow bamboo-decorated wallpaper at his precious Huntley Green, do you?"

"Well, if you think you could actually live amidst all this," Nell retorted, gesturing toward several cabinets loaded with fragile bric-a-brac, "let me tell you that you would soon change your mind. How do you suppose you would sleep in such a cluttered room?"

"You just said it was enchanting!"

"And so it is, my dear, here in the Pavilion. That doesn't mean I should like to achieve a similar result in Upper Rock Gardens, I assure you."

Rory looked for a moment as if she might like to continue the debate, but suddenly her cheeks glowed with an extra touch of color, and the sparkle in her eye was enough to inform Nell, even before she followed the direction of the girl's steady gaze, that Rory had discovered her target for the evening.

X

Nell experienced a sense of astonishment when she realized that the focal point of Rory's rapt gaze was none other than Major Gideon Talcott. She had been nearly certain that the younger girl would be ripe for a new conquest by now. But she could see no one else who might have drawn Rory's eye, and that was surely the major and no other in the crowd ahead of them.

They passed along one side of a magnificent, illuminated stained-glass enclosure that resembled a giant Chinese lantern, exhibiting the insects, fruit, and exotic flowers of the Orient, and Nell's attention was momentarily diverted from Major Talcott. By the time they entered the music room, he seemed to have drifted away in the crowd, and a glance at Rory's crestfallen expression told her aunt that she, too, had lost sight of him. Nell leaned nearer in order that her words would carry no farther than the younger girl's ears.

"You would be well-advised, my dear," she said gently, "to behave with all propriety tonight. Your copybook, you might remember, is a bit blotted at the moment."

Delicate color suffused Rory's cheeks, but she vouchsafed no answer other than a brief nod. It was enough to satisfy Nell, however. Huntley escorted them to a set of chairs near the wall, and soon afterward there came a stir from the musician's gallery as they began to make ready to play for the first set of country dances.

The prince and Mrs. Fitzherbert led the first two or three dances and then retired to an elegantly draped dais from which they could view the activities of their guests and where his highness might receive further congratulations upon his birthday. Nell, sitting out the first dance and watching Huntley and her niece, noted that Rory seemed to be giving him less than her undivided attention as her eyes moved in a continuous attempt to locate Major Talcott. When she suddenly relaxed, a secret little smile playing upon her lips, Nell knew she had found him.

He stepped up to greet them the moment they returned. "I trust your card is not yet filled, my lady," he said in his pleasant voice.

"Oh, no, indeed, sir. Why 'tis but half filled," she replied happily.

"Inconceivable." His eyes twinkled, and Nell could not be surprised when he received an immediate, glowing response. She glanced at Huntley, but he seemed unaware of any byplay, merely shaking hands with Talcott and greeting him politely.

The major took Rory's card and scrawled his name in two separate places. When he held it out to her again, she looked for a moment as if she might point out the fact that there were several other blank spaces, but she apparently thought better of the notion and merely smiled up at him as she accepted her card. The next dance was the first by which he had entered his name, so once the music began, he bowed briefly to Nell and swept Rory off to join the nearest set.

Nell looked at her companion a bit warily, wondering if he might be annoyed. Huntley glanced down at her just then and she saw not annoyance but humor in the hazel eyes.

"Afraid of me, Nell?"

"Of course not," she retorted instantly. "What a ridiculous notion, my lord. I cannot think what can have put such a thought into your head."

He chuckled, taking a seat beside her. "Perhaps 'twas the fact that you looked for a moment as if you feared I might bite."

She grinned back at him, then lifted an eyebrow ruefully. "I doubt you would bite, sir, though I confess I did fear you might be a trifle annoyed when I did nothing to intervene."

"Intervene?"

"Well, the major has been a bit particular in his attentions, and there are some who would say I ought, as Rory's chaperon, to put a stop to them."

"I, however, do not number among them," he said.

"Your partner will be wondering what has become of you,

sir," she pointed out, suddenly, and for no good reason that she knew of, nervous of his presence.

"I have no partner."

The answer flustered her. "B-but you cannot . . . that is, you must have partners, sir. You cannot mean to dance only with Rory. People would surely talk."

"They would think me an eccentric fellow?"

"Indeed. And you would not like your name and Rory's to be bandied about in public, sir."

"This afternoon you called me Philip," he said irrelevantly, and she saw from the deepening twinkle in his eyes that he was laughing at her.

Her color mounted, but she faced him squarely. "No doubt I forgot my manners in the agitation of the moment, my lord," she said.

He chuckled. "No doubt. But I prefer my name to all the blasted sirs and my lords you see fit to shower over me, my dear. Do you not think you could—by virtue of our long-standing friendship—put aside these airs of propriety at least when we are alone?"

The twinkle in his eye set her heart thumping, but she did her best to consider his request. After all, they had been good friends, although she would have used the term *long-ago*, to describe that friendship, rather than *long-standing*. Still, that was little more than a quibble, and as it would clearly be tactless of her to point out that he had not asked his intended bride to use his given name——

"Nell?"

She started, flushing more deeply and giving herself a small shake as she recognized the trend her thoughts had been taking. "I beg your pardon, sir, but you are betrothed to my niece, and it would be unseemly of me to make free with your name. Furthermore, you must find a partner. What will people think if you continue to sit here beside me when you should be joining in the dance?"

"Nell, Nell," he said in a gentle reproof, "you are too sensitive. What else should they think, but that I am biding my time before my betrothed returns by passing an agreeable few moments with her aunt?"

"But——"

"No more buts, if you please," he said, smiling now. "You have told me that I must make my interests plain, and I can think of no better way. Aurora would certainly not take it kindly if I were such a sapskull as to attempt to monopolize *her* time. I daresay she would balk at more than two dances with me. I shall be lucky, in fact, if I can get her to accompany me down to supper without a scene.''

His words made sense, but Nell could not help thinking that he might make more of a push to define his position with her niece than just to sit beside her all evening. It would accomplish little if Rory intended to flirt as much as she had done on other occasions. Not but what it would be most agreeable. She gave herself another little shake.

"Do you mean to sit here *all* evening?" she asked.

"Well, I shall dance another dance with Aurora, of course. I put my name down for the second contradanse. But aside from that, I see no reason why I should not sit with you. Unless. . . .''

"Unless what?" she asked suspiciously.

He turned a little more in his chair in order to look at her directly. His eyes seemed to be teasing her, she thought idly. They were very nice eyes.

"Unless you will agree to stop being fusty about your duties long enough to dance. There is no reason I can think of for you to plant yourself in that chair for the entire evening. I've seen the way your feet beat time to the music, my girl. You are just bursting at the seams to join the others. If you will engage yourself to allow a few of the gentlemen who approach you to sign their names on your card, then I shall endeavor to trot a few of the more likely damsels onto the floor, as well. What do you say, Nell?''

"But my mama never danced when she took me about!" Nell protested.

He chuckled. "Your mama never exerts herself without dire need to do so. Believe me, the only ladies who did not dance to the assemblies we attended in London were those who were absolutely decrepit and who attended merely to play cards. You agreed to dance with me last evening when I pointed out that your sister would never sit still just because she had her daughter in tow. So just you hand over that card, my girl. Now.'' He held out his hand imperatively. She looked at it, then raised her eyes.

It did seem silly when he put matters into such a perspective. She had taken her cue from her own mother's behavior during her come-out and, for that matter, the behavior of most of her friends' mothers. None of them danced. Mostly, they sat in a corner together and gossiped. But as she looked around now, she could see several women her sister's age, at least two of whom had daughters who had made their come-outs this year, and they were dancing despite the fact that their daughters, still unmarried, were doing likewise. Huntley was smiling down at her, and his smile was a warm one. Still, there was a look of implacability in his eyes that made her hesitate to press the matter further. Indeed, she did not know why she would want to press it further. He was quite right. Even now her feet were keeping time beneath the lace flounce of her pale blue skirts. She returned his smile and handed him her dance card.

"Very well, sir."

"Much better." He scrawled his name twice, then looked up and gave a short nod with his head. Before Nell could imagine what he was doing, several young men approached her and requested the privilege of signing her card. She gazed at Huntley in amazement.

He grinned at her. "You know most of these rattles, I daresay. MacElroy, here, asked me to do my possible. The others agreed. Said it was a dashed shame such a beauty was intent upon remaining upon the sidelines when it was clear she was meant for dancing. Couldn't help but agree with them. There, Flint, pass that card along to Braithwaite, behind you." He looked down at Nell. "I trust you are not annoyed with me," he said quietly. "MacElroy is no more than a fashionable fribble, but he dances passably well, and the others are good sorts. I am persuaded you will enjoy the festivities much more as a participant than as on onlooker."

"And you, my lord? Shall you keep your part of the bargain?"

He sighed. "I shall. Not that that means I shall be dancing as much as it appears you will be. But I shall endeavor to do more than merely hold up one of these so elegant walls. And to keep an eye on my prospective bride, as well," he added with a little smile.

The rest of the evening seemed to pass quicky for Nell. Only twice did she lose sight of Rory for any length of time. Upon the first of these occasions, she had a strong sense of having failed in her duty and spent several anxious moments searching for her before she saw her approaching on Huntley's arm and realized that he had merely taken her to find some refreshment. Upon the second such occasion, her anxiety was not so great, for she was quite certain that Rory would reappear within moments, as indeed she did. If Nell was not particularly pleased to see that this time, as she made her way through the crowd of merrymakers, Rory was accompanied by her current favorite among the Prince's Own, she was too glad to have her charge restored to her to say anything. It was only as the pair drew nearer that Nell realized that Rory was looking oddly subdued, while her large partner wore an air of sternness that she had not seen before.

She said nothing to indicate that she had noticed anything out of the way, and the major politely excused himself, saying that he must find his next partner. Rory was silent, cheering up only when her own partner came to claim her hand for the minuet. Nell was engaged to dance it with Mr. MacElroy, who strolled up but a moment later, apologizing for keeping her waiting.

" 'Twas this demmed lace," he moaned, showing her the delicate edging of his cuff. "M' last partner had a demmed bracelet, kept catching in it. Beg pardon, Miss Lindale, but knew you'd understand."

Nell grinned at him and assured him that she had not been waiting long. There was scarcely a dance after that for which her hand was not engaged, and by the time Huntley informed her that he had called for his carriage, her feet hurt and she was beginning to yearn for her bed. Rory had been enjoying herself hugely, however, so she had disliked suggesting departure before. She had not seen hide nor hair of the major and could only be thankful that her niece was enjoying herself without flirting any further with him.

Rory agreed quickly when Nell told her that Huntley was ready to depart. She smiled at friends as they passed and retained her gay attitude until they were actually inside the carriage, when she slumped back against the squabs and went silent. The coachman gave his horses the office, and the carriage lurched forward.

"Rory, dear," Nell said after a silent moment or two, "do you feel quite the thing?"

"I expect I'm just tired, Aunt Nell," the girl said quietly. "It was a very nice evening."

" 'Tis no wonder if you're tired,'' Huntley murmured. " 'Twould be even more wonderful if there is a scrap of leather left to the soles of your slippers. You must have stood up for every dance.''

"Yes, I think I did,'' Rory answered politely. But then her voice changed oddly. "At least, nearly every one.''

In the light from the carriage lamps Nell could see an expression of unhappiness flit across the younger girl's face. She wanted to ask her about it, but decided the timing was not good. Better to wait until they were alone. Instead, she drew Huntley into conversation with herself, letting Rory have a semblance of privacy for her own thoughts. He responded easily enough, and they discussed the various gentlemen who had followed his lead in asking Nell to dance, laughing together over MacElroy's snagged lace.

Pavingham was waiting to admit them to the house, and Huntley stepped inside to bid them good night. Rory was still silent, but Nell thanked him warmly for escorting them, and he turned to take his leave.

"My lord, wait.'' Rory's words were spoken low, but he heard them and turned back, an expression of polite inquiry on his face. Nell stared at her niece, then realized Rory was looking with some misgiving at Pavingham, who lingered in the hall waiting to put out the candles behind them.

"Shall we go into the saloon?'' Nell asked, looking directly at her niece.

"Oh, no—that is . . .'' She glanced at Pavingham again. "Oh, very well, perhaps it would be better.''

"Tea, Miss Nell?''

"No, thank you, Pavingham. His lordship will be leaving directly. Perhaps, however, you will inform Madge and her ladyship's Sadie that we are returned.''

With Pavingham satisfactorily disposed of, she turned her attention to Rory again, drawing her gently into the green saloon and waiting until Huntley had shut the door behind them. Then another thought occurred to her.

"Do you wish to be private with his lordship, my dear? I shall go upstairs if you like.'' She glanced at Huntley, who looked only puzzled.

"No.'' Rory nearly clutched at her arm. "I want to speak to both of you. I-I behaved badly this afternoon, and I must make you both m-my profoundest apologies. I-I didn't know what would happen. Please believe me. But I made such a figure of myself, and I know that you, at least, my lord, were prodigiously angry with me. And, Aunt Nell, you have been so kind to me. To serve you such a trick when you trusted me . . ." She broke off, looking perilously near to tears, and Nell stepped quickly forward to place a reassuring arm around her shoulders.

"There, there, dear heart," she said quietly. " 'Twas nothing that cannot be mended. Even his lordship has said so." She glanced beseechingly at him, astonished to see amusement flickering in his eyes. But he responded quickly enough.

"Indeed, Aurora, you have not ruined yourself or anyone else," he said lightly. "You behaved badly, but I daresay you will have learned a valuable lesson from it all and will never do such a foolish thing again."

Rory stiffened but recollected herself immediately and murmured something about how good he was to see the matter in such a light. Then she turned to Nell.

"Will you excuse me, ma'am? I-I find I can scarcely keep my eyes open."

Nell nodded. "Of course, dear. I shall come with you. Good night, my lord."

"One moment, if you please, Miss Lindale. Aurora will not mind if I detain you for a moment or two. Good night, Aurora."

Rory didn't hesitate to leave them, and Nell turned back to Huntley the moment the door had shut behind her. "Well, sir, I scarcely like to think what Pavingham will think if he returns to find us closeted together like this."

"Worried about your reputation, Nell?"

She twinkled up at him. "No, my lord, about yours. I am a respectable spinster lady, you know. 'Tis your credit that would suffer were my servants to think you were trifling with me."

He chuckled appreciatively. "I had hoped for praise from you for my deft handling of that little situation."

"Praise, sir?"

"Indeed. I followed your orders, I think, by saying nothing more about the business. However, I did not notice that she was particularly appreciative to be let off easily. Did you say something to her earlier that led to that affecting little scene?"

"No, indeed I did not," Nell replied, wrinkling her brow as she thought back over the evening behind them. In her mind's eye she saw a picture of Rory returning to her side upon Major Talcott's arm and, remembering their expressions, had no difficulty determining the fact that he was responsible for the apology they had just received. She glanced uncertainly at his lordship. "I-I daresay she simply decided that an apology was in order."

"Just as I expected," he pointed out. "Told you so from the outset. Aurora is not completely thoughtless, merely a bit spoiled. I daresay the incident has been preying upon her mind since this afternoon, and it just spilled over once we were all together and could be private."

"Perhaps you are right, sir," Nell returned, keeping her thoughts to herself. "And it was kind of you not to scold, when I know you must have been longing to do so."

"Nothing of the sort," he retorted. "Your brother is the only one I've got harsh words for now. Aurora, though she ought to have known better than to drink the stuff, had no means of knowing what would happen to her. But he knew perfectly well and deserves to be soundly thrashed."

"You . . ."

He chuckled. "Don't worry. I'll give the lad a rare dressing, but nothing more. That much I can promise you. I am not given to violence, my dear."

Nell was nearly as certain as she could be that the business had not been entirely Kit's doing, nor that of his friends. But she could imagine no good to be gotten out of arguing the point with Huntley just now. Besides, Kit could take care of himself, and one of Huntley's thundering scolds would do him no harm, so without further discussion, she bade his lordship good night and took herself up to her niece's bedchamber.

Upon being told she might enter, Nell pushed open the door to discover the Lady Aurora wrapped in a fluffy confection of ribbons and lace and seated at her dressing table, while Sadie meticulously brushed out the long, golden tresses.

"What a very fetching night dress, my dear," Nell said, reaching out her hand to take the brush from the maid. "Here, Sadie, I'll do that. I wish to speak privately with her ladyship."

"But, I always see my lady to bed, miss."

Nell caught Rory's eye in the looking glass.

"You may go, Sadie," the girl said quietly.

Accepting the silver brush from the maid's reluctant hand, Nell applied it rhythmically to the silky golden curls. "Thank you, dearest. I thought we should have a little talk."

"Are you still vexed with me, Aunt Nell?" Rory looked a trifle anxious as she waited for the response.

"Not vexed, precisely," Nell replied, "but I am disturbed and think we should perhaps discuss the matter."

"Well, I think everyone is making a great piece of work about nothing," said Rory sulkily. She began toying with the hairpins on the dressing table before her, absently making patterns with them, then she glanced up again, catching Nell's eye in the mirror. "Was it truly awful? I don't care about Huntley's opinion. He's always stuffy. But Gid—— But you," she corrected herself quickly, "are not. So if I truly vexed you, I am sorry for it. However, I have already appologized, so I cannot think why we must discuss the matter any further."

"Rory, you know perfectly well that you behaved very badly, and that there is still a good deal that ought to be said. Why, if Mama knew anything about it, she would very likely suffer one of her spasms, so we are fortunate that no one happened to be there who knows you are her granddaughter. I assure you, if she were to hear of it, it would distress her very much." She paused to see what, if any, effect her words were having. Rory bit her lip, which Nell took to be a good sign. She went on gently. "Huntley believes you had no notion how the spirits would affect you. Is he correct in that belief?" The young girl's gaze shifted back to the hairpins, and the color in her cheeks deepened by at least two shades. "I thought as much," Nell said. "You are too intelligent, my dear, not to have guessed how it would be. What did you drink?"

"Two very small glasses of champagne," Rory answered readily. "Mr. Seton's sister and her husband were partaking of a bottle when we arrived and offered some to us. I did not think it would matter if I had a little."

"And the gin? Where did you come by that, Rory?"

Rory tried to look innocent but failed entirely and turned her eyes away again when Nell merely returned the look with one of patience. "Mr. Seton had a flask in his coat pocket. I only had a bit—maybe three or four swallows. The first burned, you know. It was much worse than the champagne. That only tickled my nose. But Kit and Harry said to try again—that's when I choked, which they found vastly humorous. They said the second and third swallows would go down much more easily. And they were right. I thought it very peculiar that the first would be like swallowing fire and the others so much softer. Why do you suppose that is?''

''I have not the slightest notion,'' Nell replied, trying to retain her stern attitude and finding it difficult because her sense of the ridiculous was stirring. ''Rory, I know you were only curious, but you did know that it was foolish to drink such stuff.''

''You sound like Huntley.''

''He was very much annoyed. You are lucky to have escaped his displeasure so lightly, my dear.''

''I did expect him to bellow a bit more tonight,'' Rory confessed. ''But I don't think he really cared much. It would have been different if I had made a scandal, of course.''

''How can you say that when you know he is to be your husband?'' Nell demanded. ''Of course he cares. He lost his temper earlier because he cares, and tonight he was gentle because of his belief that you had no clear understanding of how the stuff would affect you.''

''Do you truly think him such a slowtop as all that, ma'am?''

The question caught Nell off guard. She blinked, the brush hovering in midair. ''A slowtop? What a thing to say, Rory. Of course he is no slowtop. I think his understanding is superior.''

''Well, so do I,'' Rory replied flatly. ''So, how can you think he believed such stuff? Moreover, when he bellowed at me, he said nothing about my innocence. He was angry that I had made a spectacle of myself, that I had perhaps endangered my reputation, but it was not he, after all, who pointed out that I might have done myself an injury if I had been so unfortunate as to fall off that stupid wall.''

''I collect, then,'' Nell said dryly, ''that Major Talcott did point out that fact.''

''Yes, he did.'' Rory sounded nearly defiant, and her look as much as dared Nell to make something of it.

Nell smiled. ''I'm glad he did. And that you seem to have

had the good sense to believe him. Do you think you would have believed Huntley if he had said as much to you?''

The shrug that was her sole reply told Nell her thrust had gone home. But what good it had done she was at a loss to discover, and she could scarcely credit herself with having brought Rory to a clearer understanding of the impropriety of her behavior on the esplanade. If anyone had done that, the credit must go to Major Talcott. From what Nell could read in Rory's expression now, and despite any thoughts Huntley might have expressed to the contrary, the fact that the major had been displeased to hear of her of her antics was the only thing that had been preying upon her mind when she had made her apologies earlier.

Therefore, when Nell took herself off to her own bed-chamber, it was not to sleep but to lie in bed with a good many thoughts for company. Chief among these was a growing belief that her niece was too young altogether to be thinking about marriage. Particularly marriage to such a man as Huntley. He had already suggested that he found her tiresome. She certainly resented his slightest interference in her life, while something in her very nature seemed to stir his exasperation. And, clearly, something in his stirred her to anger, bitterness, and yet more childish behavior. If he were unwise enough to take her to task over some issue or other, she rebelled or sulked. Yet, Major Talcott had only to express displeasure and to look stern, and she was offering apologies to everyone. Nell had the oddest notion that Huntley might have demanded an apology till doomsday without getting one.

She turned that thought over once or twice, examining it more closely. It seemed to underscore the fact that Rory was not yet ready for marriage. Perhaps the thing to do was to discuss the fact of her youth with Rory herself. Surely, if she could be brought to see that it would behoove her to wait a year or two, it would be a simple matter to convince Cross-ways and Clarissa. Well, Nell amended silently, perhaps not Clarissa. She would no doubt be longing to get her daughter firmly wed to someone of solid means, and Huntley was ideal for her purpose. But even so, if Rory herself balked at the notion, Clarissa would at least hesitate. And Crossways, besotted as he had always shown himself to be over his beloved eldest daughter, would not think twice about calling off a wedding that was not to her liking. Then Huntley might look about for another suitable choice. It was clear enough to one who knew him that he had already begun to entertain second thoughts about the wisdom of marrying someone as young as Rory.

Nell had no doubt that much of the blame for their difficulties rested in the disparity between their ages. No doubt Rory compared him to her father, from whom she was unused to encountering any restraint, and consequently she resented Huntley's efforts to curb her more outrageous starts. Major Talcott, on the other hand, was several years younger than Huntley. The fact that Rory responded when he chose to lay a hand to the rein was, Nell told herself, merely an indication that she tended to respond more positively to reproval from gentlemen nearer her in age.

XI

Nell's theories suffered something of a setback the following morning when she entered the breakfast parlor to discover her brother and her niece engaged in a spirited and uncomplimentary exchange of personalities, while her mother watched them, her vinaigrette poised but forgotten as she tried to make head or tail of their debate.

"What in the world is all this row!" Nell demanded when there was a pause long enough to allow her to make herself heard. All three persons at the table looked up at her in astonishment. Lady Agnes found her tongue first.

"Do you know that Aurora was so foolish as to attempt to walk along the sea wall by the esplanade yesterday, Nell dear? Really, I cannot think you were wise to permit such a thing."

"Nell did not permit it, Mama," Kit said indignantly. "Nor did I. 'Tis merely that this uncivil baggage here seems to think she can do as she damned———"

"Kit! Your language! And at my breakfast table, too. You must not, dear boy. My nerves!" The vinaigrette was put instantly to use.

"My apologies, Mama. Nell, will you please explain the matter to her, and tell this—this. . . ."

"That is quite enough, Kit," Nell said, firmly stifling a chuckle. "Mama, there is nothing to explain. Rory did a foolish thing, and the matter has already been discussed. There is no need to pull caps over it any more. As for you, Kit, I wonder that you will have introduced such a topic to Mama's breakfast table, for the incident certainly brings little credit to you." He looked away, and she went on more gently, "I hope you remember that Lord Huntley wishes to

134

speak with you this morning. It would be as well for you, I think, if you do not keep him waiting."

"What! Does he expect me to call upon him at his house?" Kit tugged at his neckcloth, a good deal taken aback by the suggestion.

"I think he would have more respect for you if you were to go to him rather than wait for him to come to you. You would not wish him to think you poor spirited."

He mulled over her words silently, but she knew he had taken her point when he looked up with a slight grimace. "I daresay you are in the right of it, Nell, but I doubt I shall much enjoy the visit."

"I hope he gives you pepper," Rory said rudely, spilling a liberal spoonful of sugar into her coffee.

"That will be enough out of you, miss, or you'll see who gets pepper," Kit promised, rounding on her in a flash. "I told you what would come of your silly experiments, but would you listen to me? Oh, no. Said you could dashed well take care of yourself and didn't need an uncle not yet dry behind the ears to tell you how to behave. If I had ten minutes with you in private, my girl, your own shell-like ears would ring sorely for those words. And that's God's own truth of the matter, believe me."

Rory flared up in immediate indignation, but any retort of hers was stifled at birth by her grandmother's vaguely wondering why it was that no one ever troubled to explain matters to her.

"For if the rest of you comprehend this conversation," she said peevishly, "I can tell you that it is more than I do. I've not had the slightest notion what is what since I came into this room, Nell, and discovered these two in the midst of an argument that sounded much like the sort of brangle you and Kit were used to engage in when he was still in the nursery. Your papa was used to become very much displeased by such behavior, and I confess 'tis prodigiously uncomfortable."

"Well, I'm sorry if we distressed you, Grandmama," Rory said with a sigh, shooting an oblique glance at her uncle. "There is nothing to it, of course, except for Kit's suffering from one of his distempered freaks and wishing to take his feelings out on someone else. I was the only one here when he came down, you know, so it fell to me to be his victim. I promise you," she added kindly, "I shan't regard it, and I hope you will not be grieved over his lack of good manners. It comes of being a gentleman, I expect. I have noticed before that even the best of them behave much as they please in their own homes, without the slightest regard for anyone else's comfort.''

Lady Agnes nodded in vague agreement, but Kit looked as if he might well explode. Laughing, Nell recommended that he put a sock in it. "For you will never make poor Mama believe it was anyone else's doing now, Kit. You have been piqued, repiqued, and capotted, I fear. And a good loser, according to words I've heard you quote myself, knows when to cut his losses and leave the table. Do you intend to ride this morning, Rory?''

Kit glared but subsided into his chair, and Rory broke into a cheerful smile, promptly acknowledging that she did indeed mean to ride and that it was for that very purpose that she had donned her riding habit before coming down to table.

"I see that you did," Nell replied, looking over the little she could see of what appeared to be a dashing riding dress. It was stylishly cut from deep blue kerseymere, with two rows of tiny gold buttons down the front. Around her lovely throat, Rory had twisted a lace-trimmed neckcloth in a fashion similar to one of the men's simpler styles. Her lovely hair had been combed smoothly away from a center part and was confined in a blue-net snood at the nape of her neck. Tiny sapphire earbobs glinted amidst her golden sidecurls, and a matching pin nestled in the folds of her neckcloth. "You look charmingly," Nell said. "But you ought to have sent me word that you wished to ride today. Now, you must wait while I change, whereas if you had warned me, I might have been prepared, you know.''

"Oh, you needn't feel obliged to go with me, Aunt Nell," Rory said hastily. "I have my own mare and my groom, you know. I shall be perfectly all right by myself.''

"Nonsense," Kit put in before Nell could speak. "Chit like you's got no business jauntering about town by herself, with or without a groom. Better with, of course," he amended, "but devilish improper either way. You wait for Nell.''

"He's right, my dear," Nell said quickly when the storm warnings flashed in Rory's eyes. "You really cannot ride about Brighton alone. It would be most improper.''

"Well, but I didn't mean to trot down the Steyne or

anything like that," Rory protested. "I thought I might just ride toward Kemp Town and then maybe along the beach or up along the Downs."

"The Downs! Well, of all the crackbrained, totty-headed——"

"Kit, hush," Nell ordered, stifling her amusement at Rory's determindedly casual attitude. "There is no reason that she should not ride on the Downs. There are a number of very good trails, and I should be most happy to go with her. But you must not go alone, Rory. He's in the right of it there. It would not only be improper, but it could also be dangerous. You have heard us mention the military encampment, I'm sure. There are a good many common soldiers attached to it who cannot be trusted to behave as we would wish. And there are others, too."

"What sort of others?"

"Smugglers, for one," Kit answered her. "And footpads, and all manner of the scaff and raff. Not desirable company for a delicately nurtured female, I promise you."

"Stuff," Rory retorted. "I should like above all things to meet a real smuggler and discover how he goes about his business. But surely that could not happen so near the military encampment."

"Bless you, child, even the military get their rum as cheaply as they can. Aye, and cloth, lace, and whatever else appeals. They are scarcely more saintly than the rest of us, after all."

"But I thought it was the duty of the military to assist in the apprehension of smugglers," Rory protested.

"That's the job of the preventative officers, just like it is in Kent," Kit retorted. "The military don't meddle unless they're called upon to do so, and then only with half a heart, since they think the import duties as ridiculous as we think them."

Nell applied herself to her breakfast, lending only half an ear to the conversation that followed. Kit and Rory seemed to be more in charity with each other, and Lady Agnes had laid aside her vinaigrette. She wondered if Rory had hoped to meet her major. It was fairly clear that she had had some such plan in mind, but Nell would see to it now that, even if they rode to the Downs, they would ride nowhere near the encampment of the Tenth Hussars, so a chance meeting was unlikely. Perhaps the morning would pass without any unfortunate incidents.

Kit seemed in good spirits when he excused himself from the table, and she found herself hoping Huntley wouldn't be too hard on him. It sounded very much to her as if her brother had simply found it impossible to curb Rory's behavior and had received no support from either his friends or the so-called adults present. A glance at Rory now showed her to be in some sort of brown study, so Nell turned her attention to Lady Agnes.

"That's a very fetching cap, Mama. Is it a new one?"

"It is," her ladyship replied, smoothing the article in question. It was indeed becoming to her, being all creamy lace and blue ribbons that very nearly matched her eyes. Her morning gown was also blue, with a deep flounce and knots of green ribbons round the scalloped edges of the hem. It was cut high to the throat and long to the wrist with edgings of the creamy lace everywhere.

"What do you do this morning, ma'am?" Nell asked.

"Why, as to that, I cannot say," was the reply. "Yesterday ought to have been vastly fatiguing to one of my delicate constitution, you know. But the oddest thing is that I feel fresh as a nosegay this morning. Sir Henry suggested he might like to take a stroll along the Steyne, and I tell you, Nell, if I feel as well in an hour as I do now, I just might join him. And I didn't even get my full night's rest, mind you."

"Dear me. Were you out raking all night, too, Mama?"

Lady Agnes chuckled. "Nothing so energetic as that, my dear. But Sir Henry found himself without a feather to fly with, I'm afraid."

"Without— Never say you were gaming ma'am, for I shouldn't credit it!" Even Rory seemed to have come out of her brown study and was gazing curiously at her grandmother. "He never took you to a gaming house."

"Of course not," returned her ladyship with a twinkle. "We gambled right here. And I trounced him, as Kit would say."

"Silver loo?"

"No, cribbage."

"Cribbage for money, ma'am. I have never known you to do that before."

"No, but you must admit, my dear, 'tis sadly flat to march one's counters about for no purpose, when one might be profitting greatly by their activities."

"Or taking an unhealthy loss, ma'am. It does not seem at all like you to risk your blunt on the gaming table."

"But I nearly always win at cribbage," her ladyship pointed out. "At least when I play with Sir Henry. So there is very little risk, you know. And we play for only shilling points, so I shall not lose the house or even one of the carriages if I am rolled up."

"Rolled up? Mama, such language," Nell teased. Lady Agnes only smiled placidly, however, so she took her leave and went to change. Less than fifteen minutes later she was ready. Her riding habit of twilled cotton was not nearly so dashing as that of her niece, but its russet hues became her well, and Nell knew Rory's look of admiration when she joined her in the entry hall was unfeigned. The younger girl had donned gloves of soft kid and a dashing little hat with an ostrich plume, and, like Nell, carried her riding whip. She explained that she had already ordered the horses brought 'round.

They were waiting, held steady by Nell's own groom and a link boy. Nell looked at Rory. "I thought you said your groom would attend you."

"Oh, he will meet us later," was the casual response. "I daresay yours will serve us both for now. May we ride straight to the Downs?"

Wondering what she was up to now, Nell thought it prudent to keep a still tongue and merely nodded. She let Peter help her into the saddle, gathered her reins, and waited patiently until he had performed the same services for her niece and had mounted himself. Then she signaled him to fall behind, and they turned toward Edward Street. It was easily half an hour's ride before they had left the town behind them and were able to enjoy a canter on the Downs. But the panoramic view back over Brighton to the sea was such that even Rory expressed her pleasure.

Nell breathed deeply of the crisp fresh air and gave her horse its head, letting it out for a full gallop, her skirts flying. Rory was not slow to follow her, and for some fifteen minutes they rode furiously. Then, reluctantly, Nell drew rein. Rory rode up directly behind her, breathing hard.

"Oh, Aunt Nell, I haven't done that in such a long time. It felt wonderful!"

"Yes, it did, didn't it?" Nell grinned. "One may do that

sort of thing up here, but only when one is quite unobserved. The ladies of Brighton, and even some of the gentlemen, have a tendency to deplore such hoydenish behavior.''

"Oh, I know. Mama was forever pinching at me about riding like a Diana. It was all very well for hunting, she said, though we scarcely ever joined in a hunt. Papa does occasionally, but he says it is no place for young ladies, especially since I wasn't even out and so couldn't go to any house parties. But Mama says in London one may never ride so, only sedately in Rotten Row at specified hours of the day. I am so glad she sent me to Brighton instead, though I was furious with her at the time, of course.''

"You wanted to go to London?''

"Well, of course I did. Doesn't everyone?''

"I suppose. I went, you know. But I was rather shy and didn't know many people, you see. I enjoyed the summer here, where I knew everyone, much more.''

"Did you know Huntley in London or here?''

"Both. He came here with the prince, but I had first made his acquaintance in London. We became excellent friends, for he was very kind to me.''

"Oh, he is kind enough, I expect, when one has not managed by some means or other to displease him.''

"Rory,'' Nell said suddenly, "do you truly wish to marry him?''

"Well, of course I do. What a perfectly ridiculous question, when it is all settled. Why should I not wish to marry him?''

"More to the point,'' Nell countered, looking directly at her, "I cannot conceive of a single reason why you *should* wish to do so. I know it is hardly my place to say anything, but I cannot help having noticed that you feel none of the tenderer feelings toward him. I expect he cares for you, of course, but——''

"Not a rap,'' Rory declared. "I told you that before.''

"Then, how can you wish to spend the rest of your life with him?''

Rory looked a trifle daunted by Nell's particular phrasing, but her chin came up, and she soon had herself well in hand. "It is truly a wonderful opportunity for me, Aunt Nell. Surely, you would be the first to wish me a splendid marriage.''

"There can be no doubt of that, my dear. But I would wish you to marry someone you could care deeply for.''

"Love, you mean," Rory said with a laugh. "Goodness, Aunt Nell, I never expected you to be a romantic. Mama says that's all very well and good in books, mostly rubbishy books. But she says a girl has to think ahead past smiles and soft words to proper gowns and sufficient servants to make one comfortable, and elegant carriages with well-bred horses to drive behind, and . . . well, all that sort of thing. I expect you have never clapped eyes on Huntley Green. I have not either, but my papa assures me that it is a seat worthy of an earl and his countess. And I shall very much enjoy being a countess, Aunt Nell."

"But Huntley means to spend most of his time in Kent, my dear. You have always talked as if you yearn for a gayer life than that."

"Oh, I do, and Mama says I needn't bother my head about it, that Huntley will do as I wish him to do. Moreover, if he should not wish to accompany me to London, I shall simply go by myself. Mama says a good many married ladies do just that and that they have a cicisbeo or two to take them 'round if their husbands cannot do so. I think it sounds like good fun, so I daresay I should prefer it if Huntley did remain in Kent."

Thus outlined, the prospect made Nell shudder, and it occurred to her, not for the first time, that Rory's mama had talked a great deal of nonsense. The more she thought about it, the less she liked the idea of the forthcoming marriage. Rory deserved to find that life had more to offer than fine carriages and worldly titles, and Huntley certainly deserved more than a wife who wanted only his money and position. For the next twenty minutes or so they rode together in near silence, while Nell searched her mind for some means by which her niece could be brought to value his lordship as she knew he ought to be valued.

When a rider suddenly appeared from a small grove of trees and seemed to be hurrying straight toward them, wrenching Nell from her thoughts, she was conscious of a wish that she had a pistol by her or that she had commanded Peter to carry one. However, one look at her niece's smiling countenance caused her to relax once more.

"Is that your groom, Rory?"

"Yes. I expect he finished his errand sooner than he expected," she replied glibly.

"Indeed." Nell managed to keep her tongue before more words tripped off it. She had no doubt that the groom had been sent to carry a message from his mistress, but there would be time enough to make her opinion of such behavior known if the message had been answered. Whatever answer there was was gleaned from only the groom's brief nod, but Rory seemed well enough pleased by it. Nell decided to test the matter by suggesting that perhaps it was time to begin their return journey. The suggestion was dismissed abruptly.

"Oh, no, ma'am. Why, 'tis such a splendid day. I should like to try another trail. What do you say to that one yonder?"

Nell agreed without comment but began keeping a weather eye peeled for the major, thinking he would no doubt soon join them. She was not disappointed. Less than a quarter hour later a splendid bay galloped over the small rise ahead of them, and its rider could be easily recognized as the tall Hussar officer. Rory, waving madly, nearly stood up in her stirrups, thus causing her mare to sidle nervously.

"Rory, for heaven's sake, what are you about?" Nell demanded, feigning astonishment.

"It is merely Major Talcott, Aunt Nell, and he has seen us, too, for he is riding directly toward us."

"How fortuitous," Nell said, her tone dry to the point of being sardonic.

Rory glanced at her suspiciously, and Nell returned the look steadily. The younger girl hunched one pretty shoulder and twisted her lips into a slight pout. "Oh, very well, it is not a chance meeting, as I expect you know well enough. I asked him to meet us here." She looked directly at Nell, as if she was gathering courage. Then her chin came up, and she licked her lips and plunged to the heart of the matter. "I wanted to see him quite desperately, Aunt Nell. Please try to understand. He was so angry with me last night because of that stupid business on the esplanade. I told him myself, thinking to amuse him. Only"—she paused, drawing a ragged breath— "only he didn't find it amusing at all. He said I had behaved dreadfully and not at all as he should have expected me to behave. Also, he said he had thought I had better sense. And, oh, Aunt Nell, I do, and I mean to tell him so and also to tell him that I apologized to everyone, so he won't be angry with me anymore."

"But why should it matter that he might be vexed? That

young man is nothing to you, and you didn't care a rap for the fact that Huntley was displeased.'' Watching her niece closely, Nell realized that the thought as she had expressed it hadn't struck Rory before. She seemed taken aback, but she brushed the words aside impatiently.

"I don't know *why* it should matter. I only know that it *does* matter. It matters a great deal that he should think well of me. Please, Aunt Nell, when he gets here, could you possibly be so obliging as to fall a bit behind so that I may speak to him properly? Surely it will not be so dreadful if you keep us in sight.''

Nell's first inclination was to deny the request, but she thought better of it. After all, the major's influence so far had been only beneficial, and at least he would not step beyond the line of what was pleasing. She could even hope that he might succeed in deterring Rory from future outrageous behavior.

She watched as, taking her reluctant nod for encouragement, Rory spurred the mare and sped to meet him. He turned his mount when she reached him, and Nell was thus left nearly a quarter mile behind. It did not worry her particularly, because it was fairly open country, and she did not fear losing sight of them.

Upon hearing a halloo a few moments later, she turned in her saddle and saw a horseman approaching at speed. She had no difficulty whatsoever in recognizing the broad-shouldered, loose-limbed gentleman atop the large roan-colored stallion moving with such liquid speed through gorse and over small shrubs as if he were on the prince's own grassy racetrack. Reining in, she half-turned her mount and waited for him to draw even with her. A sudden thrill of pleasure shot through her, speedily replaced by dismay as she glanced back over her shoulder to discover that the major and Rory had disappeared over a small rise. As she looked back again, Huntley waved, and she marveled at how he seemed to be part of his mount. Like a centaur, she thought, watching him draw closer. The stallion was still moving at great speed, and she could hear his hooves pounding the hard ground. By all rights, she ought to have been terrified at the possibility of being ridden down, but the thought never so much as occurred to her, and she seemed to sense the very moment when he would draw rein, the very moment when the stallion would come to a plunging halt only feet from her. Both grooms, having drawn up a short distance behind her, sat their horses, gaping.

"What a magnificent animal!" Nell breathed. "He is truly splendid, Philip."

"Never mind that," Huntley snapped. "What the devil are you doing out here alone?"

She looked at him then. She had been so intent upon his beautiful horse that she had not realized he was angry until he spoke. But if she was to go by the look of him, he was very angry, indeed. Nell drew in a long breath, watching him much as if by doing so she hoped to calm his temper as well as her nerves.

"I am not precisely alone, my lord."

"I can see that, girl. I'm not a ninny. But I am not referring to two sapskull grooms who would be of little use to you if you were to encounter ruffians of either the military or civilian variety. However, I was informed that Aurora would be with you."

"Who . . ." Then she remembered Kit, and realized he had probably mentioned that Rory had been dressed for riding. In that case, of course Huntley's anger was nothing more than annoyance that she had seemed to misplace Rory again. The notion restored her normal presence of mind, and hoping to divert his attention until they should at least come in sight of the other couple, she glanced at him quizzically. "I do hope you have not seen fit to murder my brother, sir."

A reluctant smile lit his eyes then, and he relaxed in his saddle as he drew the huge stallion in closer. "I didn't. I like him. But I did get a round tale and gave him some good advice, so I daresay Aurora will find it a bit more difficult to get 'round him next time." The smile touched his lips. "This little tangent will not answer, you know. Where is she? Don't tell me she has been naughty enough to give you the slip."

"No, but I fear you will not like what I have done, and so I did not like to tell you straight away."

"Thought you weren't afraid of me."

"Don't be nonsensical. 'Twas merely that I didn't wish to incur your censure, and I do fear that by allowing Rory to speak privately with Major Talcott, I may have done just that." He said nothing, and she stared at him fixedly. "Well, you might say something," she said at last. "Are you vexed?"

"No, Nell, merely surprised. That Talcott fellow seems mighty stubborn, doesn't he?"

She nodded, but then her conscience pricked her. "It was not his notion to meet us here, Philip. I am afraid Rory sent him a message. In fact, I think she had it in mind originally to come here in search of him. I scotched that by insisting that she must not ride anywhere alone. But though I realized she was up to mischief, it truly never occurred to me that she might arrange an assignation or that he would come to meet her if she did."

"You underestimated them both, it seems." But he smiled down at her, and she knew he was not angry. She smiled back. The two grooms had dropped back some distance, and Rory and the major were still beyond their range of sight, so she felt quite alone with him again and conscious of that odd feeling of shyness.

"I am glad you are not angry, Huntley," she said at last, rather briskly. "Rory wanted to tell him she was sorry about her behavior yesterday. It seems she told him the whole last night, expecting him to be amused by the tale. He was not, and that is why she was so subdued on the way home and so apologetic later."

Huntley was silent long enough to make her fear that she had annoyed him after all, but when she looked up at him, she saw that he was only deep in thought. It seemed a long time before he turned his gaze toward her, and there was a look in his eyes that she could not decipher when he did. It was gone seconds later, replaced by a rueful gleam.

"It appears likely that I shall have to have another talk with that young man before we are any of us much older," he said. But for once his tone was not grim. Indeed, Nell thought he sounded much as if he regarded the prospect as a gloomy one.

XII

Whether or not Huntley did speak to the major, Nell had no way of knowing, but she suspected that he must have done so, for during the week that followed the excursion to the Downs, although she and Rory chanced to meet Major Talcott on more than one occasion, his attentions seemed less particular than those of Rory's other countless admirers. Huntley made good his promise to escort them whenever Nell pressed him to do so, and as time passed, she found that less and less persuasion was necessary. Indeed, he had a tendency to meet them at functions even when she had neglected to request his escort.

The one factor that nearly convinced her that he must have said something to the major, however, was that the latter, unlike the myriad of others, did not pay morning calls in Upper Rock Gardens.

Huntley himself came often, though he spent most of his time conversing with Lady Agnes or Nell. Harry Seton came nearly every day, and so did a number of other fashionable gentlemen. And not all of the others came merely to visit the Lady Aurora. At least two showed a decided preference for her aunt.

Some ten days after their excursion to the Downs, the two ladies found themselves entertaining no fewer than six gentlemen callers. Four of these were gathered about the Lady Aurora, nearly overwhelming her with their compliments and maneuverings. But if she hoped for assistance from her aunt, she was to be disappointed. Nell had her hands full.

She was seated upon the low sofa in the window bay, flanked by her two most recent admirers. Upon her right sat Mr. MacElroy, precise to a pin in buff pantaloons, shining

Hessians, a gaily embroidered rose-colored waistcoat, and a coat of bottlegreen kerseymere so tight-fitting that it must have necessitated the efforts of at least two hefty footmen as well as his valet to squeeze him into it. His neckcloth was intricately tied and so stiffly starched that he could scarcely move his head. Therefore, he had been forced to sit on the very edge of the settee with his whole body skewed toward Nell in order to converse with her.

Her other visitor, by comparison, was relaxed to a point that her father would certainly have castigated as behavior unbecoming a gentleman. He was Sir Thomas Maitherstone, who, somewhat to Nell's dismay, had proclaimed himself a poet and requested her permission to dedicate his latest set of odes to her beauty. Sir Thomas had presented himself in Upper Rock Gardens attired in a loose-fitting drab coat, buckskin breeches, riding boots, and—worst of all—with a checkered handkerchief knotted around his thin neck. His appearance was such, in fact, that Pavingham had declined to show him into the drawing room without first seeking permission from Nell. She had granted it willingly, for Sir Thomas amused her, but she could scarcely help being startled by his appearance.

Her expression must have given away her thoughts, for he promptly began to defend himself on the grounds that a man ought to be valued for more than the clothes he wore. Since Mr. MacElroy had been enjoying the pleasure of having Nell's attentions all to himself until Maitherstone's entrance, his reaction to this statement—utter sacrilege in his opinion—was perhaps more pointed than it might have been. Despite Nell's attempts to guide the conversation along civil lines, she soon decided that no effort of hers, short of expelling them both from the drawing room, would prevail. They were extraordinarily polite to one another, but a constant stream of verbal thrusts ensued, continuing until she might cheerfully have knocked both their heads together.

The opening of the drawing room doors provided a welcome diversion, but Nell was conscious of a sharp stab of disappointment when it was merely Kit and Lady Agnes who entered. Her brother shot her a quizzical look and she responded by lifting her brows in mock helplessness. Kit grinned but turned away toward the group surrounding Rory.

"Good gracious!" exclaimed Lady Agnes as she followed

him and took the seat reluctantly offered to her by one of her granddaughter's admirers. "What a crush! Nell, dear, have you ordered refreshment? I am persuaded these gentlemen would appreciate some of your papa's Malaga."

Since nearly every gentleman present had been there for at least twenty minutes by then, and several had been there a good deal longer, Nell had hoped that the lack of refreshment would recall them to their senses and send them on their way. But to a man they expressed approval of Lady Agnes's suggestion, and so Pavingham was soon treading his stately measure from one to another with a tray of glasses and a sparkling decanter. In the midst of this cheerful scene, Jeremy pushed open the drawing room doors again and announced Lord Huntley.

Startled, Nell glanced up, an involuntary smile of welcome lighting her eyes. Huntley looked swiftly around the room, his gaze sliding over Rory and her entourage, past Lady Agnes, until it came to rest upon Nell herself. She rose to greet him, and her quick movement brought her two companions scrambling to their feet. Huntley glanced from one to the other, and when his gaze met Nell's, it was brimful of amusement. Her own eyes twinkled in response.

"You know, Mr. MacElroy, of course, sir, but I do not know if you are acquainted with Sir Thomas Maitherstone. This is the Earl of Huntley, Sir Thomas."

"We haven't met," Huntley admitted, holding out a hand to the younger man, "but you are Lord Edgbaston's nephew recently down from Cambridge, I believe. His lordship mentioned you only last evening." He lifted his quizzing glass.

Sir Thomas, blushing under such open scrutiny, acknowledged the relationship. His discomfiture seemed to be caused as much by Huntley's mention of his noble relation as by his lordship's slow examination of his person. Nell took pity on him.

"Sir Thomas is a poet, my lord," she said, preserving her countenance with difficulty.

"Is he indeed?" Huntley polished the quizzing glass with his handkerchief. "I daresay that accounts for it, then."

"Accounts for what, my lord?" Sir Thomas inquired with a hint of defiance in his tone. Mr. MacElroy hid a smile behind a lace-edged, monogrammed handkerchief.

"Why, for that certain air of otherworldliness which seems

to enfold you," replied Huntley in a bland drawl, lifting the glass again. "I am informed that such an air is *de rigueur* among poets. Have you written an ode to Miss Lindale's eyes yet? I am persuaded they deserve to be preserved in rhyme."

"I have," replied Sir Thomas warily. "Comparing them to dark liquid sapphire pools. And another to her lips. They are like——"

"Rosebuds or ripe cherries, if your previous display of originality is anything by which one might judge the matter," Huntley said, ruthlessly interrupting this discourse. "Insolent puppy," he added moments later when Sir Thomas had taken a hasty departure. "Did he actually have the effrontery to make you the object of such dismal stuff?"

"I'll have you know, my lord, that he has written separate odes to my eyes, my lips, my hair, my chin——"

"Good God! As bad as that? I've a mind to speak to that young cockerel. Bad enough that he should appear in a lady's drawing room dressed all by guess, but——"

"Just what I said myself, Huntley," put in Mr. MacElroy, lisping slightly as was his unfortunate habit. "Not that the young cub would see reason. Actually said a man's clothes were unimportant. Unimportant! Did you ever hear the like?"

"You still here, MacElroy?" Huntley inquired gently, raising his quizzing glass again as if he had only just noticed the other gentleman.

Undaunted, Mr. MacElroy assured him that he was indeed still there, and even preened himself a bit beneath the moving glass. "Was enjoying a comfortable coze with Miss Lindale until that demmed popinjay imposed his company upon us. Matter of fact, my lord," he confided, "I'd consider it a kindness if you was to take yourself off and leave us to finish our conversation."

"Daresay you would at that," Huntley agreed. Suddenly the movement of the glass halted, and he peered at his victim more carefully. "I say," he said, much concerned, "do you know you've got smut on your waistcoat? Good thing I chanced to notice. Only think how you'd feel when you discovered it yourself, very likely after visiting any number of people who wouldn't care to direct your attention to it."

"Yes, by Jove!" Dismayed, MacElroy looked down at his stomach. There was indeed a tiny smudge of some sort, but not one that would be readily apparent to any but the sharpest eye. The discovery seemed to overset him entirely, and after stammered apologies, his speedy departure left Huntley in sole possession of the field.

"For shame, sir," Nell scolded as he took his seat beside her and crossed one elegantly clad leg over the other. "I'll have you know you have robbed me of my two fondest admirers. I am Sir Thomas's inspiration," she added soulfully.

"The devil you are," Huntley replied, grinning. "And MacElroy? Do you inspire him as well?"

"Goodness, I hope not," she chuckled. "I should dislike very much to have been the inspiration for that outrageous waistcoat." He made no response, and she regarded him searchingly. "Did you have something you particularly wished to discuss with me, sir, or did you merely desire to clear the room?"

"Nothing of vast importance," he replied, eyeing the group around Lady Agnes and Rory. "It is merely that I have seen little of you these past few days and wondered if all was going well."

"She has been up to no mischief that I know about, sir, which is not to say there hasn't been some." She grinned at him. "We met the good major on the Steyne yesterday, but when he only bowed in passing, her air of disappointment was enough to convince me that there have been no more assignations, though we are forever running into him at parties, of course."

"Well, that's all right. I was afraid she might be fretting you to flinders."

She twinkled at him. "I do not fret so easily, sir. Besides, we have been too busy. There was a riding party yesterday, and we have been sea-bathing and to several private parties. Rory had not been into the sea since her last visit, you know, and she was so astonished to discover that old Martha Gunn is still operating the ladies' bathing machines that she quite forgot her sulks."

"Well, I daresay she will soon forget the major, too," Huntley said comfortably. "They both know, after all, that nothing can come of their relationship. Even if Aurora were not contracted to me, her parents would never consider such an alliance, you know. Talcott is a younger son, I believe, and your sister would never countenance giving her daughter to a man without solid prospects."

Nell did not question his reasoning. Though it was inconceivable to her that a man who could afford a majority in the Prince's Own Regiment could have been born without a shirt, she knew the major's claims could never rival Huntley's in her sister's eyes. So, instead of debating with him she turned the subject to one she considered more suitable to the time and place.

"I have been wanting to thank you for your kindness to Kit, sir. I know you said you had not been harsh with him, but I certainly never expected you to exert yourself so much on his behalf as he assures us you have."

"Nonsense," he replied, coloring a little beneath his deep tan. "I've done very little of consequence and nothing at all out of the way, I assure you."

"Oh, of course not," she agreed promptly. "It must be quite a normal thing for you to take a green young man under your wing and to provide him with the entrée to a club he'd not have dared to set foot in on his own."

"Well, that may not have been such a great service," he confessed with an apologetic smile. "The play there is nearly as deep as any at Brook's or even White's in London, but it is better for him to drop his blunt in an honest game than a dishonest one. And those clubs he's been frequenting with young Seton are little more than hells that specialize in separating unwary young chubs like Kit from their brass. He'll come to no great harm at Alcott's."

"Well, it was kind of you, sir," she insisted, "and you can scarcely say it was to save his groats that you presented Kit to the Prince of Wales."

He chuckled. "I daresay you'll come to wish I'd never done that, either. But at least I can see to it that he acquires friends of a different stamp than those rattles I've seen him with. Someone ought to have introduced him about long before now."

"I cannot think who might have done so," Nell replied, wrinkling her brow. "Crossways might, of course, only I daresay it wouldn't occur to him unless Kit asked him, which he wouldn't, not being in the habit of applying to him for anything. And it would never occur to Sir Henry to do so, because he still thinks of Kit as a schoolboy, despite all Kit's attempts to prove how grown up he has become. Perhaps it would be different if he had gone up to Oxford or Cambridge."

"He ought to have gone. It would have been good for him."

"But he is not at all inclined to be bookish," Nell explained, "and he has no interest in a military career either, though both Mama and I can only be glad of that. He prefers a sporting life to anything else, and I daresay that once Sir Henry places his affairs in his own hands, Kit will retire to the property Papa left him near Patchem and settle right down. Until then, however, he is bent upon cutting a dash, and Sir Henry is bent—with Mama's encouragement, of course—upon seeing to it that he has as little of the ready to waste as possible. You have had a beneficial influence in that quarter as well, I'm pleased to say."

"The devil I have! I've scarcely exchanged three words with Sir Henry Sinclair. Doing it too brown, Nell."

She laughed. "No such thing, sir. It's the truth. Mama has a very strong sense of economy, though I've never understood how she came by it unless it was through fear that my father would outrun his fortune and thus prove to her relations that she had married beneath her station. But, whatever the reason, she exerts enough of an influence over Sir Henry that Kit's allowance has been extremely small. And since Sir Henry thought him a mere schoolboy and disapproved of his friends into the bargain, nothing Kit could say seemed to make any impression at all."

"What of you? Did you say nothing?"

"Oh, I exerted myself to change Mama's views, but it was to little avail. And Sir Henry merely pats me on the head and tells me it is not expected that a mere female should understand the workings of the financial world." Her fingers curled as she said these last words, and Huntley grinned at her.

"Poor Nell."

"Well, no one would like being spoken to in such a way. But, of course, once he realized that you had taken Kit under your wing, he saw immediately that Kit's allowance must be increased. And his generosity was such that Kit is practically in alt."

Huntley frowned and turned a searching look upon her. "You must find it a trifle frustrating that after all your efforts on his behalf, I should succeed without the merest effort and without, for that matter, even knowing I'd done anything out of the way," he said sympathetically.

Nell shook her head, smiling at him. "Oh, no. How could I be so selfish? I'm truly grateful to you, sir. I'd nearly come to my wits' end and was beginning to fear that, out of pure exasperation, Kit might work some mischief or other. Especially in view of all the attention being lavished on Rory once she arrived." She paused, gazing down at her hands, then gave him a straight look. "I'm afraid I even feared he might have encouraged her to drink too much that day in hopes that she might be sent home in disgrace."

"Well, you can put that maggot straight out of your head," Huntley said. "I'm certain such a thought never entered his head. Aurora behaved badly, and though I think he ought to have stopped her, I do undertand that he, at least, believed himself unequal to the task. Is that young fop with his arm draped over the back of her chair her latest conquest, by the bye?"

Nell glanced over to the other group, noting the elegantly dressed, if unmannerly, young gentleman to whom Huntley referred.

"He is only one of many, sir. I doubt she is very intimate with any of them."

"I should hope not."

"No, indeed," Nell replied with an innocent look. "You've much more to fear from Jeremy."

"And who, pray tell, is Jeremy?" The heavy brows quirked, but she knew he had taken her measure.

"Why, our footman, sir. He and Rory are thick as thieves."

"Cut line, Nell. I know Aurora well enough to be certain I need have no qualms about a mere footman."

She chuckled. "Perhaps not. But they are firm friends, nonetheless, on account of Ulysses." He looked puzzled, so she explained patiently that Ulysses was Rory's kitten. "The one you allowed her to bring home in your carriage from the esplanade that day, sir. You were afraid of fleas," she reminded him. He nodded, calmly recommending that she get on with her tale. She dimpled at his stern tone but obeyed him willingly enough. "It seems that the care and feeding of Ulysses have pretty much fallen to Jeremy's lot. And he is so besotted over Rory that he does her slightest bidding without question. Why, I do believe that if she was to command that he sleep with Ulysses, Jeremy would even do that. I have discovered them more than once head to head in conference over Ulysses' needs, and I daresay my incorrigible niece has confided more to him than she has any business to confide to any servant.''

Huntley agreed that she was very likely right, but Nell could detect not the slightest degree of annoyance in his tone. They conversed amicably for some moments more before he took leave of her and moved to speak briefly to the two ladies on the sofa. His farewells seemed to provide a signal of sorts to the other gentlemen, for they followed nearly upon his heels, taking Kit with them and leaving the three ladies alone at last.

Lady Agnes announced that she for one was ready to lie down upon her bed. ''All that conversation has given me the headache,'' she declared. ''I should have known better than to exert myself.''

''Poor Mama,'' Nell said, twinkling at her. ''Shall I ring for Mathilde to bring you a dose of hartshorn and water?''

''I shall go up,'' replied her ladyship with dignity. ''You were very cozy with Huntley, my dear. I hope he wasn't put out by all the young men he found here. We could scarcely forbid them the door, when I know most of their mamas!''

''Don't distress yourself, ma'am. Huntley and I discussed Kit and Rory. He was not at all put out, I promise you.''

Lady Agnes accepted her at her word and went upstairs to tend her headache, but Rory eyed her uneasily and, the moment the doors had shut behind her grandmother, demanded to know if Nell had spoken the truth about Huntley's not having been annoyed.

''For I cannot think why else you should discuss me, though I have told him I'll not stand for his interference in my life!''

''Rory, only listen to yourself,'' Nell pleaded. ''To speak in such a way of a man who has been more than kind to you is most unbecoming.''

''Well, I don't care. I can't think why he came to Brighton after promising I should enjoy myself. He is always hovering about, watching me, and bellowing when my activities displease him.''

''Since we have scarcely seen him in three days, I don't know why you would say such a thing,'' Nell said. ''Come now. Admit you are being unfair.''

But the most she could get by way of a response was a

sulky look and a shrug of one pretty shoulder, so Nell left her niece to her own devices and went upstairs to be sure Lady Agnes was not really unwell. Since she found her lying down upon her bed with a down comforter pulled up to her chin and a cold cloth laid over her brow, one might have expected a dutiful daughter to feel some anxiety. However, Nell was inured to such scenes and did not so much as turn a hair at the sight of the haughty Mathilde lighting pastilles on her ladyship's dressing table.

"I see you are in good hands, Mama. Is there anything you wish me to do for you before I leave? I mean to write a letter to Clarissa this afternoon."

"No, no, my dear," her ladyship replied weakly. "Mathilde will see to everything. I daresay I shall be well again in a trice, so say nothing to worry Clarissa, I beg you."

"Of course not, ma'am."

Nell let herself out and went to her own sitting room, where she set out paper, ink, quills, and her favorite pen knife. These preparations completed, she sat down at her writing table and stared at a blank piece of paper for some time before she stirred herself to write the greeting. Then, she sat and thought. Her intention had been to assure her sister that all was going well and that her beloved daughter was enjoying her Season in Brighton. But Nell wasn't by any means certain that either statement was a true one.

In the first place, she was more convinced every day that a marriage between her niece and Lord Huntley would be a mistake. More than that, it would be a disaster. And in the second place, she wasn't at all persuaded that Rory was enjoying herself, having in fact suspected for several days that the child was bored and frustrated. Since the boredom could not possibly be the result of a lack of activity, Nell had to search for another reason, and since Rory's attitude reminded her much of Kit's when he had felt confined by his lack of funds and by the seeming lack of understanding that surrounded him, Nell thought it entirely possible that Rory felt confined in Brighton.

Taking advantage of their growing friendship, she had attempted on more than one occasion to discuss her thoughts with Huntley, but she felt she had made little headway. Although he could be so understanding of her own feelings, and seemed to have a nearly magical knack for dealing with her brother, his advice with regard to Rory was generally, in Nell's opinion, hasty or thoughtless, and sometimes even downright pig-headed. His inclination seemed to be to blame everything on Rory's youth and to assume that she would outgrow any behavior of which he disapproved. Nell's notion that Rory felt confined, he termed ludicrous.

But it was not. Nell knew that her niece was used to enjoying an amount of freedom at home that simply wasn't possible in Brighton. Even so benevolent a rule as Nell herself imposed was too restrictive for Rory's tastes. Huntley said merely that she had been spoiled. Nell agreed but could not see that it mattered much one way or the other, since she could scarcely make much of an imprint in a few weeks when the damage had been done over a period of so many years. And in the meantime, and much more to the point as far as she was concerned, her niece was unhappy. And Nell could not imagine that marriage to Huntley, however admirable he was, would improve that situation.

Finally, after several false starts, she pushed the letter paper and quill aside and decided to see if her niece would enjoy going for a drive or perhaps even for a ride. Finding that Rory was no longer in the drawing room, Nell went back upstairs. She was not in her bedchamber, either, but Sadie was straightening up the room, and the gown that Rory had worn earlier was spread out upon the bed.

"Where is your mistress, Sadie?"

The maid's rosy countenance took on a martyred expression. "I'm sure I couldn't say, miss."

"Don't take that tone with me, if you please," Nell replied firmly. "Her ladyship must have given some indication of her intention when she changed her gown. What dress did she wear?"

Sadie looked mulish. "My lady said I was not to tell."

"Sadie," Nell warned, "listen carefully to what I say, because I shall only say it the one time. I should be very sad to have to turn you off, but if you continue with this unfortunate attitude, I shall do so. And do not think it is beyond my power, for I assure you it is not. Lord Crossways would not like to hear that you abetted his daughter in misbehavior, perchance even into danger. Your mistress still has little knowledge of the sort of thing that might happen to her here, and if she has not got a proper escort, wherever she is, something dreadful could happen.''

"She is in no danger," Sadie muttered sullenly.

"Be that as it may, you have no way of knowing. And the fact remains that you will either tell me this minute where she has gone, or I shall send you straight back to Crossways to explain the matter to his lordship.''

Sadie paled. "Don't do that, miss. She didn't say where she was going. On my honor. But she did wear her habit, and she sent word to Joe at the stables to bring her mare around.''

Nell had feared something of the sort since she had first seen the morning gown on the bed, but she wasted no time telling Sadie what she thought of a maid who would assist her mistress in such an escapade. There was no time to be lost. Hurrying to her own bedchamber, she tugged the bell, and began changing into her riding habit as quickly as she could manage it. When Mary came to see what was wanted, Nell refused any assistance and sent her instead to order her horse brought 'round.

"And just where might you be going, Miss Nell?" asked that worthy henchwoman placidly.

"The Lady Aurora has taken her horse out, Mary, and I fear she may have ridden up to the Downs," Nell replied quickly, knowing better than to try to snub Mary.

"That wicked baggage," returned the maidservant, not mincing matters. "But you'll not be going after her yourself, Miss Nell."

"Of course I shall," Nell snapped. "She cannot be left to her own devices, Mary. She doesn't realize what might happen up there.''

"But you do, miss, and the proper person to go chasing after that one is his lordship. You should sit yourself down and write a proper note to him. That's what.''

"Oh, Mary, by the time we track his lordship down, anything might happen to Rory! He could be anywhere in Brighton, and if he is at the Pavilion, I'm not by any means certain we *could* get a message to him. There is no time, however, so please do as you are bid. Please, Mary.'' The last was said coaxingly, and although Mary grumbled, she obeyed, and she must have sent a linkboy fairly flying, for when Nell came downstairs ten minutes later, Pavingham informed her that her groom was waiting outside.

She scarcely waited for Peter's assistance and ignored his protests entirely when she informed him that they were headed for the Downs. It occurred to her that, once again, she had forgotten to tell him to arm himself, but she trusted to her own resources if they should encounter trouble. Half an hour later, she had reached the place where she and Rory had ridden before, but she could see no sign of the girl.

"Can you see fresh tracks anywhere, Peter?"

"Lord, Miss Nell, there be fresh tracks everywhere. This be a popular place to ride 'n all." He scratched his head, looking perplexed. "What be we alookin' fer, Miss Nell?"

"The Lady Aurora's horse, Peter. Could you tell his hoofprints from any other horse?" But Peter shook his head. "Very well, then, we must simply ride until we find her," Nell said firmly, turning her mount's head toward Brighton Camp. "I daresay that if we continue in this direction, we shall come up with her before long."

"But, Miss Nell, we be headed——"

"I know, Peter, but it cannot be helped. We simply must find her ladyship."

Nell spurred her horse, cutting off further protest. It was still several miles to the camp, and she hoped against hope that they would find Rory before reaching it. If they did not, she would have to send Peter to look for Major Talcott. Certainly, she could not go in search of him herself. And she hoped Peter would not have to go either, because she would not enjoy waiting alone for his return. Her courage nearly failed her altogether at the thought that such a thing might be necessary, but she bolstered it again by indulging in a silent rehearsal of all the things she would say to her niece when they found her.

XIII

An hour's search revealed no sign of Rory on any of the trails they had taken before, so with reluctance Nell turned onto a path that led downhill toward a thick wood. She knew the military encampment was located just the other side of the wood, and involuntarily, halfway down the hillside, she slowed her horse, casting a hesitant glance at Peter. He stared back at her unencouragingly. With a small grimace she looked away, determined to find her niece. But even as she moved to use her spur, a shout from behind gave her a pause, and glancing over her shoulder, Nell saw a horseman pounding down the hill at almost reckless speed. Recognizing him at once, she gave a sigh of relief and drew rein.

"He looks like the very devil, he does," Peter observed dispassionately, drawing in beside her.

Once Huntley realized they had seen him, he slowed the great stallion to a safer pace. Nell, watching him, hoped he had only been concentrating on the terrain, and that that accounted for the deep furrow where his heavy brows came together, but when he glanced up again, she knew Peter was right. Her sense of relief faded quickly, replaced by an unfamiliar shiver of fear. She met his angry gaze steadily, however, when he pulled up near them. He did not speak to her, but turned to Peter.

"Leave us. I shall see your mistress safely home."

"Aye, m'lord." Without so much as a look at Nell, Peter turned away, leaving her feeling slightly affronted. He was her servant, after all, and should not be so quick to obey another.

"My lord, you cannot simply send him off. What would——"

"What would people think, Nell? Is that what you were about to ask me?" His tone was such that she was glad he didn't wait for a reply. "Do you dare to ask such a thing after careering off on a wild goose chase with only a groom for escort?"

"A wild goose chase?" Her eyes lit, and she forgot his anger for the moment. "Then she is safe? Where was she?"

He grimaced. "She was riding on the beach not half a mile from the men's bathing area, skirts flying, hair streaming out behind her like a damned gypsy."

"Merciful heavens!" Nell gasped. "Did anyone see her?"

"Only half a dozen or so of the men who accompanied his highness to the beach this afternoon," he replied with a touch of sarcasm. "That's all. Thankfully, I doubt if anyone recognized her except for myself. I had my curricle, so I simply left the bathing party and drove along the Marine Parade until I spotted her idiot groom waiting near the dunes by the new royal crescent. I took his mount and went to fetch her."

His words made it all seem very matter-of-fact, but Nell had an instant vision of what was no doubt a pounding chase. And there was equally little doubt as to what Rory's reaction must have been when he caught her. On the other hand, if there had been a quarrel, it was no wonder he was in such a flaming temper now. Nell gazed at him searchingly. His lips were drawn together in a thin line, and his eyes seemed to be sunk deeper than ever beneath the heavy brows. She swallowed carefully.

"I-I daresay you saw her safely home again, sir."

"I did. And I don't mind telling you, I said a few things to her that she won't forget in a hurry."

"Oh dear," Nell said, frowning. "I wish it may have done some good, sir, for I expect she deserved every word. However, I——"

"She deserved a good thrashing," he retorted, not one to understate matters, "While as for you, my girl——"

"Me!"

"Yes, you, and don't look so wide-eyed," he said grimly. "Why do you think I sent your groom away? I mean to say a few things to you, Miss Lindale, that I am quite certain you would prefer to hear privately."

"Well, I cannot think what you might wish to say, sir," she replied, concentrating on the back of her horse's arched neck as she turned him uphill. "Nor can I stop you from saying whatever you like. However, your horse should not be kept standing while we talk. Shall we start back?"

"We will ride to the elm grove at the top of the hill. By then Jack will be ready to rest for a few moments."

"But we must get back to town, sir! Everyone will begin to wonder what has become of us."

"Then they must wonder. I have a good deal to say, and I desire your full attention while I say it. You had no business to come up here by yourself, you know."

"You have no authority over me, my lord," Nell retorted.

"We'll just see about that."

Silence fell between them, although Nell wanted very much to tell him to his head that he could just keep his tongue between his teeth. She had no wish whatever to hear what he had to say to her, for she knew only too well that she had acted rashly in letting her anxiety over Rory's well-being make her forget about her own. It had seemed such a simple matter merely to ride up here, find her, and take her home again. And Peter had seemed sufficient escort for such a purpose. It was not until the possibility had arisen that she might have to be separated from Peter that she had recognized any difficulties, but they had been brought home to her in full force then. When she had seen Huntley riding down the hill toward them, she had felt as though a full cavalry regiment was coming to her aid. Though she had seen his anger and had briefly thought it aimed at her, once he had begun speaking of Rory's escapade, she had assumed his temper was the result of that and nothing else. Now, it appeared that there was a good deal more to the matter than that.

They reached the grove of trees, and Huntley dismounted, dropping Jack's rein to the ground, then turning to help Nell from the saddle.

"Truly, my lord, there is little to be served by stopping here. We must——"

"You are coming out of that saddle," he said, favoring her with a stern glare. "It would be wise for you to cooperate."

She returned the glare. "Very well, sir. I can see that you are quite determined upon this course."

He grasped her around the waist and lifted her easily from the saddle. When he released her, it was only to replace his hands upon her shoulders, and Nell feared from his grim expression that he meant to shake her. That is, she suspected the little shiver that raced up her spine must be one of fear, but even as the thought occurred, she knew she was not afraid of him. Whatever he might do, whatever he might choose to say to her, she was certain he meant her no harm. She stared up at him, waiting for whatever would come next, and when he simply released her and turned away, she felt a wave of disappointment that startled her. Before she had time to examine the extraordinary feeling, he turned back. She watched him, interested to note that his teeth seemed to be clenched. Certainly, his hands had curled into fists.

"Damn it, Nell," he said softly, his voice obviously under rigid control. "You must know how stupidly you behaved today."

"I was worried about Rory," she said, amazed that her own voice seemed so steady. "If I didn't stop to think properly, surely, under the circumstances, no one can blame me."

"The devil they can't!" he snapped, his quick temper not eased in the slightest by her studied calmness. "One idiotic action can scarcely excuse another. You had no business to go haring off like that, and you know it. What would your father say to all of this?"

"Since he is in no position to say anything——"

"Don't quibble, damn it! I'm having enough difficulty to keep from shaking you, or worse."

"Very well, sir!" she replied in the same tone, placing her hands on her hips. "Eight years ago my father would have said very much what you are saying now, but that was eight years ago when I was a girl like Rory. And I promise you, sir, I had planned a number of such things to say to her when I found her. But Clarissa, Crossways, and you as well, Philip, chose to make me responsible for her. And since she *is* my responsibility, when she disappeared, I came to find her. It is unfortunate, perhaps, that it did not occur to me she might ride anywhere but here——"

"It was damned foolhardy not to consider other possibilities!" he declared, unimpressed. "But it was even more foolish of you to go in search of her without so much as informing anyone other than a housemaid of your purpose. Before you can accept responsibility for Aurora's behavior, you must learn to act responsibly yourself, Nell. Your actions today indicate that you have not grown much wiser than the green girl I met eight years ago.''

She opened her mouth, but the words she meant to utter stuck painfully in her throat. Having accepted the fact of his anger, she had expected that he might say things she would as lief not hear, but she had not expected anything he said to hurt her. And his last words had hurt. Her throat closed up even more, and the tightness seemed to creep up the side of her face and behind her eyes. She felt her chin tremble and realized with some astonishment that she was on the verge of tears. Her hands, placed as they were on her hips, felt suddenly ridiculous. I must look like a fishwife, she thought bitterly. But she seemed unable to move them. She could only stand there, staring at Huntley, fighting back the stupid tears.

''Nell?'' He said it twice before she heard him, and then she only tilted her chin to a more defiant angle, glaring at him through tears that sparkled on her lashes. Huntley took a step nearer, anger replaced by concern. ''What is it, Nell? What did I say to make you look like that? Damn it, don't cry!'' He reached out a hand and laid it gently upon her shoulder, as though he would draw her nearer, but she pulled away from him, her hands dropping to her sides at last.

''I won't cry,'' she said grimly, clutching at her skirts. ''I am not a stupid watering pot. Nor am I as silly as Rory, damn you!''

He made no immediate reply, and if there was amusement in his expression, Nell was too angry and too concerned with controlling her tears to notice it. After a moment he asked gently, ''Did that hurt so much?'' Angrily she turned her back on him, but he stepped closer, his hands upon her shoulders again. ''I never meant I thought you as silly as your niece, Nell. Only that you did not act very wisely today. Now, turn around, look me in the eye, and tell me, if you dare, that I'm wrong.''

Her shoulders shook a little under those gentle hands, and two wrenching sobs escaped her before she forced herself to breathe deeply in an attempt to regain control of her ragged emotions. Huntley said nothing at all, nor did he move, and after a moment or two her breathing steadied, though her nerves did not. He was too close, yet she did not want him to move away. It was almost as if she hoped to gain the very strength to face him from the warmth of those hands upon her shoulders. Realizing the thought was an absurd one, she took another deep breath, wiped her hands on her skirts, and turned, looking up at him through her damp lashes, the picture of contrition.

"You are not wrong, my lord." She spoke gruffly, but his gaze held hers for a long moment, and she could not seem to turn away. The tension thickening between them quickened her pulse, but more than that, she was aware of a look in his eye that she had seen a time or two before, almost as if he felt some pain or other. Whatever it was, she was conscious of a need to comfort him. "I may not be as silly as Rory," she said quietly, watching him closely, "but I deserved a trimming just as surely as she did. If your words upset me, 'twas only because I knew I had acted foolishly and was annoyed with myself. I own, I have often ridden up here with only Peter's escort, but never so near to the camp as this. That was indeed foolhardy."

"You are not to come here alone at all, Nell," he said sternly, reaching into his waistcoat pocket for a handkerchief, with which he began to mop at her cheeks. "And do not dare to tell me I have no authority over you," he added when her mouth dropped open as though she would protest. "It is my belief that, in your father's absence, you have become as fond as your niece of having your own way, and if no one else will take it upon himself to curb your high flights, as your friend I must. I don't mind telling you that this little escapade of yours frightened me witless. Here, blow your nose."

She had been holding her tongue only until he had quite finished, intending to declare her independence, her maturity, and anything else that might be necessary to convince him that, while he might be in the right of it over the way she had dealt with things today, he still had no right, even as a friend, to dictate to her. But his last words put a period to that little speech before it was begun. Instead, she took the handkerchief from him and obediently put it to good use. Then, clutching it in one hand, she looked up at him again, her head tilted a little to one side. "Did I truly frighten you, sir?"

His jaw tightened, and he turned slightly away, drawing in a long, slow breath. Thinking he was exerting himself in order to keep from treating her to the benefit of a few more blistering words, Nell touched his arm.

"Please, Philip, I——" Whatever else she might have said was lost as she found herself suddenly crushed against his broad chest. She struggled briefly, but it was useless. He was too strong. With a little sigh she relaxed, putting her trust in fate. He was muttering into her curls now, something to the effect that she had frightened the very liver and lights out of him. The phrasing tickled her sense of the absurd, and she chuckled against his waistcoat, only to find herself thrust suddenly away, his grip bruising her shoulders as he peered anxiously down at her.

"Here, you aren't crying again, are you?" Her eyes twinkled as her lips parted slightly, and he groaned as if he could stand no more. "Damn you, Nell," he muttered, pulling her into his arms again and lowering his head to claim her lips in a ruthless kiss.

Astonished, even stunned as she was by this sudden display of passion, it never once occurred to Nell to resist him. The feelings coursing through her would have made such a response seem entirely ridiculous. Instead, she followed her instincts, meeting his demands with a passion that matched his own, offering no resistance, even when his tongue moved against her teeth, demanding entrance. She seemed to know instinctively what he wanted from her, and she responded willingly, trusting him still to do nothing that would harm her.

If she had been capable of rational thought, she might have been amazed that she could respond so easily to Huntley's passion, for although she had been frequently in his company of late, she had continued to think of him primarily as a comfortable escort, a dear friend. If she had begun to turn to him more and more for advice, she would have said—had anyone remarked upon it—that it was only because he was so readily available to her.

Her thoughts on that or any subject, however, were not rational at the moment. Indeed, as Huntley's hands began to move over her body, following the curve of her waist and hips before moving upward again, Nell was lost, suspended in a world of wondrous sensations. The roughness of his coat seemed unique and somehow fascinating beneath her fingers, and her hands began to roam just as his were doing, seeking new textures, delighting in the feel of his hard, muscular body. She was hardly aware of the actual course they took, however, for her senses were overwhelmed by the magical feelings his kisses and the touch of his hands stirred throughout her own body. His hands moved gently over her soft breasts, and she gasped, pulling slightly, involuntarily, away from him. At once his arms encircled her, crushing her against his chest again, and she felt the stirring of his warm breath against her curls.

"Oh, Nell, forgive me," he murmured. "Or send me to the devil for a hypocrite. To think I dared to preach responsibility to you! I ought to be horsewhipped."

She drew in a long breath, not daring to examine her own upended sensibilities, but forcing all her energies of concentration onto his dismay instead. He was her best friend, and he must not be allowed to castigate himself. Not for something which had seemed, incredibly, to have happened quite naturally and which had clearly been pleasurable for them both. Not that it wasn't rather pleasant to have the boot on the other foot for once, to see him angry with himself instead of with Rory or with her. The thought steadied her still-reeling senses.

When she moved a little within his arms, he loosened his hold, thus enabling her to look up at him. It took some effort to appear calm, but the hint of a mischievous twinkle lurked deep in her eyes. "If I were the green girl you accused me of being some moments ago, sir, you might indeed deserve to be punished. Although," she added musingly, "I cannot think who might attend to the matter for me. Kit, perhaps? Or, no, that would be if there were to be a duel, in which case you would, of necessity, delope, and all would be well, because although he is expert with a shotgun, poor Kit could not hit a mail coach at ten paces with a pistol. But for horsewhipping, one is supposed to send one's lackeys. Is that not so?"

His lips twitched slightly, but he managed to answer evenly enough. "It is the recommended procedure."

"Well, then, what are we to do?" She tilted her head. "Peter has already shown a detestable willignness to obey your slightest command without so much as asking my leave, which, you will admit, hardly encourages one to believe he would support any effort to effect your punishment. Moreoover, there is the difficulty of your size. His head scarcely reaches your shoulder. And if you are thinking Kit's groom might be more equal to the task, let me tell you, you are quite out, for Ned is a mere scrap of a fellow. And Trilby, my coachman, as you know perfectly well, is well past the age mark. So we are at a stand, I'm afraid.''

He laughed, tweaking one of her curls. "Nell, are you never serious?''

"Yes, of course I am, but not when others talk fustian.''

He grimaced again. "It's not fustian, and you know it. I had no business to do what I did, but oh, I wish that I had and that Fate had not served us such a devilish trick.''

The last few words made her tremble, but she forced herself to ignore their possible meaning as she placed her hand upon his arm and looked him straight in the eye. "Dear friend, you did nothing that I did not allow you to do, and I never once feared for my honor or my dignity. Indeed,'' she added, managing a nearly roguish smile, "I must be an abandoned woman, for I enjoyed myself hugely. And if I do not regret what happened, why then should you?''

"Ah, but you are still an innocent, my dear, regardless of the fact that you think yourself such an old cat. The fault is mine. I should not have let it happen.''

"But it did happen,'' she pointed out. "Between two good friends, and it is over now and done. We should be thinking ahead now to how you mean to deal with Rory, should we not?''

"Deal with Rory?'' He seemed puzzled.

"Well, surely this proves that you must not marry her, Philip.''

He cast her a pain-ridden glance, but she said nothing further, and at last, staring at a point beyond her shoulder, he spoke. "I have realized for some time now and for several reasons that my betrothal was an unfortunate mistake. However, that knowledge, though frustrating, makes little difference. I am contracted to her. Had I known after my brother died— But it is so senseless to look back, to wail over what might have been. Indeed, it is pointless. My honor is at stake now, so there is nothing to be done.''

"How Gothic!'' Nell did nothing now to conceal the sudden anger she felt, but when he only regarded her with that expression of helpless pain, she realized it would be fruitless to debate the matter with him. A gentleman of honor, such as she knew him to be, could never call off his betrothal. It was a simple enough thing for the lady to do—ladies being considered a fickle lot—but it was never an acceptable act for a gentleman. Privately Nell thought that a stupid custom, for certainly a gentleman could make a mistake (as, indeed, Huntley had done) just as easily as a lady might.

Pressing her lips together she let him help her back into the saddle and, during the ride back into Brighton, made little effort to respond to his occasional conversational gambits. Her mind was too busy for desultory chitchat, and though he looked as if he could use some more comforting, she had no wish to offer him soothing words. Her emotions were too much in turmoil.

Where she had once thought marriage to Huntley would be the making of her niece, now she knew it would be total disaster for both of them. And for others, as well. Herself, in particular. The thought showed an alarming tendency to linger, but for the moment and despite her still-tingling senses, Nell made every effort to repress it. It was not in her nature to dwell upon what might have been, but it was certainly in her nature to attack present difficulties head-on in order to clear the way for what might be. Therefore, it made better sense to deal with the situation at hand than to attempt to make sense of Huntley's cryptic references to the past. A little resolution was clearly required if matters were to be rearranged satisfactorily.

She thought at first that Huntley himself, if he truly wished to be free, might simply make a push to discuss the matter with Rory and convince her to agree to a mutual dissolution of the betrothal. But upon thinking it over, she realized it would be useless to suggest such a course to him. He would refuse, insisting that to make the suggestion would be every bit as insulting to Rory as it would be to jilt her without discussing the matter. And in the normal course of events, of course, it would be. But from what she had seen of her niece lately, the events were anything but normal. She had a suspicion that, with very little encouragement, Rory would welcome an end to her betrothal, that she had already discovered a preference for men—perhaps even for one man—nearer her own age.

Clearly, then, Nell herself would have to discuss the matter with her. Briefly, she considered the possibility of informing him of her intention, but she discarded the notion almost the moment it entered her head. He would forbid that course as well, and then she would be at a standstill. And Nell meant to do something. She could not simply let matters take their course, for if she did, Huntley would end up married to Rory, and they would all be miserable.

At that moment and seemingly of its own accord, her memory jumped back to the interlude in the elm grove. His behavior had shaken her a good deal, but never had anyone made her feel as Philip had made her feel in those brief moments. Certainly, she could not deny her own body's responses. Of course, she was, as he had pointed out, rather inexperienced in such matters. She cast her now silent companion a speculative glance. Perhaps he had only given way to the sort of passion men—if what one had heard was true—indulged in without really thinking it meant anything. She had certainly never thought before today that he might carry a tenderness for her. Oh, there had been a time all those many years ago when she had thought he cared for her, when she had even hoped— But it had come to nothing, and had probably been only friendship even then. No doubt she had been too strong-minded for him. But then other memories of the elm grove intruded, and stirred by a small, delicious tremor deep within herself, she was forced to consider the possibility that he might be rather strong-minded himself from time to time. And looking at his glum countenance now, she could not believe he had no strong feelings for her. Before the thought settled, however, she remembered how easily he could be ruled by his sister's strong words, a couple of crystal vinaigrettes, and by his own wretched sense of honor. It was all disturbing, even frustrating. Moreover, it was all mere pointless speculation, unless the betrothal could be ended.

When they reached Upper Rock Gardens, Huntley rather disconcertingly bade her farewell on the doorstep, declining an invitation to step inside for a few minutes. Then, when Nell said, somewhat hesitantly for her, that they would look for him at eight to escort them to Mrs. Calvert's drum, he clapped a hand to his head and looked at her ruefully.

"I forgot," he said, "and I told Aurora it would be best if she remained at home this evening. Never gave a thought to the fact that I would be spoiling your pleasure, as well."

"Merciful heavens, next you will say you sent her to bed

without her supper!'' Her equilibrium fully recovered now, Nell regarded him in fond exasperation. ''Typically Gothic behavior, if I may say so, my lord. It will serve no useful purpose to keep her at home tonight, and it may do harm. There is, despite your assurance to the contrary, a slight possibility that one of those gentlemen with the prince might have recognized her today. She is an extraordinarily beautiful girl, after all, and has drawn a good deal of attention. If she does not put in an appearance tonight, any suspicion of that sort will be confirmed. We must go.''

He nodded. ''I confess, I hadn't thought the matter through carefully. Very well, you may tell her you cozened me into changing my mind. And, Nell . . .''

She looked up curiously but found only warmth and a hint of sadness in his expression. ''Sir?''

''You see to it that that baggage keeps out of mischief,'' he ordered. ''My patience is wearing thin, and it will do her no good to turn me into a tyrant before she's saddled with me for life.''

She grinned at him, dimples showing in both cheeks, but she vouchsafed no reply. Her mind was made up. If Huntley hadn't enough resolution to see the betrothal ended, then she would simply have to attend to the matter herself. Bidding him farewell with the firm intention of having the matter well in hand by suppertime, she went in search of her niece.

XIV

Nell did not have far to search. When she pushed open the door to the yellow bedchamber, she beheld her niece curled up on the French seat in the window bay, staring out at the back garden, her arms folded along the back of the seat, her chin resting upon her hands. The gray kitten curled up in the folds of her skirt opened one eye but closed it again upon seeing Nell, and after a momentary hesitation, Rory lifted her head and looked over her shoulder. Her expression gave little away, but there was a hint of defiance in her voice when she spoke.

"I suppose you have seen Huntley."

Nell shut the door. "Indeed I have, and such a lecture as he read me you would scarcely believe!"

"He scolded you, Aunt Nell?" Rory sat up a little straighter.

"He certainly did. I'd no notion the man possessed such a temper." She stepped to the window seat and sat down, peering rather anxiously at her niece. "Are you all right, my dear?"

Rory grimaced, then pulled Ulysses into her lap, stroking him gently. "I expect he told you what happened," she muttered.

"Yes, of course he did, and I must say it was foolish of you to ride so near to the men's bathing area, but I explained that I had forgotten to warn you against it, so he has come down out of the boughs. You've no need to fret any further."

Rory looked up through her heavy lashes. "Is that why he was angry with you, ma'am? Because I don't think he should be."

Nell chuckled. "Good gracious, no. I took a foolish notion into my head that you had ridden to the Downs, and so I rode up thinking to meet you. Only of course you hadn't, and so when Huntley found me I was alone, for of course he sets no store, as you know to your own cost, by a mere groom's escort. So he ordered poor Peter off home and gave me the devil of a trimming.''

"Oh, Aunt Nell, I'm truly sorry!"

Nell's eyes twinkled. "Don't refine too much upon it, my dear. I assure you, I don't. Very likely he was annoyed at having his bathing interrupted and merely took the opportunity we offered him to ventilate his feelings.''

Rory's slim fingers fiddled with gray fur until Ulysses uttered a faint mew of protest, whereupon she relaxed her hands and looked at her aunt. "I hope he doesn't ventilate such feelings often, ma'am. I, for one, don't like to be bellowed at.''

"Dear me," Nell said, "did he bellow?" She gave it some thought. "He does have a sad habit of doing so from time to time. However, I am persuaded——" She bit off the words she had been about to utter, realizing there would be little profit to be gained from insisting that his lordship's bark was a good deal worse than his bite. Instead, she patted the girl's hand sympathetically. "I expect you are not accustomed to bursts of temperament from those around you. You know, my dear, the more I learn of your Lord Huntley, the less I believe him to be the man for you.''

Rory shrugged. "There is nothing to be done, however.''

"You could end the betrothal," Nell suggested baldly. "You would scarcely be the first young woman to change her mind.''

The golden eyes widened. "Oh no, ma'am, surely you must see that I cannot. Mama and Papa would be so disappointed. Mama, in particular," she added with a small sigh. For a brief moment she gazed wistfully out of the window, but she rallied quickly and managed a smile when she turned back to Nell. "Besides, I shall quite like being a countess and having lots of money. I daresay that will make up for the rest.''

Resolutely Nell swallowed the sharp retort that sprang to the tip of her tongue, but it was clear that ending the relationship between Rory and Lord Huntley might not be so easy as she had first thought. For one thing, she had forgotten Clarissa, who would be most unlikely to whistle a fortune the size of

Huntley's down the wind without a fight. And Rory herself was obviously more enamored of the title and the money than Nell had first supposed. If there were only someone else whose eligibility would match his lordship's. But there was not. She dismissed Major Talcott with little more than a brief thought. Although she was perfectly certain that her niece had a strong interest in the gentleman, she had seen little indication of late that he returned that interest. And even if he did, his fortune could scarcely compare to the earl's. She continued to consider the matter far into the afternoon and even while she prepared for the evening ahead, but she could think of no course of action that would answer the purpose.

Huntley, arriving promptly at eight, gave her a quick, searching glance, then seemed to relax when she smiled at him. A moment later Nell, knowing full well that he had somewhat mixed feelings about her mother's fragile constitution, hid a grin at his visible attempt to conceal astonishment when Lady Agnes informed him that she meant to accompany them.

"Is it not courageous of her, sir?" Nell asked, quizzing him. Lips twitching, he replied that it was, indeed.

"I think it is splendid," Rory said cheerfully as she settled herself in the carriage.

"Well, Mrs. Calvert is a particular friend of mine," Lady Agnes explained earnestly when Huntley handed her up to sit beside her granddaughter, "and there will be a card room set up, you know, so I shan't exert myself beyond what my constitution will bear. I hadn't really thought I should go, but dear Nell thought it would do me good to get out, you know, and Sir Henry concurred, so here I am. It is good of you to lend us your escort, Huntley."

"The pleasure is mine, my lady," he assured her, indulging himself in a twinkling glance at Nell as he climbed in to take his place beside her on the forward seat. The warmth behind the twinkle sent her senses reeling again, and it didn't help when his hand brushed inadvertently against her skirts. Plunged suddenly into her own thoughts, Nell took little notice of the conversation as the carriage moved through the streets of Brighton.

Mrs. Calvert had cleared her drawing room for dancing and had turned her first-floor saloon into a card room. Greeting them upon their arrival, she announced in her placid manner that a late supper would be served at eleven in the dining room. "Agnes, my dear, we are delighted to see you. We had quite decided you would be unable to afford us the pleasure of your company."

"What 'us'?" Huntley inquired in a low voice as he escorted the ladies toward the drawing room. "She invests the word with nearly regal overtones."

Only Nell heard him, and she turned laughing eyes to his. "There is a Mr. Calvert, my lord," she told him, her voice catching a little when she realized how closely they stood together. "Rather a quiet, somewhat elderly man. I believe we would find him in the card room if we were to look. Oh, Mama," she added, speaking slightly louder, "there is Sir Henry. I didn't know he meant to be here this evening. We should have invited him to make one of our party."

"Oh, he thought he might just look in, you know," Lady Agnes replied vaguely, signaling Sir Henry, however, with her silk fan even as she spoke.

A few moments later Sir Henry had taken Lady Agnes off to the card room, and Rory's hand had been solicited for the first dance, so Nell found herself alone once more with Huntley. His nearness was still disturbing, and she searched her mind rapidly for a safe topic of conversation. "Have you seen the prince, sir?" she asked at last. "Was he annoyed with you for leaving his bathing party?"

There was a brief pause as his eyes met hers, but then, seeming to shake himself, he smiled. "Prinny is in high gig," he said, taking a seat beside her. "You know old Smoaker, of course."

"Certainly," she replied gamely, "though I have never met him. He is as much a legend as Martha Gunn. He's been the prince's dipper for years."

"Well, he's a crusty fellow and has a reputation for being very strict with his charges," Huntley said, "but today he outdid himself. According to Prinny, when he went into the water this afternoon, he ventured out a bit farther than he usually does. Next thing he knew, old Smoaker was squawking at him to come back. Prinny ignored him, of course, so what does the old fellow do but dash in after him and drag him out by the ear!"

Laughter came easily, and she said, "It sounds precisely

the sort of thing he would do to any other gentleman, but it is scarcely the sort of treatment the prince is accustomed to.''

"Oh, Prinny was highly diverted," Huntley assured her. "Marlborough said at dinner that Smoaker explained himself by grumbling that he warn't going to let the king hang him for letting the Prince of Wales drown hisself, not to please nobody!''

"You must have been sorry to miss such a scene," Nell said, still chuckling. Then a note of contrition touched her voice. "I hope it has not made you more displeased that we should have——"

"What's done is done and no use talking about," he said brusquely. "Will you dance?"

Though Huntley's mind, like her own, seemed to be elsewhere a good deal of the time, the evening passed agreeably enough. Nell, keeping a close watch over her, thought Rory seemed distracted, too. She smiled and even flirted, but her heart didn't seem to be much in it. She seemed to have her eye on the entrance, and when she casually mentioned that Huntley might take her down to supper if he'd a mind to, since no one else had asked her, Nell's suspicions were aroused. She said nothing, however, and the three of them went down to supper together. Afterward Huntley volunteered to see that all was well with Lady Agnes, and Rory and Nell walked back to the drawing room.

"I do hope Grandmama is not overdoing things," Rory said. They had neared the doorway, and she raised her voice slightly in order to make herself heard over the sound of the musicians tuning their instruments.

"She is no doubt enjoying every moment," Nell replied, smiling.

"Well, I must confess I've noticed she rarely lets her health interfere with anything she tru——" Rory's voice seemed to catch in her throat. Nell, noting the way her eyes lit up and following the direction of her gaze, saw Major Talcott coming toward them from the main entryway. "Good evening, sir," Rory said with a brilliant smile. "We had nearly given you up."

"Forgive me, my lady," he said smoothly, grinning at her and then bowing to Nell. "I was unavoidably detained."

"Invasion, sir?" Rory's eyes twinkled, and dimples appeared in her cheeks.

The expression on Talcott's face and the warmth in his eyes when he responded to this sally made Nell regard him with a good deal of speculation. His attention was fully engaged, however, and he did not notice her searching look.

"Only smugglers," he said. "The Land Guard has asked our help in searching out a particularly stubborn lot of them. Seems their activities have been on the increase in this neighborhood since the prince and his friends came to town."

Rory smoothed the lace on her sleeve somewhat guiltily. "Is that really so dreadful? I think the duties are loathsome."

"So do most of my men, I'm afraid." Talcott had not missed her gesture, but he said nothing about it, for Huntley approached them from the card room just then. "Good evening, my lord."

"Major Talcott has just been telling us he has been looking for smugglers, Huntley," Rory informed him. "Is that not thrilling?"

"Indeed," Huntley replied, shaking hands with the major. "Locals?"

Talcott nodded. "We think so. The Land Guard has asked merely that we send out the occasional night patrol, hoping to deter their more outrageous activities. It's good practice for my men, although so far I'm afraid their interest in actually capturing any smugglers is slight at best."

"Huntley does not approve of smuggling," Rory said with an oblique, pouting look.

"I should think not," replied the major, to her evident dismay. Nell hid a smile, her sense of the absurd suddenly tickled by the memory of her niece's oft expressed wish to meet a smuggler and the thought of what the major's opinion of such a desire would no doubt be. He was still talking, his tone firm but gentle. "I know you and most of the other ladies think it's exciting to purchase smuggled goods, particularly laces and other fine materials for your gowns"—he smiled pointedly at Rory— "but a good deal of the money from the smuggling operations goes to support the French war effort, you know. And it's not only gold, but information as well that gets out of this country by way of the smugglers."

"Surely, the gentlemen would not do anything to betray England," Rory said to him. Then, when his eyes narrowed a bit, she added on an airy note, "They prefer to be called gentlemen, you know. Either that or free-traders. And so long as the high duties on tobacco, salt, laces, and particularly brandy continue——''

"I should like to know how you come to know so much about it, miss," Huntley put in repressively, "but I daresay the major has better things to do than to discuss the issue with you."

"Because I am a mere female, sir?" she challenged.

"Because this is neither the time nor the place for it," he countered. "The musicians have begun to play again. Do you wish to dance?"

"Yes, but I have already accepted Major Talcott's offer, thank you," Rory replied without a blink. "Will you excuse us?"

Huntley scarcely waited until they were beyond hearing before he let out an exasperated sigh. "Where on earth does she come by her absurd notions?"

"Don't be ridiculous, sir," Nell said, unable to resist teasing him. "She has grown up in Kent, after all, where free-trading has been a way of life for years. I daresay Crossways hasn't a barrel of brandy on his estate that hasn't come into this country duty-free. Do you mean to tell me you pay more for yours at Huntley Green?" She thought guiltily of the cellars in Upper Rock Gardens.

Huntley grimaced. "I doubt that a penny's worth of duty was laid out for the brandy in my cellars," he admitted, "though it was not my doing, but my brother's and my father's before him. Damn it, Nell, I am not a prig, and I know perfectly well that many of the 'gentlemen' make a much better living by free-trading than they could make otherwise. However, it *is* against the law, and there are better means of fighting the import duties than by encouraging the smugglers. Talcott is right about the damage they do."

"Well, I daresay our local lads have little to do with that side of the business," she returned pacifically.

"That has nothing to do with the matter. Perhaps," he added, regarding her sternly, "you might tell me just how it is that Aurora is aware of their preference for the term *gentlemen*. I can accept the fact that she might have heard reference in Kent to free-trading, although it is unlikely that such a topic would be bandied about Crossways' drawing room or schoolroom, but she talks as if she is more intimately acquainted with the business than that."

Although she was perfectly well aware that the lace on Rory's gown—and that on her own, for that matter—had been delivered to the kitchen entrance of Number Twenty-seven less than a week before, Nell thought it wiser to profess ignorance than to confide the information that several of their own servants had relatives in the trade. She had little doubt that Rory, with her romantic soul and her love for Gothic novels, had learned a good deal in Kent before ever coming into Sussex. Nevertheless, she knew also that Rory—though insisting it had been on Ulysses' account—had spent more time than was proper with Jeremy, and Jeremy had at least two cousins that Nell knew of among the 'gentlemen.' Very likely, the young footman had added much to whatever knowledge Rory had had before coming to Brighton.

She said nothing of this to Huntley, but set herself to coax him into a better mood instead, and by the time he escorted them back to Upper Rock Gardens, she was able to congratulate herself that she had succeeded very well in her efforts. It was not part of her developing plan of campaign, however, to shield him from her niece's shortcomings, and in the days that followed, Nell was very busy.

There were moments when she tended to picture herself in the impossible position of second to two parties who had engaged to fight a duel, rather than to marry. But whereas the first duty of a good second was to effect a reconciliation between his principals, Nell no longer retained the slightest vestige of a desire to reconcile them, or even to help them learn how to go on better together. Instead, she meant to part them as quickly and cleanly as possible, for whenever she thought about the possibility of a marriage between them, her teeth seemed to clench together of their own accord and her thoughts showed an uncontrollable tendency to fly back to that afternoon on the Downs. Whenever that happened, it was almost as if she could feel his hands on her again, as if she could feel the very sensations his kisses had stirred throughout her body. He simply could not marry Rory.

In consequence, she sympathized openly whenever Rory complained of Huntley's behavior, and even contrived to keep a still tongue in her head when his advanced age and fusty manners were mentioned. And whenever she found herself in his lordship's company, she took whatever opportunity offered to point out—albeit with a becoming air of reluctance—any of her niece's shortcomings that he might previously have chanced to overlook. With such tactics as these, it was not long before she was persuaded she was making progress.

Clearly, Rory was beginning to think less and less of the advantages of being a wealthy countess and more and more of the disadvantages of having a husband who would treat her more like a disobedient, even tiresome, child than like a wife. And Huntley, though he continued to insist that his honor counted for more than any future discomfort, was certainly beginning to concentrate with more misgiving upon the disadvantages of acquiring a very young wife.

It was not just her youth, of course, as Nell realized rather quickly during her campaign. It was, more specifically, Rory's upbringing. Again and again she managed to bring into ordinary conversation the fact that Huntley could scarcely hope to undo the work of years in weeks or even months.

One morning during the course of her campaign she agreed to accompany Rory and her maid to the shops along the Steyne, and when Rory became engrossed in the selection of new fabrics in a particularly stuffy little shop near Donaldson's Library, Nell took the opportunity to step outside for some fresh air. Not two minutes had passed before she found her elbow in a firm grip.

"Have you now taken to wandering the streets entirely alone, Miss Lindale?" Huntley demanded as he turned her to face him.

Admirably concealing her delight at the encounter, she answered saucily, "You will have all the fops ogling us, my lord, if you continue to maul me about. Rory and her Sadie are just inside that shop, but I found the air oppressive and stepped outside for a moment, so you are quite out, and I will thank you to keep your reproofs for those who require them."

"For those who attend them, at any rate," he replied, grinning down at her with a warm look in his eyes that stirred her to her very toes. "I should have known you would not come here alone, my dear. However, I was startled to see you here without Aurora. Should have realized she'd be somewhere close at hand, no doubt purchasing some expensive trifle. Every time I see the two of you here, she has at least a parcel or two. Does the chit never cease wasting the ready?"

Nell nearly jumped to Rory's defense before she saw the advantages of the topic. Not, she was forced to admit to herself, that he was far out. "She does spend quite a lot," she said thoughtfully, avoiding his eye.

"The devil of a lot if what I've seen of her gowns is anything to go by! Crossways must make her an enormous allowance."

"Oh, you know how it is, my lord," Nell replied casually. "She is the eldest, and the apple of his eye. He put no limit on her spending and merely said to send him a Dutch reckoning."

"But both your mother and your sister possess an excellent sense of economy," he protested. "I should have thought that Lady Crossways would have drummed such notions in Aurora's head."

"Indeed, one would think so," Nell agreed. "However, I fear Clarissa spoils Rory quite as much as Crossways does. No one has ever said she couldn't have anything she had set her heart upon."

She saw that he was thinking deeply and let the subject rest, believing it unnecessary to pursue it further. Nevertheless, when Rory and Sadie came out of the shop, each carrying large bundles, she could have hugged them. Huntley said nothing beyond pointing out that they ought to have brought a footman with them if they meant to make such numerous purchases, but Nell informed him that Trilby was down the way, waiting only for their signal before bringing the carriage to collect them, so there was little more that Huntley could say.

In the week that followed, she was well pleased with the progress of her campaign and content to let matters take their course. Rory's depression mounted by leaps and bounds, and Nell was persuaded that one look at her downcast face would convince even Clarissa of the cruelty of forcing the marriage with Huntley. The child was really too young, in her aunt's opinion, to marry anyone, and it would not hurt her to wait another Season or two. Besides, she would no doubt thoroughly enjoy making a splash in London the following spring. And Clarissa would not count the expense by then, not with two more daughters soon to emerge from the schoolroom. Their come-outs would be less expensive, after all, if Rory was well established and able to assist them. It was not until the

Monday evening following Mrs. Calvert's drum that Nell had cause to reexamine any single portion of her careful reasoning.

The two younger ladies had planned to attend the assembly at the Castle Inn, as they generally did on Monday evenings. However, Huntley begged off, on account of his presence being commanded for dinner at Mrs. Fitzherbert's house, and so when Rory pleaded a headache at supper, Nell readily agreed that an evening spent at home would no doubt do them both a great deal of good. They retired to the drawing room with Lady Agnes, leaving Kit to enjoy his glass of port in solitary splendor. Lady Agnes immediately lit a branch of working candles and drew out her fancywork. Nell asked Rory if she would like to play a game of backgammon.

"No, thank you, Aunt Nell," replied that young lady, stifling a yawn. "I believe I shall just thumb through the copy of the *Ladies' Monthly Museum* that came in the afternoon post, and then go up to bed. Oh, thank you, Jeremy," she added as the footman entered with Ulysses. She took him, and the kitten promptly began to knit a place for himself in her lap. "Has he had his supper?"

"Yes, m'lady. And taken care of other matters as well," replied the young footman in an odd tone. Glancing at him, Nell noticed his eyes were still on her niece and that a somewhat intent look had replaced his usual boyish grin. She hoped he was not getting notions above his station.

"Oh, good," Rory said, blithely unaware. "I'll have Sadie bring him down to you when I go to bed."

"Yes, m'lady." He gave a small sigh of resignation, then turned to Lady Agnes. "Will there be anything else wanted, ma'am?" She declined, saying only that they would want the tea tray brought in by nine o'clock and that he'd best see Mr. Kit didn't drink too much port before setting out for wherever he meant to spend the evening. Jeremy bowed again and paused only long enough to stir up the fire before leaving the room. Lady Agnes looked up at Nell, who was just finding her place in the book she was presently reading.

"I must say, my dear, that Kit has been in much better spirits of late."

"Indeed he has," Nell agreed.

"Yes, Sir Henry is well pleased with him. I daresay all these new coats he's been wearing have cost the earth, however."

"Don't let it trouble you, Mama. I am persuaded Sir Henry will not let him outrun the constable," Nell said with a smile.

Surprisingly, Lady Agnes did not pursue the matter, though Nell had certainly expected at the very least a few more comments upon Kit's recent, clearly more expensive lifestyle. Instead, she said merely that she was certain Sir Henry knew just what he was about, and the conversation continued sporadically until all three ladies became engrossed in their separate occupations. There was little noise after that beyond the occasional turning of a page, the crackling of the fire, or a rustling sound when Lady Agnes searched for something in her workbasket. Neither she nor Nell paid much heed when Rory closed her magazine, gave another, somewhat ostentatious yawn, and announced that she simply could not keep her eyes open another moment. Lady Agnes wished her a good night, but it was not until she had reached the doorway that Nell even looked up.

Then, smiling, she said, "Are you off to bed, then? I hope your headache is better."

Rory passed a hand across her forehead. "I expect a good night's sleep will do the trick, Aunt Nell."

"Of course it will."

"Do you want some hartshorn, dearest?"

"Oh, no, Grandmama. That stuff doesn't agree with me. Sleep is all I need, I promise you. Goodnight."

She left, and Lady Agnes raised an eyebrow. "She has not been looking at all well lately, Nell. Do you think she is ailing?"

"No, Mama, merely fagged. We have been going a rapid pace, you know."

Lady Agnes agreed to it and went back to her fancywork. Kit came in a few moments later and announced that he was off to visit friends, and then the ladies were left alone again. Nothing disturbed them for quite half an hour, at which time Pavingham entered the room, and one look at his expression showed that he was big with news. He carried a packet which he handed to Lady Agnes.

"From Parkhurst, ma'am, by special courier."

Lady Agnes's brow wrinkled slightly. "Good gracious, whatever can Agatha want that requires the expense of a courier?" Pavingham vouchsafed no reply, but neither did he leave. A chief advantage to being an old and trusted servant was that he might expect to have his curiosity appeased. "Merciful heavens!" her ladyship exclaimed as she scanned the first lines of the missive.

"What is it, Mama?" Nell demanded.

"Your aunt is ill," Lady Agnes replied, her lips thinning into a narrow line as she read further. "This is written at her request by her man of affairs. He writes that she is not expected to live out the month. Oh, Nell!"

Nell jumped up from her chair and ran to kneel beside her. "Mama, you must go to her at once. I shall help you make the arrangements."

"Go to her! I should think not," Lady Agnes replied indignantly. "What good could I do by going to her? I only hope she has not died already. I do not *want* to be forced back into black dresses. I am fed to the teeth with mourning!"

Nell repressed a gurgle of laughter, and gave her mother a hug. "I'm persuaded it cannot be so serious, ma'am. Only think how often you have apostrophized Aunt's man as a doomsday parson and given thanks that Sir Henry handles your affairs. Why, only last year he wrote that Aunt had an inflammation of the lungs when it was nothing more than an epidemic cold. No doubt we shall receive a letter in due course stating that she is quite herself again."

But Lady Agnes was not comforted. "No, we shall not. Last year he did not send his message by special courier. Moreover, it would be exactly like Agatha to die just now when you are finally beginning to go about again and might even be so fortunate as to find yourself a husband. Was there ever a family so cursed?"

Nell did what she could to cheer up her afflicted parent, but nothing would do but that her ladyship must write immediately to inform her elder daughter of the impending tragedy.

"For even if that dratted man thought to write her, you may depend upon it that he sent the message to Crossways, for he can have no way of knowing they are gone to Chatham. But I shall not send the message by courier. The regular mail will do well enough." She added that she might just as well attend to the matter at once and asked if Nell would be so kind as to fetch her letter paper and a quill from the table in her boudoir. Nell agreed, choosing to take the back stairs since they were closer. She was a little surprised to meet

Sadie on her way, but since the maid was carrying the little gray kitten, she would have thought little more about it had it not occurred to her that Sadie was looking the very picture of guilt.

XV

"What is it, Sadie?"

"Oh, nothing, miss," the maid replied nervously. " 'Tis merely you startled me, me not expecting to see you on these stairs. I been putting m'lady's things away and was just taking Ulysses here down to his bed."

"Is your mistress still awake, then?" Nell asked, thinking that if that were the case, she would just step up and tell Rory about Aunt Agatha's illness and make sure she was comfortable for the night. But her question appeared to agitate Sadie still more. She seemed, even in the dim light of the stairwell, to have gone quite pale.

"Oh no, miss, she be asleep!"

"But if she is sleeping, surely you wouldn't just be coming down from straightening her things," Nell objected, watching her closely now. Sadie bit her lip.

"I was quiet, miss," she muttered defensively.

"Maybe so," Nell agreed, "but I think I will just step upstairs and see for myself that her ladyship requires nothing further tonight."

"Oh, please, miss," Sadie gasped. "My lady will be so angry with me. Pray, do not go up!"

"Well, what is this, then? Have you been up to mischief?" A dozen thoughts passed through Nell's mind, and she remembered the other servants had been determined to teach Sadie her place. She had heard nothing more of the matter, but perhaps she would have to look into it. Then she realized Sadie was denying that she had done anything, and it occurred to her that the maid rarely spared a thought for anything but her mistress's needs. It was not Sadie who was likely up to mischief. Suddenly Jeremy's intent looks earlier in the drawing room took on new meaning, and misgivings stirred, developing rapidly into a deep sense of foreboding as she gazed with narrowed eyes at the maidservant. "Is the Lady Aurora truly sleeping, Sadie? Mind you do not lie to me, for I do indeed mean to go upstairs."

Sadie's lips trembled. "N-no, ma'am."

Nell sighed. "Where is she, Sadie?"

"I dunno." She saw quickly that Nell disbelieved her, and raised her hand in a quick gesture of protest. " 'Tis the truth, Miss Nell. She never told me. I only know she went out looking like the very spit of mischief and wouldn't say a word about where she was bound."

"Good God!" Nell exclaimed. "An assignation!"

"No, ma'am," Sadie stated positively.

"How can you be so certain?"

"Because she was dressed in boy's clothes, Miss Nell."

With a gasp of pure shock, Nell leaned against the banister, clutching at it for support. "Boy's clothes. Where on earth—"

"She had them from home, miss. Often wears 'em out riding. Even Lord Crossways don't know. My lady cursed Lord Huntley when he insisted she always take a groom, for of course she didn't dare wear those clothes where anyone else might see her, lest her mama or papa find out."

Nell remembered Rory's own casual reference, soon after her arrival in Brighton, to her habit of donning boy's clothing when it suited her purposes, and decided the girl must not harbor similar fears with regard to a mere aunt. Her face paled. "Dear God, does that mean she will have gone somewhere all alone now?"

"No, ma'am, for she couldn't saddle her horse alone, and at home she carried the clothes in a satchel until she was well away from the house. I expect she's taken that Joe boy into her confidence. He fair dotes on her ladyship."

"Then he is as much of a nodcock as you are, Sadie," Nell said, not mincing matters as her temper flared again. "I promise you, you have not heard the last of this, for I shall have a deal to say to you later. But now the important thing is to find your mistress before she finds herself in the basket." She had been thinking rapidly and realized that there was very likely at least one person in the house who *would* know where Rory had gone. "Don't cry, Sadie!" she snapped as she realized tears were beginning to course down the maid's cheeks. "We've no time for such nonsense. Go immediately and desire Jeremy to step up to my mother's boudoir. Tell him to hurry."

"Yes, miss." And Sadie fled, leaving Nell prey to all manner of worrisome conjectures. She very much feared she knew exactly what Rory had taken it into her head to do. Had she not mentioned her interest in the free-traders time and time again? Would it not be exactly like the little wretch to follow her own wishes if she had found some means by which to do so?

Nell was very nearly wringing her hands when Jeremy entered the boudoir some moments later, looking anxious. "Sadie said I was to come up straightaway, Miss Nell, and she sounded all of a twitter. Be something amiss?"

"Indeed, something is amiss," Nell agreed, eyeing him speculatively. "The lady Aurora has gone out, and we do not know where she has gone. I thought she might have confided in you."

"Me, miss?" But he tended to avoid her gaze, and she could see that his thoughts were giving him little comfort.

"What is it?" she demanded. "Come now, Jeremy, if you know where she is, you must tell me."

"She never told me she was going out, Miss Nell, and that's God's own truth. I did fear she might have taken some fool notion into her head when you didn't go to the assembly tonight, but she swore to me she'd do nothing foolish. Howsomever——"

"Out with it!" Nell, her fears rising with each passing moment, wanted nothing more than to shake him. "Now, Jeremy!"

"Well, her ladyship's been right curious all along about the gentlemen, Miss Nell, 'n she's always askin' a fearful lot o' questions."

"Good God! I knew it! But what sort of questions? Where on earth can she have gone?" She had expected something of the sort from the moment Sadie had mentioned boy's clothes. But it was no use to congratulate herself on her insight. She must do something to prevent Rory from dashing headlong into catastrophe.

Her intent to get to the bottom of things was clear, and Jeremy grimaced, then let out a long sigh. "There be a boat coming in tonight, and m'lady pestered the life out of me to tell 'er where they'd be landing.''

"Merciful heavens!" Nell exclaimed. "Surely you were not idiotic enough to tell her!"

"Well, that's just it," the lad confessed reluctantly. "I never meant to, Miss Nell! 'Twas like she bewitched me. And when she said she only wanted to have a look from the clifftops, I gave her pepper, Miss Nell. Said it was fearful dangerous even to be thinking of such stuff, 'n that I couldn't speak even for my own cousins an they discovered a pretty young thing like herself out 'n about on the cliffs. She said I'd no business to be talking to her like that, me being a mere footman 'n all, but she promised she'd do nothing foolish. I-I believed her—thought she meant she'd stay at home. Not," he added more wretchedly, "that that will save my groats when Cousin Jeb comes to hear of it.''

"Where has she gone, Jeremy?" Nell struggled to keep her voice calm, though she wanted to stamp her feet and shout at him.

He looked at her in astonishment. "Lord, Miss Nell, I can't tell you that. Best I can do is go after her myself. Haven't I just said there's a boat landing tonight? It'd be worth as much as your life—aye, and mine—an I was t' tell you.''

"Jeremy," Nell said, her voice dangerously calm, "you have done enough damage already. I shan't allow you to do more, so if you do not tell me instantly where she has gone, I shall send for Lord Huntley and for Major Gideon Talcott of the Tenth Hussars to discuss the matter with you. If my wretched niece has taken you even half as far into her confidence as I believe she has, you will know that neither gentleman will deal lightly with you. I shall give you precisely five seconds to choose which course you will follow.'' She folded her arms beneath her breasts and waited, scarcely daring to breathe and terrified lest he prove stubborn enough to force her to send for Huntley. She had no doubt of his lordship's ability to get at the truth, but they could ill afford the extra time it would take.

But Jeremy had gone quite pale at the mere mention of the two names. He had met his lordship, of course, and Nell had no doubt that Rory had provided him with an excellent description of the large major as well. He cleared his throat twice.

"Well, Jeremy? I am waiting."

"Yes, ma'am." He eyed her unhappily, then capitulated. "They be landing at Black Briar Cove, Miss Nell, which be about three miles along the coast road, Rottingdean way."

"I know the place," Nell said, sighing in relief. "What time will that boat land?"

"Not till midnight or after, but there'll be lookouts posted long afore that."

"Does Rory know?"

"Aye."

"Will they harm her, Jeremy? She's wearing male attire, probably in the belief that it will somehow protect her, but will it fool them at all?" Nell made no attempt now to conceal her anxiety.

Jeremy shifted his feet. "Depends, miss, but I doubt it, and probably it be best if it don't, if they see she's a lass. Either way, if one of my cousins is on look-out and if she mentions my name, they might only send her off with a flea in her ear. But she might not mention me."

"Why ever not?"

He looked sheepish. "I told her they'd not like me telling her so much, that they'd be like t' murder me if they found out."

"I've a certain degree of sympathy for such feelings," Nell muttered, thinking quickly. "You must go as fast as you can to Mrs. Fitzherbert's house, Jeremy. I'll write a note for Lord Huntley, but you will have to show him the way. He's not so familiar with this part of the coast as we are."

Jeremy was staring at her in dismay. "I cannot! I'll go myself, Miss Nell, but 'tis no place for a gentle-bred lady like yourself, and I cannot take his lordship there."

"You shall!" Nell snapped. "What's more, we shall send word to Brighton Camp, just in case all does not go well." Jeremy looked mutinous, and Nell stamped her foot at last. "Be sensible, Jeremy! If we hurry and bring her back before that boat lands, no harm will be done to anyone. But if we dither, anything might happen."

"No harm done! I suppose the major and his patrol will just turn about and go home again if no one has landed yet," he added sarcastically.

"Perhaps not, but your people will be safe enough if the boat hasn't beached before the soldiers get there," Nell pointed out, "and if there is a spot of difficulty, well it's no more than they're accustomed to, after all. But you would not wish, any more than I do, to put the Lady Aurora in jeopardy, now would you?"

Jeremy muttered something that Nell could not hear, but she was wise enough not to demand that he repeat it. Instead, she scrawled a brief note to Huntley and another to be delivered to Brighton Camp.

"If either gentleman cannot be immediately found, he must be tracked down," Nell said firmly. "Get Mr. Lindale's Ned to take the message to the camp. You are to go for Huntley yourself." Just saying his name stirred emotions deep within her. He would be angry, but he would help her, and she could not imagine any way by which they might successfully keep word of the night's business from him. She took a deep breath, steadying nerves that showed an alarming tendency to jump about. When she spoke again, her voice at least was under control. "Mind, Jeremy, no dawdling. I shall go on ahead, just in case you cannot find him immediately. In any case, he will want his horse, so there will be some delay at best."

"You can't go after her, Miss Nell! That's daft!"

"No doubt," she retorted crisply, "but I certainly cannot remain here with my knitting while my niece may be in danger of her life. Now go, Jeremy. Oh, wait!" she called as he turned on his heel. "First take this letter paper to Lady Agnes. She must be wondering what has kept me such an age. Tell her anything but the truth. Now, hurry!"

The moment he had gone, Nell hurried to her bedchamber and threw on her riding habit. Grabbing hat, gloves, and whip, she hurried down the back stairs and by way of a narrow passage at the back of the garden to the stables. Jeremy and Ned had already departed on their errands, and she was thankful to see that Peter had her horse and his own saddled and ready to go.

"Are you armed, Peter?"

"Aye, mistress. Me pops be under me coat, all handy like."

"Good. You know Black Briar Cove?"

He allowed as how he did, and helped her into the saddle.

Moments later they were cantering up Edward Street to the Kemp Town Road. Nell knew it would have been faster to take the Marine Parade, but they'd have been far more likely to meet someone who knew her, and that would have been disastrous.

There was no moon, and once they were past Bedford Street, there were no more lamps to light their way. But there was a blaze of starlight overhead, for the night, though moonless, was clear.

After half a mile or so the bulk of the hospital loomed on their left, and another half mile brought them to the new Lewes Crescent and Kemp Town proper. They passed the brewhouse and the Bush Hotel without incident and came at last to the coast road.

After riding in silence for some time, Peter said over the sound of their horses' hoofbeats, "Almost there, Miss Nell. Best draw up and walk from here."

Nell agreed, wondering how he knew where they were and glad she had not come by herself. At night the whole coast road seemed unfamiliar, and the cliffs here overhung the beach in such a way that any activity below would be well nigh impossible to see from above. She wondered how Rory had expected to find the place, or if, indeed, she had even attempted to do so. If this was another wild goose chase, Huntley would murder them both. Now the thought of him sent a little shiver up her spine. He was bound to be furious with her no matter what came to pass, but hopefully the fact that she had sent for him would count a little in her favor. She hoped so. Though she didn't fear his anger, the thought of it made her uncomfortable, and she would so much rather please him. A sigh escaped her as she realized the unlikelihood of pleasing him by her actions this night.

"We'll leave the horses here," Peter said quietly, helping her dismount. "I been thinkin', ma'am. Best ye let me see what's what afore we both find ourselves in the briars."

But this Nell would not allow. She had hoped that Jeremy and Huntley would have caught up to them by now, but since they hadn't, she had no wish to be left behind to face Huntley on her own before finding Rory. Peter, knowing better than to waste his breath arguing with her, merely snorted and motioned for her to stay behind him.

There was little cover along the clifftop other than occasional large rocks and bits of scrub brush, and since the brush had more a habit of catching Nell's skirts than of offering concealment, she was soon wishing she had taken time to find some old clothes of Kit's to wear. Really, she thought, as she hastened to keep pace with Peter, gentleman's attire was far better suited than a lady's for sneaking up on smugglers.

Two rocks large enough to be called boulders loomed ahead at the very edge of the cliff, and Peter stepped between them, then seemed suddenly to disappear. Nell, hurrying after him, realized he had found the pathway down to the beach, but as she peered over the edge, her heart seemed to miss a beat. She could see only dark shadows. The sound of the sea was louder than ever, and she could make out white foam edging the dark swell of the water below, but she could see no path, and though she could hear him, she could not see Peter either. She called softly to him.

"Here, Miss Nell," came his voice a little to her right. " 'Tisn't bad. Just zigzags down the face. Mind where you step, but there be little difficulty."

Easy enough for him to say, she told herself, thinking Peter must have eyes like a cat. Then she had another thought. "Peter," she whispered, "I was warned there would be look-outs posted. Where do you suppose they will be?"

"One of 'em be just ahind of ye, miss," came a gruff voice from beyond the larger boulder. "Don't 'e move, now. There's a good lass."

Nell went quite still. There was no sound at all for a moment except for a tiny stirring of stones below her and to her right. Then the gruff voice came again.

"Like an ant hill it be tonight. Shoulda sent out proper invites, we should, what wi' all the gentry folk astoppin' by t' see 'ow we does business."

Nell let out a breath of relief. "She's here, then," she said. "You found a young lady and her groom on these cliffs tonight. We have come in search of them. Please, where are they?"

"A gentry mort, 'e say?" A large shadow emerged from behind the boulder. "Dressed like a cove, she were? In breeches?"

"That is my niece, a very foolish young woman," Nell said with as much dignity as she could muster. "Where have you taken her?"

"Pleased t' show ye, ma'am, if ye'll lead the way down 'at path there."

"Oh, but I can scarcely see to find my way," Nell protested.

"Where's the cove as was wi' ye, ma'am?"

She sighed in frustration. She had hoped he hadn't noticed Peter. "Below me somewhere," she said.

"Got pops on 'im, 'as 'e?" Nell was silent. "Hear me, cove," the voice went on, "we doesn't want no fuss, and we doesn't want no ladies being 'urt. So just you be a good lad 'n toss them barkers o' yourn out toward Davy Jones, or it'll be the worse fer yer fine lady 'ere, an' that, I tell ye tr—ah-h!"

Nell had not heard the slightest sound, but another, even larger shadow had loomed up from behind the man and somehow his words had been cut off in midsentence. After a brief, nearly silent struggle, he went limp. Her first notion was that Peter had somehow managed to creep around behind him while he talked, but she immediately realized her error.

"Bring that rope, lad," Huntley growled.

"Thank God," Nell squeaked, her heart singing as relief flooded over her.

"We'll see if you thank God or not once I've got that blasted niece of yours safe," Huntley muttered. "Now for the love of God, keep your voice down. Peter, you there?"

"Aye, m'lord."

"Good. Take your mistress back to her horse and keep her there. And if Major Talcott and his men arrive, show them where we've gone. According to young Jeremy here, there should be only one more to account for, so we ought to have things all right and tight before the cavalry arrives."

"Philip, wait!"

"Later," he said brusquely. "Go with Peter."

His voice seemed oddly tight, but it was clear from the implacable tone that it would be the height of folly to argue with him, so Nell went obediently to stand beside her horse, twisting her fingers nervously while she strained her ears to catch the slightest sound. Though it seemed an age, it was less than fifteen minutes before she heard a scrambling at the cliff edge and could make out shadows moving near the boulders. A moment more and a slim, boyish figure came running up to her.

"Aunt Nell, is it really you? Huntley said——"

"I'm here, young lady," Nell replied gruffly. "Where is your mare?"

"Across the road. Joe went for her. Oh, Aunt Nell, it was most exciting! We were captured by smugglers!"

"It was utterly foolhardy of you to do this thing," Nell said sternly. "You might have been injured, even killed."

"Oh, no, for Jeremy's cousin knew who I was, you see, as soon as I told them my name, and though the other man was quite a nasty sort and wanted to hit Joe and me both on the head, Jeb said he would see no harm came to us. Only they didn't want to let us go until after the boat came, because they were afraid we should squeak beef, which I think means to tell someone, so Jeb and I and poor Joe were sitting by a tiny fire inside a cave, drinking coffee Jeb made in a tin pot, when Jeremy and his lordship burst in upon us. It was just like a Gothic tale! Truly, it was. Oh, don't scold, Aunt Nell. I have had such an adventure!"

"Aurora," Huntley grunted behind them, "here is Joe with your mare. I'll put you in the saddle." Nell waited, her breath in her throat, for him to begin scolding, but to her astonishment he said nothing further. A moment later he moved toward her. "Why are you not mounted? The sooner we are away from here, the better it will be for all of us."

"Indeed, my lord." She felt his hands firmly, warmly at her waist, and then he lifted her to the saddle. A moment more and he was astride the big roan stallion beside her. "I must thank you for coming so quickly, sir."

"Thank me later. The rest of that charming crew could arrive at any moment, and I'd as lief not have to explain our presence here, if you don't mind."

They had not ridden far, however, before a pair of lighted torches came into view on the road ahead and the thunder of hooves beating on the roadbed announced the arrival of the military. Major Talcott had brought Lieutenant Lord Hubert Coltrain and four of his men. The major rode ahead of the others.

"Huntley! Have you found her?"

The two groups converged, and it was clear from his reaction to seeing Rory that the major had feared for her safety. As though the others were little more than so much ambient air, he began immediately to reprimand her, and she attempted just as quickly to justify her behavior on the grounds of having enjoyed a great adventure.

"There is no excuse for what you have done tonight," he said, interrupting her without hesitation, "and furthermore, you look disgraceful."

"But I could not wear my riding habit, Gideon! It would have been impossible to creep around on the cliffs in such long skirts. And we should have been perfectly safe, had Joe not slipped while we were trying to creep down the cliffside to find a place where we might be able to see something exciting. But I do not repine, I assure you, for if he had not slipped, we might never have met a real smuggler—two of them, in fact——"

"It was a crack-brained thing to do," the major cut in uncompromisingly, and Nell waited in fascination to hear what he might say next. But Talcott had recollected himself at last, and after sternly adjuring the still protesting Rory to hold her tongue, he turned to Huntley. "The free-traders, did you find them?"

Huntley shot a rather speculative glance at the obediently silent young girl before replying. "Two of them. One is tied up near the pair of boulders at the top of the path, and the other can be found in a cave halfway down the cliff-face. You may keep them both with my compliments, but you'd probably be well-advised to let them escape in hopes that they go ahead with whatever signal they use to draw the boat in. I'm perfectly certain the others won't come in without it."

"Excellent advice, sir," Talcott agreed. "I shall send Coltrain and the others to keep an eye on things without showing themselves. But if you've no objection, I'd like to ride at least partway back to town with you." He paused, then went on with a rueful smile. "Her ladyship may be able to give me some valuable information about their plans for tonight. She deserves to have a strip torn off her for this business," he added glibly, quite as though he had said not a word to her himself, "and I've no doubt you'd like to attend to that as soon as may be, but this is of truly great importance."

"As you please," Huntley replied, his voice suddenly—and to Nell's relief—touched with amusement. "You'll prefer to ride on ahead of us, I daresay."

The major agreed, and a moment later, the grooms and Jeremy falling behind, Nell found herself, to all intents and purposes, alone with his lordship. Despite that brief flash of amusement, she braced herself. But he said nothing, and the silence grew until she was nearly squirming in her saddle.

"Are you very angry, Philip?" she asked at last. She wished she could see his face, but all she could make out was the shape of him.

He sighed. "I'm not angry. At least, not at the moment, though it may come in time." The sound of his voice so near to her was like a warm caress. Oddly comforted by it, she straightened a little in her saddle. He spoke again. "I suppose I ought to be grateful that you sent for me and didn't try to handle the thing entirely by yourself."

"Jeremy offered to fetch her back," she admitted. "As it happened, he might well have been able to manage it."

"Perhaps, although his charming cousin was none too cheerful about releasing Aurora. Unfortunately, I think she hasn't the least notion of the danger she was in."

"She said they promised not to harm her."

"They are rogues, Nell. Would you have believed that felon at the clifftop could be trusted to keep his word?" Unable to answer in the affirmative, she held her tongue. "Just so. And Jeremy's cousin is just such another. I've a good notion that my pistol carried more weight with him than Jeremy's pleas would have done. It will be saying a good deal if that lad gets out of this with a whole skin."

"Jeremy?"

"Yes, Jeremy. The others won't take kindly to his having informed on them, you know. He seems to think he can trust his cousin, but that other lout, though he never actually saw the lad, might still be bright enough to figure out how Aurora came by her information."

Nell swallowed carefully. "He certainly ought never to have discussed this business with her. I-I expect you will want to have a few words in private with her when we return, will you not?"

"I most certainly will not," he muttered, and Nell could have sworn she heard that note of amusement in his voice again.

"Sir?"

"My dear girl, I doubt if anything I say now or a hundred years from now would ever convince that child that she has been in any danger. She will only accuse me of being fusty again. I sometimes think she has no common sense whatsoever. You, on the other hand——"

"I had to come, sir," Nell cut in quickly. "I could not simply sit at home wondering if Jeremy had found you, wondering if you had found Rory. She is my responsibility, and I could not——"

"You could not trust anyone else to manage the thing," he finished on a slightly bitter note. "Is that not it, Nell?"

She opened her mouth to deny it, but honesty intervened. "Perhaps there is some truth in what you say, sir. I have not had anyone else upon whom I might depend for some years now, you know."

"You can trust me, Nell."

The words were spoken low, but she heard them clearly enough, and they sent a small thrill of pleasure through her. She rather thought that she could depend upon him if she ever needed to do so again. And perhaps, now that it seemed it might be possible, after all, to end the absurd betrothal, her own affairs and Huntley's might be in a way to being—— But the pleasant thought ceased abruptly, for she remembered what had started everything moving tonight. She glanced at Huntley. He must be told.

"My lord," she began cautiously, "I should tell you that my mother received an urgent letter from Parkhurst tonight. My aunt is very ill and not expected to recover. When I left, Mama was writing the news to my sister."

"Well, if Lady Agatha dies, I should be sorry, of course, but even if she should do so immediately, it would merely mean a year's delay, and you will not deny that it might be a good idea for Aurora to wait a year or so before being wed."

"My sister will not agree with you, sir," Nell said, repressing sudden exasperation. His damned honor! Why could he not at least suggest the possibility of arranging an end to the betrothal before everything ended in a tangle. Surely, he could see as well as she could that Talcott was head over heels in love with Rory. The man was not blind. And, after that afternoon on the Downs, Huntley surely had every reason to suspect Nell's feelings, even as she was becoming more certain of his. It was merely his wretched sense of honor constantly getting in the way. She fought down her irritation, determined to make him understand their plight, for whatever good it might do. "You have heard my mother on the subject of our family's bad luck," she said evenly, "and I can assure you Clarissa feels just as strongly as Mama does. She will be convinced that if Rory is not married at once, she will follow in my footsteps."

"Your footsteps?"

"We had six deaths in the family in as many years, sir, or have you forgotten?" Nell gritted her teeth. Was the man being purposely dense? "Clairssa will drag Rory to the altar herself in order to avoid such a fate for her."

"I doubt that such a thing could happen twice in the same family, Nell," he responded with a slight smile.

"Your belief carries no weight in this case, my lord," she retorted with some asperity. "You just wait until Clarissa and Crossways descend upon us, and see if I have not judged the matter correctly."

His brows knitted, but he said nothing, and since he seemed to be so clearly disinclined to agree with her, Nell let the subject drop. As usual, she would have to take matters into her own hands. They maintained their easy pace in silence, and a few moments later, as she watched the couple riding ahead, the faintest glimmer of an idea began to stir.

XVI

By the time she reached her bed that evening, Nell was exhausted and convinced that sleep would come the moment her head touched the pillow, but nothing could have been farther from the truth. Instead, she found herself thinking back over the events of the evening, the sudden fear when she realized where Rory had gone, and the odd sense of excitement she had felt at Huntley's timely arrival. She remembered, too, Major Talcott's anxious words when they met and the relief in his voice when he discovered that Rory was safe. Any doubts she may have entertained as to his feelings for her niece had vanished in those brief moments.

Talcott had taken his leave of them at Bedford Street, but Huntley had seen them to the stables, it having been decided that the safest way for them to return to the house was the same way by which they had left it. There had been a fearful moment or two before the two young women were safely inside Rory's bedchamber, but Sadie had been waiting to let them in the garden door, and although she said that Lady Agnes and Sir Henry were playing piquet in the drawing room, they managed to get up the back stairs without incident. Despite the fact that Rory made no move to dismiss her maidservant, it was clear that she expected a severe scold for her actions, but beyond telling her she had been a goose and warning her never to do such a thing again, Nell had said little. Instead, she observed that, as for herself, she had felt perfectly safe once the cavalry arrived on the scene.

"Oh, yes," Rory agreed. "Was it not kind of them to come to rescue me? Only I do hope Jeb and the other man escaped. I could not reconcile it with my conscience if Jeremy's cousin was to end up in prison on my account."

"Oh, I daresay even if Major Talcott found them where Huntley left them, he could do very little. After all, they had done nothing precisely illegal beyond holding you against your will, and I doubt that either his lordship or the major would wish to make anyone else a gift of that information, you know."

"Then they will be safe," said Rory, comforted once more, "for Jeremy said that no power on earth would cause them to signal the boat after all that had transpired. I explained that to Gideon, so he will not be in very great expectation of capturing the others." She sighed a little. "I must say, if they must be caught, I'd prefer for Gideon to do the catching."

Nell let the subject rest, but her niece's use of the major's given name had not escaped her notice. The idea that had been a mere embryo on the Kemp Town Road began to mature in her fertile imagination, and once she had retired to the privacy of her own bed, there was nothing to still the thoughts dancing so freely through her head.

All the ramifications of her Aunt Agatha's pending demise were making themselves clearer, one by one. In the excitement of the hours following the courier's arrival, she had considered only the effect his news would have upon her niece's future and Huntley's. She had not given much thought to her own. But a sudden vision of what it would be like to spend yet another year as a spinster in mourning beneath her mother's roof struck her now most forcibly. Lying there in her comfortable bed, Nell realized her teeth were grinding together audibly as the unwelcome vision passed before her mind's eye. It was bad enough that once Crossways and Clarissa heard the news of Aunt Agatha's rapidly failing health, they would wish their beloved daughter safely married to the Earl of Huntley as quickly as it might be arranged, and that they would not even wish to discuss the possible suitability of a marriage to Major Talcott, no matter how handsome or dashing he might be. But worse than that—far worse—was the thought of her own future as a spinster.

In another year she would be six-and-twenty, which was as near to thirty as made no difference, particularly in a world where an unwed young lady of nineteen was thought to have at least one foot upon the shelf already. And lonely spinsterhood seemed suddenly a dreadful fate, indeed. No longer did she have the slightest wish to remain at home, a comfort to her mama. Least of all if Philip was unhappily married to her undeserving niece.

The last thought slid under her guard, but though she had strenuously avoided dwelling on the matter, she had long since realized that she was less than indifferent to the Earl of Huntley. And now, with matters rapidly reaching a critical point, it was necessary to give a good deal of thought to their relationship. It was clear, too, that she could no longer afford the luxury of allowing things to move at a snail's pace.

For a time, she had insisted to herself that it was primarily a matter of helping two people who could not or would not help themselves, that she could postpone thinking about her own part of the business until the betrothal was at an end. First she had wanted to show Rory that wealth and position were not everything, and to help Huntley free himself of the obligation to which he was bound by his strong sense of honor. And if her thoughts had a disarming tendency to return to the episode in the elm grove, well, that was something she could not help. But now the time had come to consider the matter carefully and in detail, to admit, if only to herself, that she had fallen in love with the man who was expected by everyone else to marry her niece.

She knew he cared for her. From time to time she had wondered unhappily if perhaps he looked upon those memorable moments in the elm grove as little more than an agreeable diversion. She had even told herself once or twice that, had she had other such experiences with other gentlemen, that one would not stand so vividly in her memory. But then she would intercept a look of more than ordinary warmth from him, and she would know her own feelings were not misleading her. At other times she would see pain in his eyes and know it to be reflected in her own. Although, thanks to his wretched sense of honor, he had said nothing to give her certain knowledge that he would offer for her if he were free of his betrothal, all things considered, it seemed to her that he would most likely do so.

The greatest obstacle, as she saw it now, was her sister's very probable determination to see her daughter wed without delay. And since Clarissa would fear another series of family deaths, Nell doubted that any argument she or Rory could produce would convince her to allow the betrothal to be broken. Even though Rory herself might balk, Nell was persuaded that Clarissa could convince her of its advisability. After all, even if Lady Agatha died before the wedding, it would still be possible for Rory to marry Huntley quietly after a brief period of deep mourning. But if she did not marry him, a death in the family would mean her withdrawal from the social scene. She would have no acceptable way to meet anyone else. And try as she might, Nell could not believe Clarissa would entertain the notion of a marriage to Major Talcott for as long as it would take to suggest it.

Briefly she considered the wisdom of consulting further with his lordship, but she quickly dismissed the notion. Drastic action would be necessary if things were to be brought to a successful conclusion, and he would no doubt express firm disapproval of the plan Nell was now considering. Perhaps in time she might be able to talk him around, but lately he had shown that he was made of sterner stuff than she had first thought. Moreover, if there were sufficient time in which to maneuver, drastic action would not be necessary.

There were several snags in her plan, not the least of which was a possible lack of cooperation from at least one of the parties concerned. There was also the problem of keeping Huntley from discovering what she meant to do, but Sir Henry Sinclair's announcement the following afternoon that his lordship had left for London on urgent business eased Nell's mind with regard to that difficulty at least. In fact, Sir Henry's news came as such a relief that it never occurred to her to wonder what the urgent business might be or why his lordship had made Sir Henry privy to his intention even though he had not seen fit to stop in at Upper Rock Gardens before leaving town.

Since Sir Henry had called only for the purpose of escorting Lady Agnes to an afternoon card party, by the time it did occur to Nell to wonder how the old gentleman had come by his information, he had departed, and it was beyond her power to ask him. So she put the question out of her mind and invited her niece to come to her sitting room for a comfortable coze.

Rory agreed readily enough, although her manner was somewhat subdued, and once they had seated themselves in chairs near the fireplace, where the remains of the morning's fire still glowed, Nell smiled and said cheerfully, "Surely you are not still afraid I mean to scold you, my dear?"

Rory shook her head. "No, ma'am, though I daresay I deserve it, and I was utterly astonished when Huntley didn't bellow at me. Even when he rescued us from that tiny cave, he said nothing about my manner of dress or of the fact that I had done such a foolish thing. He only warned me to mind my step on the path."

"Foolish thing, Rory? Last night you insisted——"

"Oh, I know what I said, and it was true enough that it felt like a great adventure at the time. Only when Gideon pointed out how I had frightened him, well then I could see of course that I had not behaved very wisely."

"Goodness!" Nell exclaimed. "Don't tell me the major actually read you a scold!"

Rory laughed at her incredulous tone. "Of course not. He never does, you know. At least not like Huntley does. Gideon doesn't ever bellow. He does have a way of speaking, however, which makes me feel ashamed of myself in one way and . . . and, well, good in another." She paused, looking thoughtful. "I don't suppose I can make you understand what I mean, Aunt Nell, for I'm not at all sure I understand it myself, but when Huntley bellows at me, it makes me angry, and I want only to defy him further. On the other hand, when Gideon only frowns, I want to smooth the frown away, and when he is displeased like he was when I drank the gin and a little last night—only then he was glad, too, of course, because I could give him information about the gentlemen— Well, anyway, then he makes me feel sad that I've displeased him, but glad at the same time that he cares enough to be displeased. Oh dear, it all sounds perfectly idiotish put into words. Do you understand at all what I mean?"

"Rory," Nell said firmly, "you must on no account marry Huntley."

"No, I can see that now. In fact, I have been thinking it would be a good deal better if I were to marry a man more like Gideon."

"Not *like* him, you goose. You must marry the major and no other."

Rory sighed. "I should like that above all things, ma'am, only Mama would never permit it. Gideon is *not* the Earl of Huntley. She sets great store by——"

"Clarissa sets greater store by wealth than by title," Nell cut in, speaking practically. "Have you got any notion how the major is fixed? He can scarcely be an officer in a cavalry regiment, particularly *that* regiment, if he was born without a shirt."

"No, of course he was not," Rory agreed with a chuckle. "I don't know his exact circumstances, of course, but I do know that he owns what he calls a snug property in Somerset, and a house in London as well, so I am persuaded he's no pauper. Still, he hasn't got as much as Huntley, and he *is* a younger son, so——"

"So was Huntley a younger son," Nell pointed out, "so we must hope your mother considers that fact in its proper light."

"Aunt Nell!"

Nell had the grace to look contrite. "I know—an abominable thing to say, and I'm sure I wish no ill fate upon the major's brother. But the fact of the matter is that your mama, once she hears about Aunt Agatha, will lose no time in pushing forward your marriage to Huntley. I doubt we shall even be able to persuade her to listen to a catalogue of the major's qualities and virtues. And even if you can prevail upon her to let you call off your betrothal——"

"She would still refuse to entertain the notion of my marriage to Gideon, and I should be packed off back to Kent the moment Aunt cocks up her toes. Whereupon," Rory continued bitterly, "Gideon's regiment will doubtless be sent to the Continent for years and years, and——" She looked up in dismay. "Oh, Aunt Nell, we must *do* something!"

"Exactly what I thought, myself," Nell agreed. "And much as I deplore the necessity, I fear there is nothing for it but for you and the major to elope."

"Elope!" Astonishment vied with excitement in Rory's expression, and excitement won the day. "The *very* thing! Oh, Aunt Nell, think how romantic it would be! To ride off to Scotland with dearest Gideon at my side— Oh, it would be beyond anything wonderful!"

Nell's conscience suffered a brief pang at these blithe words, but she calmed it by repeating firmly to herself that there was no other way. Time was the important factor. When she suggested somewhat diffidently that the major might not cooperate, Rory scoffed, insisting that while it might not be a matter of utter simplicity, she had no doubt that she could, as she inelegantly phrased it, bring him up to scratch.

"For I daresay he won't quite like the notion at first," she admitted candidly, "however, once he is brought to see how desperate is the case, he will do whatever I ask of him."

Nell still had her doubts, especially when Rory suggested that it would perhaps be better to wait until she could see the major under natural circumstances rather than to risk setting up his back at the outset by sending for him. Since they expected to encounter him at Lady Blanchard's ball on Thursday evening, Nell forced herself to agree to the slight delay. Huntley would surely be in London for some days yet, and Lady Agnes's letter, sent off to Chatham by the morning post, could not bring Crossways and Clarissa down upon them for at least five days or more.

As it happened, they chanced to meet the major the very next day at Donaldson's Library, but Rory had no opportunity for more than a brief private word with him before he was off again. Nonetheless, she told Nell she had no doubt now as to the outcome of her campaign.

"I told him I was utterly cast down," she said when they had returned to Upper Rock Gardens, "that I had had the most distressing news and didn't know where to turn. And do you know, he offered to send immediately to his commanding officer excusing himself from duty for the rest of the day just to help me sort out my troubles? Is that not promising, ma'am?"

"Indeed it is," Nell agreed, "but why did you not encourage him to do so, Rory? We might have been well on our way to a solution to our difficulties."

"Well, we wouldn't," returned that young lady in her frank way, "for he would be—in the cold light of day, you know—more than likely to say I must discuss the thing with Mama, and offer to speak himself to Papa. But that would not serve, Aunt Nell. You know it would not."

"But will he not make the same suggestion tomorrow night?"

"No, for there will be a moon then, you see, and music in the background, and I shall be so very melancholy, and under circumstances such as those he would never deny me anything. You will see, Aunt Nell."

Nell could not share her confidence, but after two days of listening to Lady Agnes's plaintive comments on the thoughtlessness shown by her twin sister in choosing such an inauspicious moment to cash in her accounts, and to Kit's bemoaning of the fact that he, too, would be forced into mourning just when he was beginning to find his feet among the *beau monde*, she found herself hoping against hope that Rory's efforts would be successful.

Even Sir Henry, placidly reassuring, did little to lift her spirits. He had better luck with Kit, promising him that since he cared little for formal parties anyway, his activities would be curtailed very little in the event that he was, in fact, plunged into mourning again. Sir Henry even managed to cheer up Lady Agnes, though Nell hadn't the slightest notion how he had achieved such a feat.

Thinking of her mother only gave Nell more qualms; for, if by some happy circumstance, Rory did manage to convince the major to elope with her, and if Huntley was not so furious with Nell herself for conniving at such an outrageous act that he refused to make her an offer—assuming, she reflected morbidly, that he would make her one under any circumstances—and if she accepted him, she would be leaving Lady Agnes to cope alone with the management of both the large household and Kit, as well. The thought disturbed her only briefly, however, before she thrust it aside, determined to deal with it only if and when the need arose.

Upon arriving at Lady Blanchard's house on the Steyne Thursday evening, Nell found herself scanning the company quite as anxiously as her niece was doing, and it was with the profoundest relief that she saw the major coming to greet them. She knew that there was nothing whatever she could do herself to aid matters at this point. All her dependence must be upon Rory. Consequently, she accepted the offer to dance whenever it was made and was very gay, pretending she had not a care in the world beyond wondering who would be her next partner.

The look on Major Talcott's face when he took polite leave of her some time later, saying he must return to his regiment, was not such as to encourage her to believe her niece had met with any great success. But Rory, when questioned in the carriage on the way back to Upper Rock Gardens, expressed airy confidence, informing her aunt that she had done the trick.

"But he looked as grim as could be when he left," Nell protested.

"Oh, he was a little vexed, just as I thought he would be," Rory returned carelessly. "But when I explained to him that there is simply no other recourse, he agreed to meet us on the Downs at noon tomorrow."

"Us! Why does he not come to fetch you at the house?"

"Well, because . . . because I never thought of it," she answered, speaking rather quickly. "Besides, if I am with you, no one will suspect a thing, will they? And later you can just say you don't know where I've gone, and we shall be long gone before anyone suspects the truth. I could wear my boy's clothes, I expect, and ride to meet him alone, like Phoebe Hessell went to her Samuel, but you would not like that, and I think he would not like it, either. Moreover," she added with the air of candor that had become so familiar, "I think he is more likely to believe the situation is truly desperate once he sees that you have no objection to our elopement."

"Oh, Rory, I don't know about this," Nell said, as all the horrors of what she was encouraging her niece to do began to come home to her. "An elopement is a very serious step to take, you know. Your reputation——"

"Pooh, I shan't care a rap for that if I can have Gideon for a husband," Rory retorted. "And I shan't have to face Mama and Papa or Huntley until it is done, so that won't matter either."

But Nell knew that she would have to face them, and the thought gave her a sleepless night. Not that she was particularly worried about Clarissa or Crossways, but Huntley would be livid, and that fact did worry her. No matter how often she told herself that she had dealt successfully with his temper before, she could not convince herself that she would enjoy dealing with it upon this particular occasion. If she could be sure she was doing the right thing, it would be easier. But she could not. She knew perfectly well that Rory had little comprehension of the severe consequences that would attend a Gretna Green marriage. But Nell knew, and she was not at all certain she could reconcile herself with her conscience. Only the knowledge that all speed was necessary—and a lurking suspicion that Huntley would forgive her once he perfectly understood her reasons—kept her from throwing back her covers and hastening to inform her niece that she could not allow her to take such a deseprate step.

The morning and Rory's glowing, confident face helped a great deal. If the child herself was so certain of the rightness of her course, who was Nell to deny her the opportunity to seek her happiness? By eleven o'clock they were ready to depart. Nell ordered their horses brought around in the ordinary way, and if Joe wondered about the satchel his mistress ordered him to tie securely to her saddle, he said not a word. At last, their grooms trailing behind, the two ladies set out to meet the major.

Not until she actually perceived him riding up the hill from the wood did Nell truly believe he would be there. Nevertheless, when she realized that the look on his face was not one of pleased anticipation but rather the opposite, she could not say that she was completely astonished. The two grooms fell prudently behind, and beside her, Rory gave a little sigh.

"Oh, dear."

"Rory, I thought you said—"

"Well, perhaps I overstated his willingness a little," Rory admitted in a small voice.

"By the look of him, I should say you overstated it by a great deal."

Major Talcott, his brow furrowed in thunderous anger, was upon them in a trice. He spoke first to Nell, his voice under rigid control. "I am both glad and a little disappointed to see you here, Miss Lindale, for I didn't believe her ladyship when she said you were party to this ridiculous start. I had no doubt, however, that she would come herself, and feared she would not have the good sense to provide herself with an escort, which is the only reason, believe me, that you find me here."

He said nothing whatever of Nell's good sense, but it was forcibly brought home to her that Rory had grossly misled her, that young lady having believed as usual that her own wishes would prevail over any opposition. In truth, the major had flatly refused from the outset to be party to an elopement that would most surely put an end to his promising military career. When he repeated that refusal in no uncertain terms and said he would escort them personally back to Brighton, Rory spoke up at last.

"Gideon! You could not be so cruel. Why, Aunt Nell's very presence must *prove* to you that our case is desperate!"

The major's response to this near wail was to favor her ladyship with a hard look before he dismounted, dropped his reins casually to the ground, and strode over to remove her without ceremony from her saddle. Setting her none too gently upon her feet and retaining a firm grip on her elbow, he glanced balefully up at Nell.

"I trust you will excuse us for a moment or two, Miss Lindale. I have something of a private nature to say to her ladyship." She nodded without daring to speak, and watched as he practically dragged the reluctant Rory toward the nearby wood. Nell hoped he would not be too harsh, but the words that drifted back to her just before they entered the wood were scarcely encouraging. "You will be well served, young lady," the major said, more sternly than he had spoken before, "if you find yourself across my knee!"

Rory's dismayed protests faded into the distance, and though Nell strained her ears, she could hear nothing to indicate that the major had made good his threat. Nevertheless, when they returned at last, his fury had abated somewhat, and Rory walked with her head down, carrying a large white handkerchief clutched in her two slim hands. As Talcott swung her into her saddle again, Nell could see that she had been crying. There seemed to be nothing to say that might ease the situation, however, so she held her tongue and merely fell in beside them when Talcott had mounted his own horse. The two grooms, no doubt suffering agonies of curiosity, remained a discreet distance behind them.

It was clear that Rory had met her match at last, but the discovery did little to ease the pricking of Nell's conscience. The major's disapproval of their actions brought home to her more clearly than ever how rashly they had behaved. But even that mattered little, now that their plan had failed. For if it had succeeded, she realized that she would not have cared one whit whether it was proper or not. At the moment, all that mattered to her was that the future looked bleak indeed. Even the major would probably insist that Rory marry the earl. And even if he did not, surely Philip would not wish to marry a woman who had made so dreadful a mull of everything. He would no doubt retire to Huntley Green, thankful to have escaped a fate worse than . . . well, worse than anything else

Nell could name at the moment. In any event, he would be furious with her, for it never occurred to her that he would not discover what they had attempted to do.

The whole story would come out the moment he returned from London. And the thought of his anger, no doubt greater even than the major's had been, was a good deal more disturbing than she might have expected. Whenever the thought of his quick temper had chanced to cross her mind while the elopement was still in the planning stages, Nell had simply told herself that she would deal with it when the time came. But now, riding beside her niece and her niece's angry would-be suitor, it seemed as if all she could think about was the fact that Philip would be angry with her, and that she did not wish him to be.

The ride back to Brighton was a dismal one at best, but they arrived at the tall house in Upper Rock Gardens at last to discover a large traveling coach drawn up at the flagway. Talcott, giving it a speculative look, swung down and handed his reins to a link boy, announcing flatly that he would come inside with them. Rory had not looked up or spoken during the entire ride, but at these words she glanced first at him and then at the coach, and her face went perfectly white.

"Papa and Mama are here!" She looked at Nell in dismay. "Whatever shall we do now?"

At that moment, the front door opened, and Pavingham put his head out, then seemed to jump back inside again, and a moment later, Kit hurried out followed by Lord Crossways.

"What the devil!" Kit exclaimed, hurrying up to them.

Major Talcott turned to help Rory down. "See to your sister if you please, Lindale. Then, perhaps we might go inside before we begin to discuss this matter."

"Yes, by Jove, of course," Kit stammered, looking him up and down. But he hurried to assist Nell, whispering as he did, "There's the devil to pay and no pitch hot. They're all here, and the brat left a note, so they've been stewing the past half hour over whether Crossways ought to set out after them or let them go. Whatever were you about to have let her go like this, Nell? Huntley is——"

"Huntley! He's here?" Nell was certain her own face must have gone as white as Rory's, and as Kit set her on her feet, her knees seemed to go weak. He steadied her, speaking lightly.

"He's here, all right and tight, and I can tell you I've never seen the man so put out. I daresay he's offended that the chit would prefer the cavalry over an earldom, but whatever it is, someone's in for the devil's own trimming when he gets his chance. And that's a fact."

XVII

Kit's words seemed to echo in Nell's brain as she went with him to meet Crossways on the stoop.

"A fine business this is," declared his lordship, puffing out his cheeks in an expression of his vast displeasure. But his basilisk stare rested upon his daughter as he spoke, and Nell scarcely paid him any heed. Instead, numbly, she allowed Kit to take her upstairs to the drawing room.

As they reached the landing, Jeremy opened the double doors, and the sight that greeted Nell's eye was such that a lesser woman might well have picked up her skirts and run. Upon seeing her come into the room, Lady Agnes looked up reproachfully from her favorite chair, vinaigrette in hand, a glass of hartshorn and water on the table beside her. She gave a watery gasp and dabbed at her tear-stained cheeks with the ubiquitous lacy handkerchief, causing Sir Henry Sinclair, at her side, after one reproving look at Nell, to lean over her ladyship's chair and speak soothingly to her.

Clarissa, the train of her traveling dress caught up over one arm, gave the appearance of one who had been pacing anxiously back and forth before the fire crackling in the grate. But at Nell's entrance, she snapped her head up, and the initial look of anxiety in her eyes changed at once to the light of battle.

"Eleanor Lindale, how dared you do such a thing as this! To encourage my darling girl to such atrocious behavior! That you could so flagrantly betray our trust in you! Surely, you must have known she would be utterly ruined by a Gretna Green marriage!"

Before she could reply, Nell was pushed aside as, with a gasp of dismay, Rory hurried past her to cast herself upon

Clarissa's broad bosom. "Mama," she cried, hugging her, "pray don't blame poor Aunt Nell. Indeed, I have been *such* a trial to her." Realizing that Crossways had followed her into the room, she turned brimming eyes upward to include him in her plea. "I promise you, it is true, Papa. For truly and truly it was all my fault, and I could not begin to thank her for all her kindness to me. I simply cannot permit you or Mama to scold her."

"Very affecting," observed Huntley grimly from his vantage point a little to one side of the doorway, where he had been standing. Nell's attention having been drawn immediately to the group by the fire, she had not seen him. But now the others were forgotten as she whirled to face him, seeing at once that he was every bit as angry as Kit had warned her he was. Even as the thought registered, his eyes seemed to narrow more. "You have a good deal to answer for, my girl, and I doubt that your champion, however well-spoken she may be, will avail you much protection from your just deserts."

"Oh dear," Nell said faintly. "I was afraid you might be a little annoyed."

"A little—!" His astonishment at the understatement seemed to rob him momentarily of the powers of speech, but he recovered rapidly, speaking in a tone very like a controlled growl. "To say that I am a *little* annoyed is to put the matter very——"

"Eleanor Lindale, you are not attending to me," Clarissa cut in angrily, "though, I declare, I cannot find the words with which I might adequately describe my overwrought feelings. You were responsible for her well-being and must be held entirely accountable for this dreadful business. For despite what dearest Aurora may say to the contrary, you seem actually to have encouraged this appalling elopement!"

"Clarissa, please," Nell pleaded, "there has been no elopement, as you can see for yourself, and if I have behaved badly, I beg your pardon, but I only did what I thought was necessary in order to save poor Rory from entering into a marriage that was clearly doomed from the outset. I knew perfectly well that there was no time to lose, because you and Crossways were sure to come post haste the moment you discovered the news about Aunt Agatha, and just as sure to do your possible to push her into marriage straightaway."

"Well, of course, she must be married at once," Clarissa

retorted. "Why, there are still dozens of persons in our family who might succumb at any moment, and my poor darling Rory will find herself in the same unhappy situation as you found yourself eight years ago. So that is precisely why we have come. The moment Huntley told us of Aunt's illness, we knew what must be done."

"*Huntley* told you!" She turned accusing eyes toward his lordship.

He nodded, his expression still grim. "I rode to Chatham on my way to London, then caught up with them today on the Brighton Road. Thus, we arrived together to be greeted by the news of the elopement. It seems your maid had occasion to enter Aurora's room and discovered the note propped up on the dressing table. She took it directly to your mother, so I need hardly tell you what sort of scene greeted us upon our arrival."

She could well imagine it and glanced ruefully at Lady Agnes, but upon Clarissa's taking advantage of the brief pause to repeat in shrill tones that she had been most distressed to discover that her darling girl should have been aided and abetted upon such a disastrous course by one in whom a loving parent ought to have been able to place her trust, Nell picked up the cudgels again.

"To be sure, it might have proved disastrous," she agreed hotly, "but Rory would have been a good deal happier in the end than she is likely to be now. How her *loving* parents could have been so lacking in good sense as to contract a marriage for her with someone like Huntley, I shall never understand. And as for all the nonsensical notions you have drummed into her head over the years, Clarissa, well I am thankful, at least, that I have been able——"

"Thank you, Miss Lindale," Huntley interrupted harshly. "Your opinions must always be edifying, but you have said more than enough now and would be well advised to hold your tongue." Nell rounded on him, glaring defiantly, but when he met her gaze and held it, she realized she was no match for him in his present mood and subsided, letting her gaze slip meekly to the carpet. Satisfied, Huntley turned his attention next to the major, who had halted in some bemusement upon the threshold. "Talcott, I believe Lord Crossways has certain matters he wishes to discuss with you."

"That's good," the major replied, taking Huntley's words

as his cue to step purposefully toward the group near the fireplace, "because I certainly wish to discuss certain matters with his lordship." Nell, looking up just then, was astonished to see her sister and brother-in-law greet him with warm smiles. She shot Huntley a look of inquiry, but he had shifted his attention to Jeremy, who had been hovering behind the major, peering curiously over his shoulder, until Talcott had stepped so abruptly away.

"You may bring a teatray to this room in twenty minutes' time," his lordship said brusquely. "If we have any need of your services before then, rest assured that someone will ring." Flushing to his ears, Jeremy fled, and Kit, still standing near Nell, chuckled at his discomfiture, then confided to Huntley that he would just nip off while the nipping was good.

"If you think no one will miss me, that is."

"They won't." Huntley turned to Nell. "And as for you, my girl, I doubt they'll miss you either for a moment or two, so just you come along with me!"

Her protests falling on deaf ears, Nell found herself taken firmly by the arm and all but pushed out the door and across the landing to the morning room. Propelling her inside, Huntley then shut the door behind them with a snap. "Now, perhaps you will be good enough to explain this madness to me," he declared. His tone was quiet, but his eyes flashed with anger, and Nell's knees felt suddenly weak again.

There had been a time during all her earlier mental activity when she had actually managed to convince herself that it would be rather a simple matter to explain things to him once the elopement had been accomplished. But looking at him now, she was astonished that she could ever have thought such a ridiculous thing, and for the first time she realized she was truly thankful her plan had failed. To have had to face him with Talcott and Rory halfway to the Border would have been well nigh impossible. But then, she had never before realized he was capable of this sort of calm fury. She had expected him—to use Rory's apt phrasing—to bellow. And she had never minded his bellowing. Loud words were like thunderstorms. One merely waited for them to blow themselves out. But this quiet anger was another matter entirely. She had suspected a time or two recently that he might not be always as persuadable as she had once thought him to be, but now she knew she could push him only so far as he allowed himself to be pushed. He would tolerate no more. Oddly, instead of frightening or upsetting her, the knowledge seemed to give her an added sense of security. It meant he would not merely capitulate in order to avoid a scene or two. More than that, it meant she could behave naturally with him, could say whatever she wished to say, and he would protect her against her worst self.

"Well? I am waiting."

Nell licked suddenly dry lips, willing her heart to stop trying to jump out of her mouth. Protection and security notwithstanding, the next few moments were going to be uncomfortable ones. "I-I thought——"

"You damned well didn't think!" he snapped. "You simply assumed that no one but Eleanor Lindale ever had two thoughts worth rubbing together, and so you acted impulsively and senselessly, lending yourself to a damned silly escapade that would—if it it had been allowed to succeed—have ruined your niece and ended a very promising military career to boot. And don't, I beg of you, try to tell me you did it in the name of love!"

"Well, no one else was doing anything!" Nell snapped back, glad to have aroused him to a more familiar anger. "You left for London to take care of some stupid business or other, and Mama kept saying how thoughtless Aunt Agatha was being to die at such a time, and Kit was wailing about his lot, and Rory was at her wits' end, and I *tried* to tell you, but you wouldn't have it that there even *was* a problem, so naturally I felt it was all left up to me. And I'm sorry if you don't approve, but it was still the only solution I could think of that might answer the purpose, and I *did* think the major had agreed to it, and if he——"

"Draw rein, Nell," his lordship said more calmly. "Of course I believed you."

The words succeeded in bringing her up short. She stared at him searchingly. "But you said——"

"I know what I said . . . or rather, I don't know, but daresay I didn't say very much to the purpose. Your news about Lady Agatha was as shocking to me as it must have been to you. If I seemed unresponsive at the time, it was merely that I was thinking as fast as I could, trying to come up with a solution to our problem. Until that moment I had been pretty much contented to leave you to your little strategies, but once Lady Agatha received notice to quit at any moment, the element of speed became a good deal more important than it had previously been.''

She regarded him suspiciously. "My little strategies?"

He grinned at her then. "Lord, you must think I'm a nodcock! Did you flatter yourself that you were managing things delicately? I assure you, my dear, you were little less than ham-handed. But you seemed to be going the right way to work with her ladyship, so I had no wish to put a spoke in your wheel.''

"I see." Nell sighed. "Then you knew what I was doing all along.''

"I did, but I confess I thought we'd be grassed, because Talcott seemed less than passionately interested, and I was nearly certain Aurora would refuse to call off the betrothal if she didn't fancy herself romantically involved with someone else. Your sister's teachings had been too deeply engrained for anything less than love to dislodge them.''

"Well, I knew she cared for him and there were times I thought he returned her feelings, but it was not until the night she went free-trading——"

"That was when I knew we had a chance, too," Huntley agreed. "But that was also when you dropped the news about Lady Agatha into my lap. I had no chance to confirm my belief about the major that night, and since time was of the essence, I was forced to leave for London without tracking him down. But I hope he wants to marry the naughty puss, because I took a long chance, went straight to Chatham, and pleaded his cause with Lord and Lady Crossways. I knew I'd have better luck than anyone else, and so I did, but it was the very devil of a business.''

"They agreed to entertain his suit?" Nell's mouth dropped open. "You must have spoken very well of him indeed, sir.''

"Not only well enough that they agreed to consider his suit," Huntley informed her with pardonable pride, "but well enough that Crossways requested that I procure a special license while I was in London.''

"Merciful heavens!"

"Exactly so," he agreed, taking her firmly by the shoulders and giving her a little shake. The stern look had returned to his eyes. "You see, little goose, you are not the only one with a brain in your head. There are others who may be trusted to have an idea from time to time. And, if I may be permitted to say so, better ideas than yours. If I had had the slightest notion that you would attempt anything so cork-brained as this elopement of yours, I'd never have left town without at least speaking to Talcott. Thank God, he had better sense than the both of you, for I've not a doubt in the world that it was he who scotched your little plan. I'm only astonished he let it go so far as it did."

"He didn't," she admitted, staring at his waistcoat buttons. "Rory thought she could bring him 'round her thumb, and told me she had already convinced him it was the only course of action left to them. In fact, he had told her he would have nothing to do with it. He was waiting for us today only because he feared she might go to meet him by herself."

"That should have been the only way for her to get there," he said, regarding her somberly. "You'd no business to encourage her, let alone to go with her. I thought you had better sense than that, Nell. You disappointed me."

It was as if he had slapped her. Tightness clutched at the back of her throat, but even so, the sudden tears welling into her eyes caught her by surprise. She gasped a little, trying to stifle them, and Huntley's grip on her arms tightened.

"Nell, what is it?"

His quick sympathy steadied her, but it also reminded her of his weakness for feminine tears. Since it seemed only too likely that he had been gearing up to bellow at her some more, it occurred to her that that weakness might well be turned to good account. Consequently, she squeezed her eyes shut, letting the tears spill over onto her cheeks. Then she looked up at him reproachfully.

"I n-never meant to m-make you so angry," she stammered.

But instead of reassuring her as she had every right to expect him to do, Huntley looked searchingly at her for a long moment, then gave her another shake, forcefully enough this time to bring her teeth snapping together. "Don't you dare to cry, my girl," he ordered sternly, "for it won't do you the slightest good. You are no languishing miss, and if you think for one moment that I mean to encourage you to cultivate vinaigrettes and lace handkerchieves, then you'd best think again. I won't have it, Nell. Control yourself at once!"

Her eyes widened, the tears ceasing as if by magic. "Well, I like that!" she said. "I suppose I have as great a right as anyone else to cry when people say hurtful things to me."

Sudden amusement lit his eyes. "I said nothing you did not deserve to hear, and since weepy females instill nothing less in me than a desire to box their ears, I should not advise you to attempt such tactics."

"I suppose that is why you positively quail at the sight of Mama's vinaigrette," Nell accused. "And why your mama and sister can twist you 'round their thumbs with similar tactics."

"Since it would be highly improper of me to box either your mama's or my mama's ears, the situation is very different. As for my sister, if you think she weeps, you much mistake the matter. She shrieks. Incessantly. And if she lived with me, I should not stand such uncivil behavior for very long before putting an end to it. So, consider yourself forewarned."

"Forewarned, my lord?" She stared at him, almost afraid to think what he might mean by such words. Her heart seemed to have jumped into her throat again, but she did not think for one moment that fear had put it there. Unless it was fear that he didn't mean what she couldn't help hoping he meant.

"I had thought that if we could contrive to straighten out this mess, you might consent to return with me to Huntley Green as my wife."

"As your wife?"

"Of course, little goose, unless you've a preference for some other position."

She stared up at him, searching his face for some small indication that he might not mean what he was saying. There was nothing in his expression but that which made her heart beat faster. She decided to put him to the test. "I was persuaded you would be too angry with me to . . . to consider such a course. Are you certain you want me for your wife?"

"Only if you will solemnly promise never to subject me to such an affecting display of sensibility again," he said, withdrawing his handkerchief from his waistcoat pocket and dabbing gently at her damp cheeks.

"It was not the first time," she reminded him.

"No, my dear, but I have never before seen that calculating look beneath your tears. Your face, you know, is a tolerable reflection of your thoughts, and I am not so easily manipulated, regardless of what you may previously have believed."

"No, sir," she replied meekly.

"Much better. However, you have not answered my question."

"Oh, Philip," she said softly, "I love you so dearly, and I should like to marry you above all things, but are you certain you are not offering for me out of pity, fearing that I shall otherwise be left upon the shelf as a prop to my aging mama?"

"Nell, you *are* a goose," he said, kissing her lightly. "I'd never do anything so absurd. I love you." Despite the touch of amusement in his voice, she detected a tightness that she had heard only once before, and looking up at him, she could see the truth of the simple statement reflected in the heat of his gaze. A glow seemed to spread to her very toes, and she could not take her eyes from his. Returning her mesmerized look with a somewhat searching one of his own, Huntley began visibly to relax. He bent to kiss her again, and this time Nell's response made further conversation impossible for some moments. At last he said, "I fell in love with you eight years ago."

"Nonsense." But she softened the effect of the word by caressing his cheek. "You never gave anyone the slightest of hints."

"My suit would never have prospered," he said. "It would have been cruel to lead you to believe I felt more than friendship toward you, so long as your family was what it was. Only consider the problems we have had to overcome with Crossways and your sister, merely because Talcott is a younger son. And he has money and property of his own, which I did not have. I was completely dependent upon my father and then, after his death, upon my brother. I was not exaggerating when I said my sole reason for joining the military when I did was to avoid the humiliation of hanging upon his sleeve. It was bad enough to be made dependent upon Papa, but dependence upon my brother was intolerable to me. When I met you in London, I wanted nothing more than to ask permission to fix my interest with you. But I had no way to support you. The best I might have hoped for was an adequate allowance from my family. But your grandfather was a marquess, my dear. Your family would never have considered my suit while I was a mere penniless younger son. They'd have written me off as a fortune hunter. And two years ago, when I came into the property, it never occurred to me that you would not have been married long since, with a brood of children at your knee.''

''I thought much the same about you,'' she confessed, smiling up at him, wanting to banish the look of pain that had touched his eyes again as he spoke. ''Oh, Philip, how fate does play with us!''

''No more, my love.'' His look softened, and he held her close. His hands began to move gently over her body. ''We are together at last,'' he murmured gruffly against her curls. ''Your wretched niece will be well provided for, I think, so we can attend to our own affairs without a qualm.''

Nell sighed with pleasure at the thought, then suddenly wrinkled her brow. ''I do worry about Mama,'' she said. ''She depends a good deal upon me, you know. Do you think perhaps she ought to live with us?''

He made a small choking sound. ''I don't think that will be necessary, love. Lady Agnes will be in good hands.''

''I wish I could be certain of that, but Kit, you know, has not the habit of looking after her.''

''You cannot say the same of Sir Henry.'' He looked down at her quizzically.

''Well, of course not,'' she retorted, ''but he is merely her man of affairs, scarcely as close to her as a daughter.''

''As a husband, however, he will be a deal closer,'' Huntley murmured, letting his hands play teasingly across her breasts.

But she pulled away from him in astonishment. ''Philip, you must be joking! Sir Henry?''

''Indeed. Not only did I procure one special license at Crossways' request, but a second at Sir Henry's. I am a most obliging fellow.''

''Well, for heaven's sake!'' She eyed him innocently. ''Two licenses, my lord?''

''Three licenses. And at vast expense, I'll have you know.''

''Ah,'' she said wisely, watching him from under her lashes, ''and to think I once thought you a cautious man.''

He chuckled, drawing a finger lightly beneath her chin. "But I *am* cautious, my love. However, I am also sure."

"Are you, my lord?" He nodded, drawing her into his arms again. "Well, I am also sure, but I am *not* very cautious," Nell murmured into his waistcoat. "Are you truly persuaded that you wish to be saddled with an impulsive bride?"

"You may be as impulsive as you like, little one," he said, amused. "I shall endeavor to do what I can to rescue you whenever you fall into the briars."

"*Just* like a knight in shining armor!" she said soulfully, twinkling up at him. "And to think Rory had quite convinced me that you hadn't got a romantic bone in your body!"

"I haven't!" he denied, revolted.

"Fiddlesticks. But you needn't repine. I shan't tell a soul. 'Tis the duty of a good wife to protect her husband's proud name."

"Does that mean you will marry me, Nell?" His tone was deeply serious again, and there was anxiety in the hazel eyes as he waited for her response. She smiled at him.

"Yes, Philip, I will."

About the Author

A fourth-generation Californian, Amanda Scott was born and raised in Salinas and graduated with a degree in history from Mills College in Oakland. She did graduate work at the University of North Carolina at Chapel Hill, specializing in British history, before obtaining her MA from San Jose State University. She lives with her husband and young son in Sacramento. Her hobbies include camping, backpacking, and gourmet cooking. Her previous Regencies, *The Fugitive Heiress*, *The Kidnapped Bride*, and *Ravenwood's Lady* are also available in Signet editions.

JOIN THE REGENCY READERS' PANEL

Help us bring you more of the books you like by filling out this survey and mailing it in today.

1. Book title:_____

   Book #:_____

2. Using the scale below how would you rate this book on the following features.

Poor		Not so Good			O.K.			Good		Excel- lent	
0	1	2	3	4	5	6	7	8	9	10

Rating

Overall opinion of book. . . . . _____
Plot/Story . . . . _____
Setting/Location . . . . _____
Writing Style . . . . _____
Character Development . . . . _____
Conclusion/Ending . . . . _____
Scene on Front Cover . . . . _____

3. On average about how many romance books do you buy for yourself each month?_____

4. How would you classify yourself as a reader of Regency romances?
   I am a ( ) light ( ) medium ( ) heavy reader.

5. What is your education?
   ( ) High School (or less)   ( ) 4 yrs. college
   ( ) 2 yrs. college   ( ) Post Graduate

6. Age_____   7. Sex: ( ) Male ( ) Female

Please Print Name_____

Address_____

City_____State_____Zip_____

Phone # (   )_____

Thank you. Please send to New American Library, Research Dept, 1633 Broadway, New York, NY 10019.